Red Roses
FOR A DEAD TRUCKER

Red Roses
FOR A DEAD TRUCKER

ANNA ASHWOOD COLLINS

PENDULUM PRESS

Red Roses for a Dead Trucker ©2001 by Anna Ashwood Collins
First publication date: March 2002

ISBN: 0-9712538-4-6
Library of Congress Control Number: 2002100632

Cover design: Brian Booth and Kathy Kruger
Typesetting: Folio Bookworks

Printed in the U.S.A.

Published by Pendulum Press
Minneapolis, Minnesota
http://www.pendulumpress.com

10   9   8   7   6   5   4   3   2   1

To Susan L. Morrison, my fellow adventurer on all of life's highways, paved and unpaved. Thanks for taking care of all the details.

Acknowledgments

Thanks to all the truckers who took time to talk to me; Leo, Margaret and Susan Canale, my second family; former Potsdam State Professors Elsie Kristiansen and Thomas P. North for their love and encouragement; Mollie McCormick, director of music at the Jekyll Island Club, for our musical mysteries; Vi Bennett of Jesup, GA, the musical and physical embodiment of Abby Doyle; Mary Pulford, Jekyll Island, president of my small fan club; Joan Hesterberg and Jim Bentley of Jekyll, my computer experts; Christine Andreae and Marilyn Henderson, gifted mystery writers who are always willing to share their love and insights. Finally, in loving memory of those who have gone to that Truckstop in the Sky—my late husband, George W. Collins; my parents, Clarence and Clara Dickerson Ashwood; Al and Margaret Morrison, Helen Stiles and Abby Comstock.

1

Friday Evening

I didn't like those big headlights looming in my rear view mirror, bearing down on my old rental car on a twisting road in the Catskill Mountains on a cold evening in February.

Hertz and Avis no longer rented me cars because I returned them with dented fenders and bullet holes. Petty, petty. They had a hard time understanding why Abigail Doyle, respectable New York City efficiency expert, had so many mishaps with their vehicles. Actually, most of my misadventures occur in my lucrative sideline: I solve problems for rich people. Since I design systems for factories, businesses, and institutions, I often meet wealthy people who need help because they've gotten involved in dangerous situations. Sometimes I got into trouble and got as dented as those infamous rental cars.

Driving one of Lefty's gas station specials, a 1973 Pontiac LeMans, I looked for a pull-off to get out of the way of the behemoth behind me. My little Catskill rendezvous looked like it was going to be aborted.

"Abby, old girl, you'd better look for someplace to bail out before that thing eats you alive," I muttered, eyes uneasily shifting from the rear view mirror to the road ahead. I have a tendency to talk to myself when no one else is around; since I'm only forty, it's not a sign of senility.

The air horn blasted my nerves. I jerked the wheel. My tires caught in an icy rut on the shoulder of the road; my car lurched towards the ditch as the tractor-trailer forced me ever closer to disaster.

"You crazy idiot," I screamed as I struggled with the wheel, thankful that I had an old, tough car around ms as I felt it roll.

My last conscious thought as the car rolled over was the sign on the truck: We Aim To Deliver; even if you kill someone doing it, I added.

Revolving red lights flashed. Voices filtered through my mind. "There's a woman in here." "Get the door open." "We saw the lights of the car, Officer, when we went by." "Jesus, it's cold out here. When will women ever learn to drive."

"Chauvinist," I muttered as I opened one eye to see a bearded face pressed against the window, mouthing words I couldn't understand. Ah, unlock the door. I groped for the lock and pulled it up.

A blast of refrigerated air jolted me.

"You okay, lady. Where's it hurt?"

I was reassured by the State Police patch on his shoulder, "All over, Trooper, but I don't think anything is broken. I have a terrific headache."

"Okay, lady, don't move. The rescue squad is on the way." He covered me with a gray blanket. I smiled my thanks. "You should be more careful on these mountain roads," he added.

Did he think I'd just casually driven off the road through stupidity or carelessness? "The truck," I mumbled.

"What truck, lady?"

"A big one ran me off the road."

He looked at me skeptically. "Did you get its number?"

I grimaced. "I was pretty busy trying to save me and my car." I peered at him. "I've never seen a bearded trooper before."

He flushed. "I—uh—have a skin condition that makes shaving painful. Now, back to the accident: are you telling me you were forced off the road?"

I nodded which was a mistake as pain stabbed me between the eyes. "Exactly. Where's that ambulance?"

"Coming. Just stay quiet. We'll talk after the doc has seen you. Anybody I should notify for you?"

"You could call the Babbling Brook Inn outside Phoenicia and ask them to tell—to tell anyone who asks for me—that I'll be delayed." There goes my romantic weekend in the mountains, I thought, remembering that I was supposed to meet an old flame who wanted to fan some embers while he was here in the East. I hoped he was into home nursing!

The doctor finished peering into my eyes, patted my shoulder and said, "You'll live. Cuts, bruises, possibly a mild concussion. Take it easy for a few days. Maybe you should take driving lessons; you New Yorkers just don't know how to handle our slippery mountain roads." Another patronizing touch on the shoulder and he was gone, leaving me alone with Trooper Caleb Smith, my bearded rescuer, who was laboriously filling out forms.

"I'm really tired of everyone insinuating I'm just some dippy woman who can't drive. I was run off the road damn it," I groused.

Trooper Smith glanced up from his writing. "Can you describe the truck?"

"It was big."

"They're all big."

"It had writing on the side." I frowned, trying to recall the words that had flashed by me. "Got it. 'We aim to deliver' was painted on the side in a dark color. The trailer was a silver color."

"Most of them are silver-colored and quite a few probably have that motto. I'll watch for it." He looked at me closely. "You don't look so hot. Can I take you some place?"

I smiled; I'm one of those nervous smilers who smile even when they're in pain. "The Babbling Brook Inn?"

"Sure."

I enjoyed the ride as we sped down Route 28 towards Phoenicia. The car was warm and the purr of the dispatcher's voice in the background lulled me into a semiconscious state.

"Do you think it was deliberate?" I murmured.

Trooper Smith glanced at me curiously. "Deliberate? Why would anyone want to kill you?"

"I'm not just an efficiency expert; I also solve criminal cases for the very rich and sometimes I make enemies."

He eyed me warily. "Are you working on anything right now?" I shook my head and winced at the pain caused by the slight movement. He shrugged. "Probably an accident. A hopped-up driver in a hurry to get home and you were just in his way. Some of these guys are pretty reckless. We scrape their leavings up off the highway all the time. It ain't pretty what one of these monsters can do to a car."

He turned onto a single lane side road, bumped over a rickety, wooden bridge and pulled up in front of a sprawling two story wood-frame house. "Here we are—Babbling Brook Inn."

"This is it?" I studied the building. A faint light gleamed in the front window. I didn't see any cars around. "It almost looks deserted."

"You haven't been here before?"

"No. My—uh—friend made the reservation and sent me directions. I figured it would be a ski lodge where we'd sip mulled wine in front of a fireplace and admire the skiers' broken bones."

"It doesn't attract skiers. Very, very expensive exclusive and small. I heard there are only four or five suites and you have to be somebody or know somebody important to get one." He grinned at me. "I must admit I was skeptical when you said you had reservations and you were driving that junker."

"Never judge a book . . ." I smiled. "Could you just wait until I make sure my friend is here." I knocked on the front door which was opened by a tall, thin, middle-aged man. "Has Todd Mason arrived?"

"Yes. You must be Ms. Doyle; we've been expecting you. May I get your luggage?" he asked as he looked beyond me at the patrol car. "Interesting limo you have," he said with a grin. "Are you with the Governor's office?"

"Nothing so glamorous, I'm afraid. I was in an accident and Trooper Smith was kind enough to drive me here from the hospital." I waved at the trooper as he handed my overnight bag to the man who had greeted me. I felt lonely and uneasy as I watched the cruiser disappear.

I signed the register, noting that Todd's name was the only one in the book for the day. "Where is Mr. Mason?" I asked.

"In town. He had to run some errands." He locked the register in a desk drawer. "He said to tell you to make yourself comfortable; he'll be back as soon as possible. I gave you our two bedroom suite in the back. It has a beautiful view of the mountains. By the way, my name is Jack—Jack Heims."

He led me up a carpeted staircase to a dimly lit hall. The hall ran down the center of the house with doors on both sides. I followed Jack to a door near the end of the hall. With a flourish he opened the door and bowed me in.

The room was like a stage setting for a romantic play; a large living room with a cheery fire in a stone fireplace, two comfortable armchairs in front of the hearth flanking a table with a bottle of red wine in a basket, two glasses, and a plate of cheese and crackers.

I sighed. "The fire feels marvelous and I'm starved."

He nodded. "Let me show you your room." He opened a door on the left side of the room. "Here we are." He turned on a light switch and then opened another door. "Bathroom." He glanced inside as if counting the towels. "Dinner will be served when Mr. Mason returns. Is there anything I can do for you in the meantime?"

"No thanks. I'm going to take a hot bath and luxuriate in front of that fire."

After he left I hung up my jacket in my closet and looked around my room. "Not bad, old girl," I said as I flopped down on the queen-sized bed. The bed was modern but the rest of the furniture was old.

As the water trickled into the tub, I stared in the mirror, assessing the damage from the accident. I had a large purple bruise on my left hip and a small one on my forehead. I peered into my eyes. They looked more green than hazel, a sure sign I wasn't feeling well. I grimaced, emphasizing the deep smile marks. I brushed a hand through my curly, dark hair.

"You may be forty, old girl, but there's not an ounce of fat on this frame," I muttered as I stood on tip-toe. "Ah, vanity." I stuck a finger in the water. Hot.

After soaking for twenty minutes I spent another ten debating what to wear. "Pajamas and robe?" I muttered. "No, too forward. After all I haven't seen Todd for . . ." I thought about it. Not for quite awhile. Sighing, I opted for comfort, pulled on slacks and a sweater and ran a brush through my hair.

I crossed the living room to Todd's room and opened the door. His suitcase was open on the bed and an open briefcase was on the nightstand. Papers were strewn on the stand and on the floor under it.

I smiled. "Same old Todd; turns any room into a shambles in five minutes."

Returning to the living room, I opened the wine, poured a glass, sliced a piece of cheese and balanced it on a cracker. I sipped thoughtfully as I stared into the flames.

I sniffled. Romance writers have a real thing about fireplaces; don't they ever connect all that fire and smoke with runny noses and red eyes? How romantic can it be gazing into the bloodshot eyes of your lover and listening to all that sniffling.

I sneezed. "Damn, I hope I'm not catching cold. I need some fresh air."

I opened my bedroom window a crack and listened for a minute as I stared into the dark. Gee, they really have a babbling brook. In February? I laughed when I realized I was hearing water gurgling through a pipe somewhere. Must be someone else has arrived, I thought, as I closed the window and returned to the living room where I paced around, inspecting the pictures on the wall.

"Where can Todd be?" I asked aloud. "I'm starving and my head aches.

Some romantic weekend this is going to be, old girl."

I poured a little more wine and munched on the cheese. Drowsily, I watched the fire burn down and thought about the first time I had met Todd.

I had still been married to my beach boy husband, Rod Ralston, and my daughter, Jackie, had been about six. Some minor movie star had thrown a party for other minor movie stars up in the Hollywood Hills and Rod, then a beach boy specialist in the movies, had been invited. I'd gone reluctantly, suspecting it would be a low-grade orgy with the requisite marijuana smoking and cocaine sniffing.

What passed for conversation in Hollywood had bored me and I was annoyed, watching Rod put some moves on a beach-blanket bimbo. Tired of watching them nod off on the dope, I'd wandered out onto the terrace where I watched the lights of Los Angeles winking through the smog.

A voice behind me said, "Pretty at a distance."

Even then, Todd's hair had been white, startling against his unlined young face. "And what movies were you in?" I asked sarcastically.

He laughed. "None. I'm the date of one of those zombies in there. My cousin fixed me up. He thought I might enjoy a big Hollywood party." His blue eyes twinkled. "What an absolute waste of time; they sit around sniffing dope, playing backgammon, nodding off. Conversation is non-existent or incoherent at best."

He had moved closer, run a finger along my cheek and smiled. "With those cheekbones you could be a star."

I shook my head and laughed. "Well, you're certainly learning the lines out here. Those are good Iroquois cheekbones—be careful."

The evening had passed in a blur as we talked and talked, discovering we were kindred souls. We had a brief, passionate affair, but I had discovered I wasn't cut out for adultery. The logistics were too time-consuming when I was trying to support a husband and a child.

We had parted as dear friends, talking often on the phone, exchanging cards and notes, and meeting for drinks or dinner whenever we happened to be in the same city.

Todd, never married, stopped practicing law and went to work for some mysterious government agency that dealt with nuclear power or weapons; I was never sure which and he never gave me a straight answer.

I hadn't heard from him in about a year until last Friday when my secretary, Christopher Palmieri, had given me Todd's message.

With a raised eyebrow, Chris read, "Someone named Todd Mason called. I quote: Abby meet me at Babbling Brook Inn near Phoenicia next Friday night for old times, good times. It's important. Reservations are all made."

He had grinned at me impishly. "He's a confident old flame; didn't leave any number where you could reach him in case you were otherwise occupied. Are you going?"

I had winked at Chris. "You bet! How many invitations like that do I get? I know what you're thinking, but it's not like that; we're old and dear friends. I haven't seen him in a long time. Besides Valentine's day is coming." I frowned. "Humm, wonder what he means by it's important. That doesn't sound much like romance—more like business."

"Maybe he means it's important to him personally."

"Ah. Chris, you know how to make a woman feel good."

Rousing from my reverie, I checked my watch again. Almost eleven. I finished the wine and cheese. "Some romantic evening," I grumbled, wondering if I should ask Jack to bring me that special dinner he had mentioned. I was still starving.

A light tap on the door. I opened it up and confronted Jack who was balancing a tray on one hand and holding another bottle of wine in the other.

"Sorry to disturb you Ms. Doyle, but it's getting very late and Mr. Mason still hasn't returned. I thought you might be hungry so I took the liberty of bringing up a little cold supper. Mr. Mason will probably want that special dinner tomorrow night."

I held the door open for him and watched as he spread the food out on the table in front of the fireplace. Sliced turkey breast and salad. It looked great.

"Have you heard anything from Mr. Mason since he left?" I asked.

"Nothing. I can't imagine where he could be unless he, too, had an accident." Jack checked the food one more time and opened the wine. "When you're finished, just put the tray in the hall. Have a good evening. Breakfast is served between eight and ten."

I wolfed down the food, changed into pajamas and robe, and settled down with M.R. Henderson's latest mystery while I waited for Todd to return.

I was jumpy, nervous. Suddenly, I realized why—the silence and the darkness outside. In the city you're always surrounded by light and noise—life.

2

Early Saturday Morning

Midnight. A tap on the door and then it opened. A sheepish-looking Todd Mason tossed his hat into the center of the room.

"Is it safe to enter?"

"Todd, where've you been? I've been worried." I crossed the room and hugged him fiercely. "It's so good to see you." I winced and eased myself out of his embrace.

"What's wrong? Are you hurt?"

"Didn't you get my message about my accident?"

He shook his head. "What accident? Are you all right?" He laughed. "Of course, you are, you're here. Sit down and tell me about it."

I watched his face as I told him the story. He was still handsome—the white hair still startling over his young for his fifty years face, but something was different. I decided it was the expression in his eyes. Worry? Fear?

When I finished my story, I asked, "Why did you invite me here, Todd?"

"I need your advice."

"My advice. Why? About what?"

"As the Old Testament says, 'Blessed is thy advice, 0 Abigail.' She was a very wise woman, married King David while he was married to Bathsheba."

I grinned. "That doesn't sound too wise to me."

"Do you still have your little sideline?"

"Do you mean solving problems for the very wealthy or analyzing industrial functions?" I sighed. "Sometimes, I feel like criminal matters are occupying more and more of my time. I just finished a case with a nefarious general found murdered in a bunker at Fort Tilden."

Todd nodded. "I heard. It was the talk of some of the Government agencies I work with. You're not the most popular person in some quarters."

I shrugged. "Maybe if some of those agencies did their jobs better, they wouldn't have these little problems."

He gazed into the fire as he muttered, "That's for sure."

My head was throbbing again and muscles I didn't even know I had were beginning to ache. I squirmed in my chair. "What do you want from me, Todd?"

"Let's play reunion," he said.

"What do you mean?"

"You know—you tell me everything you've done for the past year and I'll tell you everything I've done." He looked at me quizzically. "Haven't you ever attended your class reunion?"

"No and I don't intend to; I don't like to discuss the past or lie about the present. I never knew you were sentimental."

Todd moved over to the mantle and stared into the fading fire. He poked at it. "Maybe I'm getting older or maybe I'm lonely and scared."

"You scared," I scoffed.

He gave me a crooked smile. "We'll talk about it in the morning. It's a long story and I can see you're hurting." He pulled me gently to my feet and hugged me. "Take all those aches and pains to bed." His lips brushed mine. "I'm glad you weren't seriously injured."

Pausing in the doorway to my room, I looked back at Todd who was staring into the fireplace. His shoulders were slumped. Feeling uneasy, I started to cross the room to him. Hearing me, he turned and smiled at me.

"Thought I told you to go to bed."

"Todd, if something is bothering you, let's talk about it now."

"No, tomorrow is soon enough." His lips were smiling, but his eyes were distressed. "It's a long story and there're papers to look at. Might be nothing you can do to help me. We'll both be more alert in the morning. Not a pretty bedtime story."

I smiled wryly. "And all this time I imagined a romantic weekend in the mountains while you just wanted Abigail Doyle, female sleuth instead of Abby the femme fatale."

He laughed. "Maybe, I have designs on both." He twirled an imaginary mustache and gave me a sexy wink, reminding me of the Todd I knew and loved.

I snuggled gratefully under the down comforter, deciding that the owner turned off the furnace at night to encourage romantic interludes. Make love or freeze to death. I stared at my door, half-hoping that Todd would come through it with something on his mind other than his mysterious problem. Abby old girl, you've been reading too many women's magazines, I admonished myself as I turned over and tried to fall asleep.

I listened to the sounds of the house—the sighings and crackings of cold wood as it expanded and shrunk in the icy air. Somewhere a toilet flushed, someone coughed, a stair creaked, a window closed. Perversely, I missed the clatter of helicopters going back and forth across the East River near my Long Island City apartment.

My apartment was the top floor of a factory, renovated and given to me by the grateful factory owner after I had made his business profitable again. The area was large enough for office space, a large living room, kitchen, laundry-storage room, and two bedrooms. He had even knocked out large sections of brick walls and installed windows so I had terrific views of Manhattan and Queens.

The neighborhood bordering the factory area was small and intimate with the business district on Fifth Street and St. Mary's Church, Convent and School at one end.

Perversely, I wished I was home in my own bed.

Just before I drifted off to sleep, I felt an almost uncontrollable urge to wake Todd and make him tell me his problems.

3

Saturday Morning

Heart pounding, I bolted upright in bed and listened; something had awakened me, a strange noise. I snaked a hand out from under the comforter to turn an the light so I could check the time. Just after three.

"Geez, it's cold," I muttered, trying to force my body out of my warm bed into that cold air to check on the origin of the noise. I concentrated. I have excellent hearing, like rabbit ears. But all I heard were the creaking sounds caused by the cold. Sighing, I turned off the light and slid back under the comforter.

The sun and sounds from what I sincerely hoped was the kitchen woke me up. Tentatively, I stuck a hand out to test the temperature. Ah, heat. I eased my aching muscles out of bed, opened my door and peeked across the living room. Todd's door was still closed. After I dressed, I knocked on his door. No answer.

As I opened his door, I called, "Hey, sleepy head, time to rise and shine." His bed was empty. The covers were tangled and thrown on the floor. Shaking my head, I piled them back on his bed. "Todd's really become a messy old bachelor. Wonder where he is. Must be down getting coffee."

Returning to my room, I glanced out the window to check the weather. I stared at the brook, puzzled by the large black blob sprawled half over the ice and half in a small open run of water in the center.

"My God!" I shouted. "That's a person. Todd!"

I pounded down the stairs and searched for a back door that would lead to the stream.

Jack emerged from a doorway and eyed me curiously. "Something wrong, Ms. Doyle?"

"The brook, the brook—Todd's in the brook. Call for help." I slammed my hand against a door. "How in hell do I get out back?"

"Follow me." We sprinted down a back hall to a side door that he shoved open for me and pointed. "That way."

I raced the hundred feet to the brook, oblivious to the chilling cold and the slippery ice and snow underfoot. I skidded to a halt at the edge of the ice.

Todd was sprawled face down, half on the ice and half in the water, his lower torso submerged. The ice underneath his head was shattered and bloodstained where somebody had repeatedly smashed his head against the ice. Blood trickled out of his mouth, his nose and his ears. His eyes were open. Those beautiful blue eyes were now sightless.

Biting my lip, using self-inflicted pain to control my emotions, I stretched out prone on the ice until I could reach his wrist. Hopelessly, I felt for his pulse, shuddering at the cold touch of his body.

I wriggled back to the bank where I crouched on my heels and stared at his body, letting my mind process the facts. Head smashed in, bruise mark on throat, left arm twisted behind back, pajama top, blue pants he had on last night.

I swiveled my head around looking for signs of a struggle, but all I spotted were what looked like drag marks coming to the edge of the ice. Dead before he was placed out here, I thought but why smash his head on the ice unless he was just unconscious when they brought him out here.

I realized cold tears were crawling down my cheeks and I was trembling from the cold and from the shock. Slowly, I straightened up, wincing from the arthritic pains in my knees. A noise distracted me and I looked back towards the house where Jack and a woman I hadn't seen before stood in the doorway.

Jack called, "Is it Mr. Mason?"

"Yes. Did you call the police? He's dead—murdered."

I watched the two closely. The woman wrung her hands and shrunk back behind Jack who just shook his head. I saw his lips move and she went inside. She returned and handed a parka to him.

"Put this on before you freeze to death," he said gruffly, looking past me at the body on the ice. "Nothing like this ever happened here before." He peered at me. "Who are you two, anyway?"

"Just two old friends having a reunion." I choked back a sob, knowing I needed to keep iron control of myself until I was alone. No time to grieve,

Todd, I apologized silently; not if I'm going to get the bastards who did this to you. "Did you call the troopers?"

"They're on their way. Shouldn't we cover it—him—up or something?"

"Don't touch anything." I glanced back at the path we had come down. "I suppose we've destroyed any evidence that might have been on the path or on the edge of the brook. Did you hear a strange noise about three?"

"I wasn't here," he said, frowning. "I don't stay in the inn. I have a cabin over there." He pointed at another path that led into a thick stand of pines. "Nobody but the guests are in the building at night. Martha and I are available to cook and serve and take care of the rooms. When we aren't needed, we return to our cabin. That's one of the reasons people come here—total privacy."

"Are there any other guests here?" I asked, shuffling my feet, wishing I had on my nice heavy boots.

"Mr. Mason reserved the whole inn this weekend."

"The whole inn," I gasped. "Must have cost him a fortune."

"It did," Jack said grimly, "and his life." He eyed me suspiciously. "You two were alone," he said pointedly.

"I don't think so," I said, describing the noise that had awakened me. "Was the front door unlocked?"

"Nope, I locked up when I left."

"Were any doors unlocked when you came to work this morning?"

He looked at me coldly. "What're you—some kind of cop ?"

"Among other things, I'm a private investigator, but more importantly, I'm—was—Todd's best friend and I intend to find out what happened here." I looked away for a moment to gather my thoughts. "Now, were any of the doors unlocked?" I asked harshly.

"That side door. I just assumed somebody was out for a walk."

"Front door?"

"Don't know. Haven't had any reason to go near it yet."

Martha, a portly woman in her fifties, hustled down the path, carrying a thermos and two mugs. "You'll need this," she said, pouring coffee while keeping her eyes averted from the brook.

"Thanks," I said. "You're Martha?"

She nodded shyly.

"She's my sister. Moved in last year when her husband was killed in a logging accident."

"Did you notice anything unusual this morning when you came to work?" I asked her, gratefully curling my hands around the hot mug of coffee. I watched her face, her eyes; she was nervous about something or painfully shy since she kept her eyes on the ground and cowered behind her brother.

"Nothing," she whispered as she thrust the thermos at her brother and scuttled towards the house.

"Your sister is extremely shy," I said to Jack who was watching her, a glum expression on his face.

He shrugged. "She's always been like that, especially with strangers. I'd appreciate it if you didn't upset her anymore."

We heard the sirens. "I'll show them back," he said.

Five men rounded the building and followed Jack down the path. Trampling all the evidence, I groaned to myself. They strung out along the bank of the creek and stared at Todd's body. The man in a blue parka standing next to me looked familiar.

I peered at him. "Trooper Smith?" He nodded. "Don't you ever take any time off?" I asked.

"I happened to be in the barracks when the call came in; I was afraid something had happened to you." He nodded towards the body. "Was that your friend?"

"Yes. Todd Mason. As you can see, he's been murdered," I said grimly.

Trooper Smith gave me a questioning look. "You're pretty cool, aren't you?"

I smiled nervously—one of my quirks—and said, "Only on the outside, Trooper, only on the outside."

When nobody moved, I asked, "Why are you just standing around?"

Trooper Smith answered, "We have to wait for a Bureau of Criminal Investigation officer. He's on his way from Kingston. When Jack called, we weren't sure what we were dealing with and I recalled what you said last night about being deliberately run off the road. When Jack said they had a body out here, I thought it might be you."

"Oh, you believe me now about the accident."

"Maybe."

I shook my head in disgust as I said meanly, "You guys realize you may be trampling all over vital evidence."

Startled, they looked down at their feet. I heard one of the troopers groan, "We're going to catch hell from Mickens."

"I'm freezing. I'm going in for a pair of boots." Relieved that no one ordered me to stay, I hurried inside to our suite.

I pulled on my snow boots and exchanged the borrowed parka for my own before I glanced out the window to make sure all the troopers were still creekside. I wanted to make a quick search of Todd's room.

Stepping inside Todd's room, I mentally inventoried it: bed sheets crumpled on top of the bed, a thick book and his reading glasses on the nightstand, a writing pad and ballpoint pen on the desk, a dark blue suit jacket hanging in the open closet along with a red and gray parka, hiking boots and dress shoes on the closet floor, a red-striped necktie draped over the mirror on the dresser, hair brush and comb, some crumpled bills, change and wallet on the dresser top, an open suitcase with dirty laundry on the suitcase rack, a camera and binoculars hanging from the back of the desk chair.

Something's missing, I thought as I walked into the room. His briefcase. I checked under the bed, looked inside the dresser drawers, and inspected the closet. No briefcase and no papers scattered on the nightstand or under it. I paused by the desk and stared at the writing pad I could just make out my name indented on the blank top sheet. He had written something to me. Did his murderer get it or is it hidden in this room? I picked up the dirty laundry and shook it. A white envelope fluttered to the floor. I picked it up. My name was scrawled on the front. Just as I was about to open it, Jack called me from downstairs, telling me the coroner had arrived.

Sticking the letter in my pocket, I hurried back to the brook where the troopers stood in a small circle watching two men in suits crouching gingerly on the ice as close as they could get to the body.

The two strangers turned when I hustled up to the troopers. Trooper Smith said, "Ms. Doyle, this is Investigator Mickens, and Dr. Farris, the coroner. Ms. Doyle found the body."

I was surprised when the young man turned out to be the doctor. He looked barely old enough to be out of high school.

The investigator, tall and trim with the look of a not so benevolent despot, looked me up and down. He nodded to me and in a gruff voice said, "I hope you didn't touch anything."

"I checked his pulse—to make sure he was dead. Unfortunately, all of us have rambled down this path and trampled around the shoreline, so we may have destroyed some clues there."

Mickens glared at everybody. He pointed at two troopers. "Move him."

I watched intently as two troopers gingerly pulled Todd's body from the water.

"He's not wearing any shoes or socks," I blurted.

"Difficult to put shoes on a dead man," the coroner said dryly. I raised my eyebrows. He shrugged. "There's a needle mark on his arm. He was probably injected with something and dead before he was dragged out here." The doctor stared up at the inn. "But why not just leave him in bed? Who was this guy anyway?"

"Can I talk to you privately?" I asked Mickens who escorted me up the path until we were out of earshot of the other men.

He raised an eyebrow as if to say talk. Shoving my hands into my pockets, I felt the letter and debated if I should tell him about it, decided not to, at least until I had a chance to read it. After all, it might be just an ordinary love letter. Wishful thinking, old girl.

"Well, Ms. Doyle, I'm waiting. What did you want to tell me?"

"I think Todd Mason worked for some secret agency or something in the federal government. He asked me to meet him here this weekend for what I thought was the renewal of an old romance, but as it turned out, he was worried about something and wanted my help."

Mickens looked at me curiously.

"I investigate crimes that interest me and that pay well. Todd probably thought I could help him and remain discreet about it." I glanced at the group surrounding his body. "But he never got the chance to tell me his problem. Trooper Smith may have mentioned to you that I was run off the road last night and I wasn't feeling too hot so Todd said that his problem could wait until this morning. I wish I had insisted on hearing him out last night."

"Are your accident and his death connected?"

I shrugged. "I don't think so, but I just don't know. I'm starting a job Monday in my regular profession of efficiency expert, analyzing the needs of a trucking company. Probably just coincidence."

"What agency did he work for?"

"I don't know. Nuclear power, weapons, hazardous waste, something like that. He always said it was just a boring job, pushing paper, analyzing costs, functions—things like that, but he did travel a lot to Europe and the Mid-East. I think he was a troubleshooter for someone."

"Show me his room."

Mickens stood in the center of Todd's room. He slowly turned around. "Anything missing?"

I chewed my lip. "His briefcase. When I arrived last night, I looked in his room. His case was open on the nightstand and papers were scattered on the stand and on the floor underneath."

Mickens walked to the nightstand and pulled open the single drawer. Empty. He flicked a few pages of the book on the stand, a non-fiction treatise on disposing of nuclear waste. "Not exactly bedtime reading," he commented. "Did you look at the papers on the floor or in his briefcase?"

"Really, officer, I'm not the neighborhood snoop," I snapped. "Actually, I wish I had examined them; I might know what is going on—might even have been able to save his life."

"Were you sleeping with him?"

"Is that idle curiosity or is that information vital to your case?" I suppressed my anger, but then I supposed I deserved that question since I had indicated the possibility of a romantic weekend. "Am I a suspect?"

He shrugged. "Everybody in or near this house is a suspect. Most murders are committed by people who know the victim. A romance gone wrong. What do I know about you?"

"For the record, I wasn't sleeping with him, I didn't kill him and I'm not a subversive enemy agent. I'm an ordinary middle-aged businesswoman who pays her fair share of taxes. If you want to know more about me, call Detective Margaret Standish, New York Police Department. She and I worked on a case together when a Corps of Engineer's general was murdered in New York."

"Whoa, lady," he held up both hands in a stopping motion. "I'm just trying to do my job. I assume you'd like his killer found, so let's help each other." He frowned at me. "Or do you plan to turn a quick buck on this case, doing your own little investigation?"

"Don't be insulting, Officer Mickens."

"Investigator."

"Investigator or whatever. Todd was my friend, one of my dearest friends and I loved him. I'll help you all I can, but don't patronize me."

Suddenly, he grinned boyishly, looking much younger than his fifty or so years. "You're cute when you're mad."

I glared at him. "I won't even dignify that sexist remark with an answer,"

I snapped as I stalked out of the room.

From the front porch I watched the men put the body bag into the ambulance. Out of the corner of my eye I glimpsed Jack and Martha peeking out a front window.

Dr. Farris and Investigator Mickens stood beside the ambulance, talking. Trooper Smith walked up the steps and took one of my hands. I smiled at him gratefully.

He squeezed my hand. "What'll you do now?"

"Drive Todd's rental car back to New York, contact his mother—get on with my life." I looked at him. "What'll happen here?"

"Doc will do an autopsy. Mickens will lead an investigation, but I don't think anything will come of it. Whoever killed him has nothing to do with the Catskills, does he?"

I shook my head. "They're on a plane to somewhere right now." I sobbed and Trooper Smith folded me into his arms and patted my back. "If only I had listened to him, stayed in his room with him, he'd still be alive," I snuffled into the trooper's chest.

"Or you'd both be dead." He held me away and stared into my eyes. "Don't fool with this, Ms. Doyle. He was killed by professionals." He glanced at Farris and Mickens to make sure they were still occupied before he added, "Mickens would have my head if he knew I told you this—I overheard the doc telling him that the head smashing was a red herring or an irrational act since some kind of injection had probably triggered a heart attack, killing him instantly."

I winced. "I don't think you people will have the case long either. Bet you a cup of coffee, the Feds will be here before nightfall." The door of the ambulance slammed. "Good-bye, Todd," I whispered.

The ambulance slowly pulled away as the troopers dispersed—one pair driving away and the other two heading back to the brook. Mickens slapped Dr. Farris on the back and laughed at something the doctor said as he climbed into his four-wheel vehicle.

Mickens gestured for Trooper Smith to join him. They inspected Todd's rental car inside and out. Trooper Smith shook his head at something Mickens said and glanced back at me. He smiled reassuringly. They walked up the driveway, one on each side of it as they examined it. A little late, I thought, with all the traffic on it since last night.

A hand touched my shoulder. I turned. Jack said, "Come in and get warm.

There's fresh coffee in the kitchen and Martha will make you some breakfast. You must be cold and starved."

"And heartsick," I added as I looked at the mountains dressed in winter white, glittering in the sunlight. "What a beautiful spot. I—excuse me—I'll be down in a few minutes." I rushed to my room before I broke down completely.

I rocked back and forth, sitting on my bed, staring out the window at a distant mountain peak. "I'll get them, Todd, I promise you," I vowed silently.

I dried my tears and went down to the kitchen. Mickens was eating breakfast. He nodded at me.

"Can I go back to New York now?" I asked as I poured some coffee. Jack and his sister had left the room when I entered. Pre-arranged by Mickens, I thought.

"Will you come back if it's necessary?"

"Of course."

"I guess nothing would be gained by keeping you here. Drive carefully."

I looked at him, wondering if that was a bit of male sarcasm or genuine concern.

I turned the car in at the Hertz office at LaGuardia airport and took a cab home. Glancing at the clock, I couldn't believe it was already early evening. Where had the day gone?

I showered and dropped into bed and oblivion.

Sunday, I got up long enough to eat a couple times and to thumb listlessly through the Sunday *Times*. No mention of Todd's murder.

I tried to reach his mother but she was somewhere in Europe.

I sipped a glass of red wine while I watched the Sunday news. Still nothing about the tragedy in the Catskills.

"The cover-up has begun," I muttered as I crawled back into bed.

4

Monday Morning

A nightmare woke me up. Ice and blood, blood and ice.

I sat up in my own bed, looked around the room, realizing the nightmare was based in fact—I had found Todd's battered body the Saturday before.

Monday mornings aren't that great usually, but this one promised to be a real downer. I stumbled into the kitchen where I poured myself a cup of the pre-programmed coffee and leaned against the counter reviewing all the things I had to do today and not feeling like even starting. I just wanted to go back to bed, pull the covers over my head and stay there until spring.

Sighing, I refilled the coffee cup. Abby, old girl, time to go to work.

I walked into my office where Chris, impeccably dressed as usual in a three-piece blue suit, was already at his desk. I kidded him about dressing so formally in my informal office where hardly anyone ever visited and I slouched around in casual clothes. I was glad I had let my lawyer, Maria Palmieri, Chris's wife, talk me into hiring him a few months ago when my original secretary had retired. He was not only handsome, he was a terrific secretary.

He smiled at me. "How was the romantic weekend?"

"Oh. Chris," I wailed, "You—don't know . . ."

"Know what?"

"Todd's dead—murdered—at the inn—Saturday morning."

"You're kidding!" he blurted. Looking at my face, he said, "You're not kidding. How terrible for you. I'm so sorry—what can I do?"

Taking a deep breath, I restrained my emotions while I described the weekend.

"I called his mother last night in Boston, but her maid said she's in London. She was going to have the Mason attorney contact his mother. As soon as arrangements are made, I'll be flying to Boston for the—the funeral." I sat down behind my desk. "I'm sure we'll be getting a visit from some kind of Federal agent soon."

Chris frowned. "You could be getting an unwanted visitor, too, if the murderer thinks you know whatever Todd wanted to tell you." He shook his head in exasperation. "Only you could go off for a romantic weekend, get run off the road by a truck, have your friend murdered, and then become a target yourself. Working for you is never dull."

"And to think, you could have gone into investment banking," I retorted. "That reminds me, we have to do something about Jackie, I don't want a repeat of that January situation."

My nineteen-year-old daughter, a student at Stanford, hadn't lived with me since she was ten, choosing to stay with her father after our divorce. I had supported both of them until she and I had straightened out our relationship at New Year's after she was returned after being held hostage to insure I investigated the murders of a general and his wife. She told me her father had convinced her that I didn't want her. I suspected he wanted my financial support more than he wanted to be a father to Jackie.

Chris interrupted my thoughts. "Do you want to tell her there might be a problem?"

I smiled. "You know how stubborn Jackie is."

"Yup, like her mother. I'll just hire someone to discreetly keep an eye on her."

"That sounds good. Let's make sure all the security devices are working here."

Chris checked the television cameras that scanned the alley and street outside the factory building. He deactivated the freight elevator so it couldn't be started from downstairs. Then, he programmed the sensor security system that covered every room.

"How about your bedroom access to the factory below?" he asked.

"I'll check it." In my bedroom I pressed the button that activated the bookcase and revealed a stairway going down to the factory. I set the alarm system for my room and returned to the office. "Okay, we're in business. Impregnable as Fort Knox."

"Do you want me to cancel your appointments today?" Chris asked.

"What's on the agenda?"

He flipped through the book. "The only important one is a meeting with your new client, Caledonia Trucking Company. Three o'clock."

"Refresh my memory, I'm drawing a blank."

"Noreen Caledonia, the company president, called a week ago. She and her brother inherited the company from their father, Russell Caledonia, Sr., who was killed in an auto accident a year ago. They have a chance for a very lucrative government contract for hauling nuclear waste." He stopped reading and looked at me. "Didn't your friend's agency have something to do with this type of thing?"

"I'm not sure exactly what." I slapped my forehead. "Oh my God, Todd's letter! I forgot to read it. Be right back."

I rummaged through my jacket pockets. Nothing. Damn, where'd I put it? I'd been exhausted when I'd arrived home, mentally and emotionally depleted; unable to cope with reading Todd's letter, I had put it away, but where? Let's see, I mused—I had taken my jacket off in the kitchen, took the letter out and stuck it in the junk drawer next to the sink. Ah, Abby . . . how can you organize other peoples' lives when you're so disorganized in your own? Simple, I replied. I get paid well to organize theirs.

I retrieved the letter.

I read: Dearest Abby, If you're reading this, something has happened to me. Sounds like a line from those bad movies your Ex used to make doesn't it? For the past two years I've worked for a little-known government agency that tracks nuclear materials. As you may or may not know, some forms of nuclear waste can be reused to make weapons and for some time now, small amounts have been disappearing. I think I've found out how and why. If anything happens to me ask my mother for the key I left you. That's strange, someone just drove in. I'll finish this later.

Tears oozed from my eyes. "Oh, Todd," I whispered, "later never came." I dabbed cold water on my eyes before I returned to the office.

"Anything in the letter?" Chris asked.

I shook my head. "What did you say Caledonia was trucking?"

"They're after a nuclear waste contract from the government."

I chewed my lip. "I thought that was what you said. Todd was working for an agency that tracked this stuff." I fiddled with the silver letter opener. "I don't believe in coincidence," I muttered.

"Chris, I'm beginning to get a bad feeling about this. First, this company calls me for help, then Todd arranges a rendezvous; I almost get killed by a truck and Todd is murdered." I stood up and stretched. "I think I'll keep that appointment, Chris. Where's the office?"

"Near Kennedy Airport—not a very safe area."

I grinned. "What'd you expect—a trucking company in Forest Hills?" I glanced at the clock. Almost noon. Where does the time go, I wondered; the older I get, the faster the hours fly. "Get me Dr. Farris and Investigator Mickens—the doctor first."

The doctor, sneezing and coughing,, came on the line. "Excuse me, I caught this dreadful cold Saturday," he said in an accusing voice like it was my fault.

"You should dress warmly instead of being so macho," I said sweetly. "Have you finished the autopsy on Todd Mason?"

"Yes." He sneezed. I waited. He coughed.

"Well," I prompted, "what killed him?"

"You'll have to ask Investigator Mickens; he's the only one authorized to give out information."

I glanced at Chris who was listening and recording the conversation. He raised an eyebrow.

"Dr. Farris, have you had some important visitors lately?" I asked. "From Washington?"

"Maybe." He coughed. "I can't talk to you." He hung up the phone.

"Replay that." Chris hit the play button. I frowned. "What do you think? Does he sound funny? Scared? Nervous?"

"He sounds like he has a bad cold." Chris reran the last line. "He sounds scared. What now?"

"Let's see if Investigator Mickens is scared, too." I fidgeted with the letter opener while Chris tracked him down. He nodded at me to pick up the phone.

"Investigator Mickens, Abby Doyle. Do you have the autopsy report on Todd Mason yet? What killed him?"

"I don't have it yet," he lied smoothly.

I glanced at Chris. "To save a lot of time tapdancing, I just talked to Dr. Farris who said you were the only one who could release it so that indicates you do have it."

He cleared his throat. "I can't give out any information to unauthorized persons."

"Have you had little visitors from Washington?" I asked, my voice dripping with sarcasm.

"Drop it, lady!" he said harshly and slammed the phone down.

"You hit a nerve," Chris said as he rubbed his ear. "That guy has a short fuse."

I swiveled around in my chair and stared at the Graham black and white etching of the Bayanna, a disreputable old coal belcher that used to ply the St. Lawrence Seaway before it sunk in the Thousand Islands area. My favorite ship. A very dear friend, Nina Dumas, had given the drawing to me to remind me of our younger days when we used to watch the ships on the Seaway and dream of someday sailing around the world on a freighter.

I sighed for that lost innocence: Nina had ended up in a nursing home, severely crippled by rheumatoid arthritis and I was too busy to take a slow boat anywhere.

"Wonder when we'll get a visit from Washington?" I muttered.

5

Monday Afternoon

I took a taxi to South Ozone Park near the west end of Kennedy Airport. The driver, who didn't speak anything remotely resembling English, made several false turns before he finally located the front gate of Caledonia Trucking Company where we were stopped by a uniformed guard.

The guard looked in the window at me. "Got an appointment?"

"Yes. Abigail Doyle to see Ms. Caledonia."

He studied the clipboard hanging on the wall of his booth, lip-reading down the list. "Okay, got it." He picked up the phone and muttered a few words into it. "Someone'll be down to get you in a minute."

I paid off the taxi. "How come all the security?" I asked.

"Thieves." His tone didn't encourage conversation.

I looked around. From the gate I could see a solid wall of trailers lined at loading docks. The warehouse was a large two-story building. At one corner a tower-like structure rose four stories, resembling an airport control tower. The windows were tinted.

The whole area appeared to be surrounded by a chain-link fence topped with ribbon wire. Occasionally, I glimpsed other uniformed people ducking between trailers. A few were leading guard dogs.

The large front gates were electronically operated. The place looked like a prison for trucks. I wondered if all truckyards were this heavily guarded. I recalled seeing some yards off I-95 on trips south and as I recalled, they were in large open areas. Ah, but this is New York, after all, where you double-chain your bicycle and remove its wheels.

The ear-splitting whine of jets taking off and landing at Kennedy almost drove me to my knees. The guard, oblivious to the racket, was staring in the direction of the warehouse.

"Don't these things drive you crazy?" I asked in a lull between planes. He ignored me. I tapped him on the shoulder. "The planes—don't they drive you crazy?"

He turned to look at me. "What?"

I repeated the question, watching his eyes closely. He was lip-reading.

He grimaced. "I already lost most of my hearing. I turn my hearing aid down unless I'm talking to someone." He touched the button in his ear. Glancing skyward, he said, "Wasn't them that did it. Big guns in Nam." He glanced towards the warehouse. "Here she comes."

"Who?" I watched a red golf cart with a jaunty yellow flag wagging from the rear fender race towards us.

"Izzy's a mute, but she hears real good. She'll take you to the office." Answering the question in my eyes, he added, "Caledonia is big on hiring the handicapped whenever they can, wherever they won't be a safety hazard. Izzy runs all the errands on-site in her cart. When you're ready to leave, have someone call me and I'll get you a cab."

"Thanks, Mr.?"

"Page—just call me Page. Everyone does."

Izzy skidded to a halt on the other side of the gate while Page pressed a button, opening the gate enough for me to walk through.

A big grin split Izzy's homely face as she pointed to the passenger seat. I couldn't help staring at her; pink hair stood up in spikes while her innocent blue eyes were lined in purple eye shadow and her lips were covered with matching lipstick. She must have weighed two hundred pounds. Here I was, shivering from the cold, and she was only wearing a pull-over sweater, blue jeans, and sneakers.

"Aren't you cold?" I asked.

She grinned and shook her head as she pinched a roll of fat, indicating it kept her warm. With her left hand she gripped the side bar and motioned me to hang on as she spun the cart around and accelerated towards the tower. I clung to the rail, fearing for my life as Izzy darted around trucks. She skidded to a halt, throwing me forward.

Shakily, I stepped out and checked to make sure all my bones were intact. "Thanks for the ride, Izzy. You should provide seat belts."

Flipping a wave and an impish grin at me, she zipped away. I turned to read the sign on the door—Ring Bell For Entrance. I did and pushed the door open when a buzzer sounded.

I entered a small alcove and peered through thick glass at another guard station where one guard monitored a bank of television screens while his partner talked on the phone. The one on the phone signaled patience. I smiled nervously as I pondered all the security I had already encountered. I wondered why. It seemed like overkill even for a metropolitan area.

The guard hung up the phone and spoke into a microphone. "Are you Mrs. Doyle?" I nodded. "Someone'll be down to get you in a few minutes."

Five minutes later, a door opened and a short, dark woman, dressed in a black long-sleeved tailored dress, entered the room, extended her hand and said, "I'm Noreen Caledonia."

We shook hands as we sized each other up. She was plump, but attractive except for the worried black eyes and the tension lines around her lips. She appeared to be in her mid-thirties. A woman who doesn't laugh much, I mused, a woman with serious problems.

"Elevators are this way," she said, breaking the silence and leading me into a bare hall.

Her office surprised me since I was expecting a high tech look. It was more like a room in someone's home. The room on the top floor of the tower had large windows looking out on a panoramic view of Kennedy, Jamaica Bay, part of Queens and in the far distance, the twin towers of the World Trade Center. Looking down, I had a terrific overview of the truck yard.

A large couch slipcovered in a tulip motif dominated one area. The coffee table in front of it contained an array of magazines ranging from Trucker's World to Forbes. Two wing chairs, covered in a solid green material, faced the couch. The area was almost like a garden with potted trees and plants on small tables scattered around the room. In front of the window a large oak desk was covered with papers and folders. Family pictures stood on the tables along side the plants. Hanging on one wall was a large reproduction of an old photograph. A burly, black-haired man, dressed in work clothes of an earlier age, stood proudly beside an old truck. The family resemblance was strong, especially in the eyes.

She motioned me to the couch while she sat on one of the chairs, facing me. We studied each other; I waited for her to break the silence.

"What do you know about trucks?"

"Not much," I confessed. "My father drove a logging truck in the

Adirondacks when I was a kid; he used to let me go with him on Saturdays." I smiled. "I thought it was wonderful being above everybody on the road—a sense of power."

"That's how I felt the first time my father took me out in his truck." She glanced at the picture on the wall. "He started out with that beat-up Mack tractor and built it into this." She stood up and indicated the yard out the window.

I watched her as she paced around the room, her shoulder length black hair swinging, her black eyes snapping fire as she thought about something; she seemed to have forgotten my presence.

"What exactly do you want me to do?" I asked.

She stopped pacing and leaned against her desk. "Let me give you some background. My father, Russell, was killed last year when he drove off a foggy mountain road in the Catskills. He left the company to my brother, Russell, Jr., and me. The board elected me president." She smiled wryly. "Russ doesn't appreciate that much, but he's just not as good a businessperson as I am. I do business with Erickson Chemical factory; Al March said you really streamlined his operation and allowed him to be more competitive."

I smiled. "I remember that job—I can still smell those chemicals."

"I want a more efficient way of tracking our trucks from pick up to disposal points and a more effective method of utilizing the trucks and improved dispatching. I want our operation to be as efficient and profitable as it possibly can be or I'm going to lose the business. I've just gotten a lucrative contract from the government and if things don't improve around here, I'm going to lose that contract before we even get started." She stared out the window. "I can't afford to lose that contract," she said in an intense tone.

I went into a trance. I had never done a trucking company. Interesting. Challenging. But something told me this wasn't my kind of job; maybe, I should pass it up. I stood up and walked to the window where I stared at the activity below. Trucks coming and going, men running around, the flash of Izzy's cart.

Noreen startled me when she asked impatiently, "Well, can you help me?"

I started to say no, but I was stopped by the pleading look in her eyes. I shrugged. "You'll have to tell all your employees to answer freely and honestly all my questions and you'll have to give me full access to your files and your facilities."

I frowned. "I'll tell you the truth—I've never done a trucking company, but I think I can handle it. What's the government contract for?"

"Removing radium from a Queens factory, part of the Superfund cleanup, controlled by the Army and they're very strict. But that doesn't concern you; I just want you to streamline our operations."

I smiled. "Let's get one thing straight, Ms. Caledonia, when I take a job, everything concerns me. If that disturbs you, we'll just say nice meeting you and good-bye right now."

She frowned at me.

I held out my hand. "Look, why don't you think it over and call my office tomorrow. I couldn't start for a few days anyway; I have a personal matter to take care of."

When I climbed into the cab outside the gate, I looked back for what I thought would probably be my last glimpse of Caledonia Trucking.

6

Late Monday Afternoon

Chris met me at the elevator door, wearing a pained expression as he took my briefcase and coat. "You have a visitor," he said with a nod towards the living room.

"F.B.I.?"

"Worse." He rolled his eyes.

"Give me a clue, Chris; I'm in no mood to play games."

"I'm sorry. She says she's Mrs. Electra Mason. Todd's mother."

"Oh God, Electra here!" I chewed my lip as I recalled my two brief encounters with her many years ago. Obscenely rich, she didn't let anyone forget it as she bulldozed her way through life. Todd had always regarded her with wry amusement from a distance, shrugging off her escapades with "that's Electra—she's a law unto herself."

"Let's just sneak into the office a minute. I need a drink."

Chris poured me a glass of red wine before he asked, "How'd it go at Caledonia?"

I shook my head. "I'm not sure we're taking the job. Noreen Caledonia and I don't exactly agree on how to do the assignment. She's in some kind of trouble, but I don't know if it has anything to do with the trucking company—she mentioned a government contract for a Superfund clean-up." I swallowed some wine. "Call somebody in the Environmental Protection Agency here, see if anything is doing in New York. I'd like some more information before I make a decision about Caledonia. What's new here?"

"I set up the protection for Jackie; she'll have very discreet twenty-four hour guards—all women. I don't think she'll even spot them."

"Dreamer. She's sharp, takes after her old mom," I said proudly. My California golden girl was showing signs of having my brains to go with father's blond good looks. "No little visitors?" I smiled. "I really thought the Feds would be here by now."

"Maybe they don't think you're important."

"Good. Let them labor under that little delusion for several days." I drained the wine glass. "Well, now or never. If you hear any screaming, don't pay any attention. Electra has a tendency to talk louder when she doesn't get her way."

Electra Mason didn't hear me enter the living room. Slender, short with an erect posture, she was standing at the window, staring at Manhattan shimmering in the setting sun. Her hands were folded behind her back. She was perfectly still except for the fidgeting of her intertwined fingers.

I cleared my throat. "Mrs. Mason, I'm sorry we have to meet again under these circumstances. I can't tell you how . . ." I stopped. She had turned to look at me. Rage burned in her intense blue eyes.

"I don't care how sorry you are. What are you going to do about Todd's death? I want his murderer found and executed."

"Excuse me?"

"Don't give me that innocent look, young lady, I know who you are— what you do. I know that Todd thought you could help him. So—what do you do but let someone kill him right under your nose." She stepped towards me and shook her finger at me. "I don't care how much money it takes, you find his murderer. If you won't or can't take care of him, I will. All I need is his name."

I felt like I was facing an old Mafia don. Vengeance emanated from her body. I wouldn't want her for an enemy, I thought, as I studied her, trying to get a handle on this new Electra. The few times I had met her she was always coming or going from some chic fun spot, a widow restlessly seeking excitement.

"Please sit down. Let's discuss this," I said, indicating the couch. "May I get you something to drink?"

"Scotch on the rocks. And don't try to placate me or humor me." She sighed. "If you two had married in the first place, Todd would probably be governor of California and still alive. He never got over you and bachelors never get elected governor."

I smiled. "You forgot Jerry Brown."

"Deliberately," she snapped. "Now, get me that drink."

I detoured to the office.

"How's it going?" Chris asked.

"Whew, this is not the giddy Electra I remember. She wants blood. Activate the recorder in the living room. I have a feeling she has some information for us."

I placed a tray with a bucket of ice cubes, a glass, and a bottle of vintage Glenmorangie Scotch on a table in front of her. She filled the glass, knocked it back and poured another one.

Following a couple sips, she said, "Good. Now, let's talk business. What was Todd doing up in the Catskills? Why were you there? What happened? I can't seem to get much information out of those hillbillies up there."

I smiled, picturing the reactions of Farris and Mickens if they could hear themselves called hillbillies. Maybe the best revenge would be to turn Electra loose on them.

"Todd called and told me he'd arranged this weekend in memory of old times. I guess Valentine's Day coming up had put him in a romantic mood." I blushed. "Or at least that's what I thought at the time." I told her about my accident, the subsequent events, and finally the details about Todd's death. "And when I returned to his room, his briefcase and the papers were missing, I don't know what he wanted to discuss with me. Do yon?"

Electra was on her third Scotch. She was like a balloon with a slow leak as the anger seeped out, deflating her intensity. Her eyes were tired and misty. Her shoulders slumped.

Turning the glass around and around in her fingers, she stared into it. "Todd had been acting strangely for the past year."

She sighed. "He visited me in Boston a few months ago; he was tired, discouraged and frightened. Asked me if he could stay in the New York apartment for a while."

"You have an apartment here?" I interrupted.

She glanced at the window. "Why yes, you can probably see it from here—48th and First Avenue. United Nations Plaza. Anyway, Todd said he had business in New York and would be spending most of his time here." She frowned at me. "I assumed part of that business was you. He talked about you all the time." She glared at me. "You were meant for each other, but you couldn't see it."

I sighed. "If he had lived, it might have worked out this time. We were both too ambitious, I guess." If Todd had been in New York all this time, why hadn't he contacted me? Why did he let me think he was still living in California? Who did he work for? What had scared him? Questions and more questions. Never any answers. I suppressed my hurt that he had been just across the river and not called me; he must have had a good reason.

"Have you been to the apartment since you returned?" I asked.

She shook her head. "I came straight here from the airport."

"You'd better stay here; I don't think you should go to the apartment."

"No, I don't want to put you out. I'll just go to the Waldorf." She looked at me curiously. "Why don't you think I should go to the apartment?"

"It might be dangerous. Todd had something that somebody wanted desperately. They killed him for it, but I don't think they got it. Just a minute." Retrieving the note from my safe, I returned to the living room and read it to her.

She frowned. "He didn't give me a key—unless he left it in the apartment. There's a safe behind his grandfather's portrait in the den. Sometimes, we left notes or gifts for each other there. He would know that I would check there first."

"Good. Do you have an apartment key with you?"

She rummaged through her purse. "Here it is." She handed it to me. "Be careful, Abby. I'm sorry I yelled at you. I know it really wasn't your fault. Todd was always a headstrong man, like his father, bless both their souls. But I won't rest until I have his killer."

I patted her hand. "I'm always careful. Now, this is what I'd like you to do. First, do nothing about a funeral for Todd." I closed my eyes and choked back tears. Just saying the word "funeral" made his death too real.

"Could you return to London or wherever you were without letting anyone know where you are? You could be in danger if they believe you know anything about Todd's business."

"Won't it look a little bizarre if I go gadding around Europe with my son—my only son—just barely—dead?"

"Do you really care what people think about you if it helps to bring Todd's killers to justice, and incidentally, keeps you safe at the same time?"

"No, I guess not." She patted her eyes with a handkerchief. "Sometimes, I'm just a foolish old woman."

I smiled. "Somehow I doubt that." I stood up. "My secretary lives in Manhattan; I'll have him drive you to your hotel. I'll be right back."

Chris was just turning off the recorder. "I heard you. What do I use for wheels?"

"Oh damn, I forgot I totaled another one of Lefty's specials."

"Lefty didn't forget. He phoned in his bill today. He also suggested in profane language that you might consider going to driver-ed school or buying a tank. I'll call a taxi and accompany her to the hotel to make sure she's safely settled in."

"Chris, you're a gem. What would I do without you?"

"Remember that the next time you threaten to replace me with a machine." He gave me a worried glance. "By the way, do I gather from the tone of your voice when you heard about that apartment that you're going prowling tonight?"

I gave him my shark grin. "The cat's on the prowl again. I need to know what he wanted to tell me. Hopefully, they—whoever they are—don't know about the apartment."

Chris shook his head. "Did you ever consider just asking the police for help?"

I smiled. "They're so stuffy about the rules. Remember Standish and how uptight she got whenever we bent one of their silly little police rules."

Chris nodded. "But—I also remember that Detective Standish saved your life."

"True," I conceded. "If I need her, I'll call her. Not that she's looking forward to my calls."

Returning to the living room, I explained the arrangements to Electra. "And give Chris information on where I can contact you, but don't tell anybody else where you'll be—not even your servants."

7

Monday Evening

I dressed in what Chris called my cat burglar outfit—black slacks, a black turtleneck and a black windbreaker. I put on the gold chain which held a sheathed stiletto that hung down my back in easy hand's reach. In case of emergencies, I preferred the knife, a throwback to my Iroquois heritage, I supposed. A knife was silent and easily concealed; I wasn't that fond of guns although I sometimes carried a thirty-eight.

I checked the outside television scanners. No activity on the street. I activated the alarm system and took the elevator down to the street.

"Geez, it's cold," I muttered, shivering from the first blast of frigid air. I jogged to the subway station where I caught the Flushing 7 line to Manhattan. Leaving Grand Central station, I walked east to First Avenue and then north.

Limos whooshed by me, carrying diplomats to and from the United Nations complex on the East River. I glanced across the river, easily spotting my building since I had left my apartment lights on.

I stood on the corner of 48th Street and First Avenue and studied the apartment building. The brown triangular building was built in a step-back style, giving each apartment a better view. A small park fronted it on First Avenue. At the west end of the building on 48th Street there was an entrance to a Kinney parking garage. Almost across the street from the apartment was a stationary police post, probably guarding some diplomatic building.

I entered the lobby, glanced around and spotted the simple security system. Guess people feel safe in this area with all the police assigned to guard the diplomatic residences.

After I handed the note to the doorman, he said, "Mr. Mason isn't home yet. He went away for the weekend. Is Mrs. Mason going to be using the apartment?" He eyed my outfit without comment; New Yorkers pride themselves on not showing surprise no matter how bizarre an outfit might be.

I smiled. "No, she's going to California or somewhere.

You know her—always on the go. I just have to pick up a couple things for her." At the elevator I turned and asked, "By the way, anybody else been here in the past couple days?"

"Not on my shift."

I stepped off on the fiftieth floor and looked around.

Two doors. One designated A and one B. Electra had told me to use the one with the A. The Mason apartment was a wraparound corner one looking east and south.

I found what was obviously Todd's bedroom. From his window I could look across the East River and pick out the smokestacks on the factory building where I lived. We were so close, I thought, why didn't he contact me before and why the charade that he was still living in California? I suppressed my hurt feelings and turned to look around the room.

Typical of Todd, I thought, smiling at the mess. Clothes wherever he dropped them, papers scattered on the nightstands, money and papers an the dresser-top. I had always wondered how someone with such a meticulous mind could be such a slob.

"Well, Todd, if anybody has searched this place, it would be difficult to tell," I muttered, staring at the ceiling as if he was really there. Maybe he was—in spirit.

I riffled through the papers. They were mostly copies of newspaper and magazine articles about Superfund clean-ups. I shrugged. Probably something he had been researching. I rummaged through the dresser drawers, finding the usual things, underwear, socks and shirts. My fingers touched a box underneath the shirts. I pulled it out.

"What's this, old girl?" I shook the sealed box. The printing said it was a Glock 9mm pistol. I wondered if Todd carried a gun—had carried a gun; I had to remind myself he was gone. I stuck the box back under the shirts.

I wandered through the apartment until I found the den. I pulled the drapes open and stared at the view of Manhattan looking south. I picked out the Chrysler and Empire State buildings, the Brooklyn, Williamsburgh and Manhattan bridges. I was a sucker for scenic views.

Sighing, I forced myself to get down to business. I sat at the desk where I inspected the contents of each desk drawer, finding nothing of interest.

I glanced at the wall across from the desk where a bearded gentleman with Todd's eyes stared at me, wondering why I was being so impolite, pawing through other people's possessions.

"You must be Grandfather Mason. So nice to meet you. Hope you've protected that safe." I giggled. Whoa, Abby old girl, you're getting slaphappy. Tired, I felt so tired. I stared at the portrait, almost fearful of what I'd find in that safe, and half afraid that I'd find nothing.

I didn't realize the apartment door had opened until I heard a voice call, "Todd, darling, you're back at last."

Rapid footsteps approached the den's door. "Darling, why didn't you call—who in hell are you?"

We stared at each other. It was like looking at a thirty-year-old version of myself. Dark curly hair, a little shorter than me, she was wearing a black skirt and jacket. And she had called Todd "darling".

"I'm Abby Doyle, a friend of Todd's. Who are you?"

"Marti Carr—Todd's— fiancée. What're you doing here? Where's Todd? He was supposed to meet me after work."

I smiled wryly as I remembered my anticipation of a romantic weekend. At least this explained why Todd hadn't told me he was living across the river from me.

Obviously she didn't know about Todd's death.

"Why don't you sit down." I indicated the chair across the desk from me. She perched nervously on the edge of the chair. I sighed. "I have some bad news for you." How in hell do I do this, I wondered.

Her eyes grew larger. "Todd," she whispered. "Something has happened to him. I know it. I begged him not to go to California this weekend."

So he lied to her, too, I thought.

"Ms. Carr, there's no easy way to do this; I'm sorry, but Todd was killed this weekend."

She stared at me in disbelief. "No, no, no," she whispered, shaking her head from side to side. "How? Where?"

"He was murdered in the Catskills."

"The Catskills!" She leaped up and backed away from me. "Who are you? What did you have to do with Todd? He never mentioned you. Who killed him? Why?" The questions tumbled out as she stared wildly at me.

I darted around the desk and clasped her shoulder. "Calm down. I'm a detective. Todd met me there to ask me for help. Do you know what he was working on?"

"No, no—I don't know you—I've got to get out of here." She shrugged my hand off her shoulder and bolted out the door before I could react. The apartment door slammed.

I wondered if I should try to catch her, but there was nothing I could do for her and I had more important things to do like open that safe. Using the combination Electra had given me, I opened the safe and found a stack of money, a jewelry box, two envelopes marked WILL—one for Electra and one for Todd—a small locked strongbox, and finally an envelope with my name on it.

I ripped it open and a key fell out. No note, just a key. Thanks Todd, I thought, for leaving me a clue. What in hell does this thing fit? I turned it over and over in my hand. It looked old. I stuffed everything except Todd's will and the key back into the safe. I put his Will in my pocket. Just before I closed the safe, I pulled the little strongbox out. I shook it. I tried the key. No luck. I carried the box to the kitchen where I searched until I found a small hammer and an ice pick. I jimmied the box open.

"Well, well—what do we have here."

I separated the color photographs and lined them up on the counter. They gave me a queasy feeling in the pit of my stomach as I looked at them. They showed various obscene poses of a naked, middle-aged white man with two blacks—one male and one female. I flipped one photo over. A date, November 10th and the initial B was written in an unfamiliar hand. At least it wasn't Todd's writing, but I wondered what he had been doing with these snaps and who the white man was. Typical of our culture, I thought wryly, assuming the white guy was the important one.

I pulled one of Todd's favorite beers, a Pilsener Urquell out of the refrigerator, and stood there drinking it and sort of looking at the photos out of the corner of my eye while I wondered what they meant.

I rubbed the bottle on my forehead. The coldness felt good.

"You weren't a blackmailer. were you, Todd? Were you protecting somebody? Who is this guy?" I sighed, drained the beer and gathered up the pictures. "I'd better take these with me. Wouldn't want Electra to find them," I mumbled.

I returned the strongbox to the safe and locked it up and replaced the painting. After a cursory search of the rest of the apartment, I decided to quit for the night; I was tired and my mind just wasn't working. I was spinning my wheels, dismayed at finding those photos and upset at finding out Todd had a fiancée. Home and bed called.

Flashing red lights caught my eye as I stepped off the elevator. The doorman, standing just inside the door, was staring at the activity on the street outside. I tapped him on the shoulder.

"What's going on?" I asked.

The street was filled with police cars, an ambulance, and uniformed cops who were pushing spectators back behind a police tape.

"Terrible, terrible thing," he muttered, shaking his head. "Somebody shot Mr. Mason's friend—just shot her down like a dog."

"What?"

"His friend—didn't you talk to her? She went up to the apartment before I could tell her you were there; she seemed awfully upset when she came down. Just ran right by me." His voice speeded up as he pointed, "And right out there in front, I saw a man approach her. She screamed and then I heard a shot and saw her fall. The man ran to the middle of the street where a car with no lights picked him up. The cop ran out of the booth to her and I called nine-one-one."

I didn't want to talk to the police. "Is there another way out of here?"

"Through the parking garage—comes out just up the street towards Second Avenue on 49th Street."

I slipped a twenty into his hand. "I'd appreciate it if you'd forget I was here. You know how Mrs. Mason hates publicity."

"Sure thing. Anything for Mrs. Mason."

I exited the garage onto 49th Street and went up to Second Avenue. I trotted back down to 48th Street and looked down the block. I could just see a black bundle on the street between the officers' feet.

That could have been me, I thought. Was it meant to be me? I tore myself away and headed for the subway entrance at 53rd and Third Avenue.

8

Late Monday Night – Early Tuesday Morning

After I showered, poured myself a glass of red wine and turned on the television, I stretched out on my bed to watch the late news.

A distressed-looking reporter said, "ABC newswriter, Marti Carr was shot to death earlier this evening in what police theorize was a street robbery that went wrong. An eyewitness said a white middle-aged male accosted Carr near the First Avenue end of 48th Street, said something to her, she screamed and he apparently panicked and shot her. The gunman ran to the corner where he was picked up by a car with no lights on. ABC is offering a $10,000 reward for any information leading to the arrest and conviction of the killer." He looked into the camera with tears in his eyes. "We'll miss you, Marti."

I'd like to believe it was a street robbery, but I suspected a newswriter working in this city would be streetwise enough to smile and hand over all her valuables. But I suppose she could have enemies, that her death had nothing to do with Todd's, that she was killed by mistake—and I believe in the Tooth Fairy.

"They meant to kill me," I muttered. "No doubt about it—she looked like me, dressed in black, coming out of that building. Did they follow me there or did they assume I'd go there sooner or later and they were waiting."

Letting my mind run on its own, I sipped the wine and stared unseeingly at the screen until the picture that penetrated my conscious mind electrified me. On the screen an Emergency Services crew and firemen were desperately working around a shattered tractor trailer. I turned up the volume.

The voice over was saying, "A truck driver and four auto passengers died in a bizarre accident earlier this evening on the Brooklyn-Queens Expressway when the truck drove off an overpass and landed on a car below. No names have been released yet."

I didn't need names; I could read the name on the cab of the truck—Caledonia Trucking, Inc.

The camera panned the accident scene showing the twisted rig and a score of officers prying frantically at a dark spot underneath the trailer. I finally figured out that spot was what was left of the car.

A man wearing a ragged overcoat and swigging from a bag-covered bottle stood off to the side watching intently. Idly, I wondered where he had come from and what he was doing at the scene. "You're making a mountain out of a molehill, old girl," I muttered. "Derelicts are thicker than roaches in New York."

I zapped the screen and closed my eyes. I wondered if Noreen Caledonia would call. Probably not. We hadn't hit it off that well and she would probably be pre-occupied by this accident.

I jumped out of bed. "Damn," I muttered. Wondering about Noreen's call had reminded me that I hadn't checked my phone messages when I had returned. Stumbling into the office, I snapped on the light and glanced at the phone. The message light glowed red; I punched the play button.

Wincing, I listened to Electra's shrill voice. "Did you find anything in the apartment? Some woman was killed out front. Call me." Her imperious voice added her room number.

The other call surprised me—Noreen Caledonia asking me to take the job and call her in the morning. Her voice sounded weary as she promised complete cooperation. I wondered if the truck accident had motivated her to hire me. Chewing my lip and staring at the phone, I still wasn't sure I wanted the Caledonia assignment; it didn't feel right to me. Oh well, I sighed, I'll discuss it with Chris tomorrow.

Slumping in my chair, I returned Electra's call. Without even waiting for me to say anything, Electra charged, "I've been waiting for your call. Did you find anything? What happened to that woman? Who killed her? Did it have anything to do with Todd's murder? What have you been doing? Why didn't you call?"

"Whoa," I yelled. "Take a deep breath and listen. Your apartment was a mess, but just the usual kind Todd made. I found a key, miscellaneous jewels and your wills in the safe. I have Todd's Will here in case you need it and they seal up the apartment." I took a deep breath. "Now, while I was there, a woman came in—the young woman who was shot outside—and said she was Todd's fiancée. Why didn't you tell me about her?"

"Fiancée? I don't understand. Todd never mentioned being engaged. He saw her once in awhile when he was in New York."

"Did you ever meet her?"

"I talked to her on the phone once when I called the apartment. She said she was waiting for Todd. I really felt they had some business together more than a romantic relationship." She paused. Her voice was puzzled when she asked, "Why would he talk about you all the time if he was engaged to her? It doesn't make sense, Abby."

I stared at the wall. "No . . . no, it doesn't. But why would she lie to me? And she was obviously upset at finding me in the apartment." You need to find out more about Marti Carr, I told myself. "When are you leaving?"

She sighed. "I'm flying to London tomorrow. Will you keep in touch?"

"Of course . . . and Electra, don't take any chances. Let me know if anything strange happens or anybody you don't know tries to contact you."

"I still want to retain you," she said, the old authority returning to her voice.

"Not this time, Electra. This one's on me . . . I want Todd's killer as badly as you do."

❧

Propping my feet up on my desk, I wondered how I could find out more about the mysterious Ms. Carr. I needed information from the police, but they were never too willing to share with outsiders. Now, who did I know inside? Standish, Margaret Standish, NYPD detective who had once tried to arrest me for the murder of a general and ended up saving my life. We had a friendly antagonistic relationship. She had a temper that went with her red hair, but she was intelligent and fair-minded—most of the time. I glanced at the clock—should I or shouldn't I? What the hell, she would only yell at me whether she was asleep or not.

As the phone rang and rang, I pictured Standish dragging all of her six feet four inches out of bed.

"Hello."

She sounded grumpy.

"Hey, Standish, how we doing? Abby Doyle here."

"Doyle, do you know what time it is?" she growled.

"Early."

"No . . . late. What in hell do you want?"

"See tonight's news?"

"No."

"An ABC newswriter, Marti Carr, was murdered and I'd like her address."

"So you can send her a condolence card, no doubt. Doyle, I thought we had an agreement—you wouldn't call me, I'd call you."

I pondered that. "But Standish, you haven't called," I said, letting a plaintive tone creep into my voice. "And we did make you a member of our environmental group."

"Honorary and I'm too busy trying to save New Yorkers to worry about some whale in South America."

"Forget the whales, Standish. I only need an address and you can call the seventeenth precinct and get it for me . . . please."

"If I do this, will you promise not to bother me for at least ten years?"

I smiled. I knew deep down Standish liked me or at least I thought she did. "Okay, okay, you got a deal. Call me right back."

Standish rang back in ten minutes and gave me an address in Greenwich Village. "What's the profit in a simple street mugging that went sour, Doyle? No big bucks here."

Standish resented my ability to command large fees to solve crimes that she had to investigate for nothing. Besides, she didn't think amateurs should interfere in police business.

"I'm doing a favor for an old family friend who knew her. No case or anything like that. She just wanted Carr's last address. And what're friends for . . . eh, Standish?"

"I wouldn't know. I don't have any. Real cops don't have friends, we have acquaintances." She slammed the phone down.

"Ouch. Gee, Standish, why are you so sensitive," I muttered into the dead phone.

After I changed into my black outfit, I retrieved my .38 from the desk drawer and checked the television monitors. The neighborhood looked cold and deserted.

I slouched on a bench in the subway train, sharing its stifling heat with a half-dozen homeless people who eyed my cat burglar outfit warily as I grinned wolfishly at them, hoping they wouldn't bother me.

Marti Carr's neighborhood was in transition; dilapidated old buildings were being gutted and turned into expensive condos for those yuppies who believed the good times would forever roll. Her building was on a side street that was little more than an alley filled with mounds of garbage and heaps that looked suspiciously like live people. In cold weather the homeless crawled under and into almost everything except a bed at the city shelters, preferring the streets to the inhumanity of the bureaucracy.

Huddling in a doorway across the street from the building, I scanned its facade. Three stories high with the buildings on either side of it in various stages of renovation, this one stood out as a shining example of the final product. Its walls had been sandblasted to a clean beige. New windows and a fancy front door advertised expensive.

I ambled across the street, noting no lights were on except the bulb over the front door. M. Carr was on one of the mailboxes. Lived alone, I guessed. The lock on the entrance door looked sturdy, one of the better brands and a real deterrent to all but the most determined of burglars. Then I smiled.

"My, my, what's this? Go through all that trouble and expense to put in a great lock and then put a decorative glass panel in the door," I muttered as I glanced up and down the street before I smashed the glass with my gun butt and reached in to unlock the door.

Marti's apartment was on the first floor. Her lock was easy. Inching the door open, I called, "Anybody home?" An orange cat minced towards me and rubbed my ankles. I shoved it back inside as I closed the door. "You're an orphan, pal," I said as I picked it up.

I found the light switch. "My, my . . . you and Todd were made for each other," I muttered as I looked at the messy living room. I picked up a pillow and dropped it and the cat on the couch. Actually, the room looked more than messy; it looked more like it had been hastily tossed by someone.

Standing in the middle of the room, I slowly revolved, letting my eyes absorb and my brain catalog the contents. If she and Todd had really been engaged, why weren't there any photos of him? Her mantle was covered with framed photos.

I sat down at the desk in the corner and studied the top of it. A stack of unpaid bills under a glass paperweight that said PAY OR ELSE, an address book, an appointment book opened to yesterday's date with Todd's name penciled in at 8 p.m. I flipped back through the book; the last time he was mentioned was the night before he met me in the Catskills. I thumbed the book forward to Valentine's Day. Todd's name wasn't there, but somebody named John was down for 8 p.m. and the notation, Windows on the World. Must be John was an out-of-towner.

"But wouldn't you go out with your fiancé an Valentine's Day?" I asked myself as I leaned back in the chair and looked around. Was there any sense in searching? Someone had already searched, but were we looking for the same thing? I sighed. I hated to paw through this mess; since I hadn't known the woman, I didn't even know where to begin.

"Just begin, Doyle," I snapped. The cat jumped up on my lap and batted playfully at my lip. "Ouch!" I dumped him on the floor and touched my lip. Blood. Great! Damn cat! It licked a paw and smirked at me.

The apartment consisted of a living room, bedroom, galley kitchen and a tiny bathroom. Every room was a mess.

Sighing, I started in the bathroom where I opened the medicine chest. You can learn a lot by snooping through someone's cabinet. Colgate toothpaste (she had all her teeth), cold tablets (everybody in New York has a cold), and that was it. No headache tablets, no Vaseline, no over-the-counter medicines. That gal had to be the healthiest specimen in the city.

I glanced at the small shelf over the toilet. A jar of facial cream and a lipstick. Not much on artifice either was our Marti, I thought. I dug my fingers around in the cream. Nothing. Well, that's where something is usually hidden in mystery stories. I wiped my fingers off on a towel.

I ambled into the bedroom with the cat stalking behind me. I resisted the urge to drop kick him into next week; he'd probably chew off my ankle.

The double bed had been stripped and the designer sheets wadded up and dropped on the floor. A photograph of a smiling, dark-haired man wearing glasses watched over the room. I picked it up. Love, John.

I began to feel better about Todd. I didn't know what Marti Carr had been to him, but I was reasonably sure it wasn't romantic. My money was on John.

With renewed vigor, I tossed the room. I didn't find anything that Todd's mysterious key would open. I dropped into a chair in the corner of the bedroom and picked up a notebook from the floor. I thumbed through it. Notes for a future series, I guessed. Berry Trucking caught my attention. Hazardous waste. I scanned the notes while I let my computer file the facts. This seemed to be my week for trucks. Maybe, I could ask Noreen Caledonia if she was familiar with Berry.

The cat meowed a warning. I heard the apartment door open; I dropped the notebook and pulled out my gun. I stared at the bedroom door and waited.

"Marti, Marti, I'm back." Quick footsteps headed for the bedroom. "Marti, I'm too tired for games . . . who the hell are you?" He stared at the gun and then lifted his eyes to mine.

I smiled. "John . . . I presume."

He dropped his suitcase on the floor, a bewildered look crossing his handsome face. The photo didn't do him justice.

"What's going on? Where's Marti? What's with the gun? Did you break the glass outside?"

I stuck the gun into my jacket pocket. "Been out of town?" He nodded. I chewed my lip. "I'm afraid I have some bad news for you. Marti was killed tonight, shot by a mugger." I watched his face.

He removed his glasses and rubbed his eyes. "Is this some kind of sick joke? Who are you?"

"No joke, I'm afraid. I'm a friend of a friend of hers. Did you know Todd Mason?"

"Sure . . . the government guy she was working with. She said it was the biggest story of her life and would get her out of the pack. Her golden opportunity, she called it." His eyes narrowed. "Did her death have something to do with that?"

I shrugged. "I don't know. Todd was also killed this weekend." I smiled crookedly. "Depends on how much you believe in coincidences. I don't. Do you know what she was working on? Why would she say she was Todd's fiancée?"

He shook his head. "I need . . . a drink. Want one? By the way, my name is John Locker . . . and you are?"

"Abby Doyle. Beer or wine is fine. How much did you know about her work?" But he ignored me and headed for the kitchen.

He settled on the couch with the cat contentedly purring on his lap. He turned the glass around and around in his hands and stared at his feet. His eyes were bleak with a hint of tears.

"Did you two discuss this project?" I asked, hoping to nudge him into talking.

"Just what are you exactly?"

"Todd's mother asked me to look into his death. I think the two are connected." He looked at me curiously. I smiled. "I'm an efficiency expert in real life, solving problems for beleaguered companies; however, once in awhile, I solve crimes, mostly for the rich people I meet in my business. They have serious personal problems and want them handled discreetly."

"But Marti wasn't rich . . . and neither am I."

"Ah, but Todd's mother is. What do you do for a living?"

He smiled wryly. "I'm a traveling salesman . . . only today we travel by plane instead of car or train. I just returned from Dallas. I sell computers."

John glanced around the room as he stroked the cat. He sighed. "I wanted to marry Marti but she wanted to be a famous writer. She thought she could parlay this story into a book, an exposé. She and Todd pretended to be engaged so no one would suspect they were really working together." His eyes pleaded with me. "Are you sure it wasn't just a mugging? They happen all the time in New York."

"If the two deaths hadn't occurred so close together, I might chalk it up as another New York incident. The other alternative is she was killed by somebody who mistook her for me." I explained the circumstances of her death.

He nodded and peered at me closely. "Yes, I can see a resemblance, and on a dark street, I suppose she could be mistaken for you."

Why did I feel that was a subtle insult?

Handing him my card. I said, "If you think of something that might help me, please call . . . anytime, day or night. Is there anything I can do for you?"

Still holding the cat, he stood up and shook his head. "No. I guess I'll take Spenser and go home." He glanced around the apartment. "There's nothing here for me any more."

But there is for me, I thought as I asked, "Mind if I use the bathroom before I leave. Long subway ride." As I came out of the bedroom, I grabbed the notebook and stuffed it down the back of my pants where it was hidden by my jacket.

I hesitated at the living room door. John was standing at the mantle, his back to me, his face buried in Spenser's fur. His shoulders were shaking. I envied him. He was crying, mourning the woman he loved. I sighed and let myself out, closing the door gently behind me.

9

Early Tuesday Morning

I showered again. So much for the mayor's water shortage. I carried a cup of coffee and Marti's notebook into my office. Eyeing the couch longingly, I opted for my desk knowing I'd fall asleep on the couch.

The notebook was interesting if you liked to read about all the things that were poisoning our planet and us. If I hadn't been depressed before, I was now. I wondered what kind of world Jackie would grow old in—even if she would grow old.

I glanced at the clock. Five-thirty. I shook the stiffness out of my muscles and ambled to the kitchen. After a boring English muffin and more coffee I returned to the notes I had made.

Thomas Berry was either a real skunk or an aggressive businessman depending on your point of view and whether you were one of his shareholders or one of his competitors.

He had started out as a teenage goon in the factory area of Utica, worked his way up to truck driver for one of the mob-controlled garbage companies, become a strong-arm expert in union-busting activities for the criminal infested garbage industry in several cities, and finally been rewarded by a lucrative hauling contract of his own when he was about forty. From then on, there was no stopping him as he built his company, married a dumb unattractive but wealthy Connecticut woman who put a little polish on him while he added a little excitement to her life.

"Poor boy makes good," I muttered as I noted his present address. Chateau du Mer, an estate overlooking Long Island Sound near Greenwich,

Conn. Berry Enterprises had its own building in Westchester county—a long, long way from Utica.

I made a note for Chris to obtain a complete background check on Mr. Berry, his wife, his company, and his associates. I wondered if Noreen Caledonia knew him—probably. Trucking was a small world.

Carr listed a number of Congressional subcommittees and dates which I assumed referred to hearings. I was pretty sure she was referring to Todd when she cited an unnamed government source, but the references weren't much help since she didn't name his agency. At one point she had scribbled on the margin, "ask T.M.". I felt like I was on the right track now; T.M. had to be Todd. I could make sure by checking dates if I could locate Todd's appointment book. I sighed. It was probably in his missing briefcase.

I leaned my head against the back of my chair and closed my eyes.

"Abby, Abby, are you all right?"

I opened one eye and peered into Chris's concerned eyes. I yawned. "Must have dozed off."

He glanced at my covered desk and the memos piled on his. "Stay up all night . . . were you afraid I didn't have enough work to do? May I get you a cup of coffee?"

I smiled. "Yes, yes and yes."

When Chris placed the coffee in front of me, I asked, "Are you up to looking at porn pics this early in the morning?"

He raised an eyebrow. "Are you serious?" I spread them out in front of him. "You are serious!" He prodded them with a finger. "Where'd you find these?"

"Todd's safe. Do you recognize the white guy?"

Chris avoided my eyes. Sensing his embarrassment, I picked up the photos, stuck them in an envelope and labeled it with the date and where I found them. "Put these in the safe."

He returned and looked at me. "You know, Abby, there's something about . . ." He shrugged. "No, I guess he just looks like any well-groomed white guy."

I smiled. "I thought I'd seen him somewhere too, but I can't remember where or when."

After I brought Chris up to date on the rest of my nocturnal activities, he glanced at his notes and asked, "Where do you want to start?"

"Caledonia, I guess. See if you can get me an appointment with her today and I'll start the trucking project; that will also give me a chance to ask her questions about Berry and hazardous waste. Get an accident report on that truck. Call that nice Trooper Smith and see if there's anything new on Todd's death. Check some of your Wall Street sources and see what you can find out about Berry Enterprises. Tell them it's a routine stock deal or something." I glanced down at my notes. "And make sure Electra gets on the plane today; I don't want to have to worry about her. Did I forget anything?"

"Sleep."

"Next week. I'll just catch a cold shower and be set for the day."

I looked longingly at my bed as I passed it. I opened the drapes in my bedroom to see what the weather looked like. The windows looked north along the East River at what had once been an unobstructed view, but now the monstrosity from Citicorp towered above everything on the Queens shoreline.

I sighed. "I suppose someday the whole borough will look like Manhattan—monoliths crammed into every square acre."

The day was gray. February is gray. I hate February. It's the longest month of the year; winter seems to have been going on forever and spring will never come. I always threaten to take a long vacation every February, but work always interferes. Next year, I promised myself.

My humor returned when I turned to my nature wall and lightly brushed a hand across a sand casting called RACE TO THE SEA. The irregular three dimensional casting by Carolyn Shaw McMillan showed several baby turtles bursting free from their shells. I smiled every time I saw it. In contrast was the Hein print of a regal peregrine falcon. Sometimes I wished I had followed some kind of nature career.

When I returned to the office, Chris was on the phone. "I see," he said with a wink in my direction. "I'll tell her as soon as she comes into the office. No, I'm not sure when she'll be in. Yes, thank you." He hung up. "Your government wants you."

I groaned. "F.B.I.?"

Chris frowned. "I don't know. Said his name was Turner, mumbled something that ended with agency and insisted he has to meet with you, preferably sometime today. He sounded mean."

I smiled. "I.R.S."

"Can't you be serious, Abby. You know this has something to do with Todd's murder."

"Don't lecture, Chris . . . I know full well what it has to do with, but I'm not ready to face this man. Stall him as long as possible. I need a lot more information before I can intelligently cope with the government. Anything else?"

"Electra promised faithfully to be on that plane and to ensure it, I hired one of Michael's limos to deliver her to the airport and watch her board. Noreen Caledonia is glad you'll take the job; she'll be available at ten-thirty."

"That's it?"

"That's all I've had time for so far. Your shower didn't take very long."

I rubbed my eyes. They felt gritty, like they were full of sand. "Do you think I was supposed to be the victim last night?"

Chris shrugged. "It wouldn't be the first time that someone has tried to dispose of you."

"I'm just so angry at Todd."

Chris looked startled. "Excuse me?"

"For getting himself killed, for not talking to me before. I had so much to say to him." I stared at my desktop. "That's what people never tell you . . . when someone you love dies unexpectedly, it's not sadness you feel—it's anger . . . rage. You're just so angry at that person for leaving you behind, so angry about all the things left undone, unsaid . . . and what's worse, I don't even have time to mourn him until this is over."

I looked at Chris. "Do you think I was wrong . . . not letting Electra bury him? I don't even know what she's feeling; I can't even comfort her."

"You do what you have to do, Abby."

"I always do what I have to do," I muttered. "Okay. Chris, let's get on with this. Oh, one other thing . . . call Lefty, ask him for another car."

Chris groaned. "Oh no . . . you know he's going to be furious."

"I know, I know. But promise him I'll take real good care of this one."

10

Tuesday Morning

Waiting outside for Lefty to deliver another one of his special rentals, I reviewed what I knew and concluded it wasn't much.

I studied the car banging down the street, praying that it wasn't one of Lefty's. The saddest excuse for a car I'd ever seen lurched to a stop in front of me and Lefty hopped out, grinning. "Well, how ya like it.?" He patted it fondly on the front fender.

"What is it?"

He looked hurt. "This here is your basic police car, a 1985 Chevy Caprice. Indestructible. Over 150,000 miles on it and still purring. Built like a tank. Even you can't hurt it."

"I don't want to buy it, Lefty, and I'm kind of in a hurry. Chris called a cab for you."

I jumped into the Chevy and drove away. I glanced around the interior, noting the hole where the patrol radio used to be, the worn leather seats where overweight cops had squirmed in boredom, the heavy duty spotlight, and various holes where other pieces of police equipment had been removed.

I touched the accelerator and the old warhorse leaped ahead—recalling days of pursuit glory in its old tin heart, I fantasized as I noticed people moving aside for my battered blue and white. I grinned, wishing I had a siren and flashing light.

Page raised an eyebrow at my wheels as he gestured, "Go right in, Ms. Doyle. Izzy will lead you to a parking space and take you to the office."

"Thanks, Page. I was really looking forward to another ride with Izzy."

He rolled his eyes.

I was escorted into an almost empty office one floor down from Noreen's in the tower. A trestle table covered with files had been set up on one side of the room; across from it was a bare desk. Another small stand held a coffee maker and all the fixings.

Ms. Caledonia is going out of her way to make me comfortable, I thought; maybe, this job won't be so bad after all. I looked out the window at the loading docks. If someone could explain what was going on down there, I might be able to spot inconsistencies from here, I thought; I wasn't looking forward to standing around that yard in the February wind.

"Is this all right?"

Turning, I smiled at Noreen Caledonia. "It's more than I usually get, Ms. Caledonia."

"Call me Noreen."

"Fine. Call me Abby. We'll be working closely together." I placed my brief case on the desk. "Oh, I'm sorry about your driver last night. I saw it on TV."

Tears filled her eyes. "Jack had been with the company for ten years and his wife, Flo, joined us three years ago. Jack had a perfect driving record. Terrible, terrible accident."

"Two were killed?"

"Oh, no . . . Flo wasn't with him last night. He was just moving a semi-trailer to another area."

"Anything of value in the trailer?"

"Empty. The police think he took the exit ramp too fast." She paused, staring out the window, her eyes dark and brooding. "I can't believe Jack would have made such an elementary mistake. Every good driver is aware that an empty trailer can fishtail, especially on slick roads and at too high a speed."

I chewed my lip as I replayed the accident scene in my mind. "Have you had many accidents lately?"

"Why do you ask?" She looked at me curiously.

I shrugged. "I need all the available information to do a good job for you."

"Come up to my office." I followed her up the stairs where she paused at her secretary's desk. "Bring me the insurance file for the past year."

An hour later, I looked up from the file. "Is it my imagination or has your company had more than its fair share of mishaps—some of them pretty bizarre. Like this one." I thumbed back through the pages. "Here it is . . .

Canton, New York . . . railroad tie thrown off an overpass, hit windshield, glass shatters, driver blinded, loses control of truck. Sheriff's department put it down as a childish prank." I frowned. "I don't see a child or even two being strong enough to lift and throw a railroad tie—do you?

She shook her head. "Todd told me you were sharp."

"Todd! Todd Mason?"

She nodded. "He told me to call you . . . to hire you—not to make the business more efficient, that was just a cover, but to find out who is trying to destroy the company." She gave me a searching, doubtful look. "When I heard about his death, I wasn't sure what to do. You were there. I thought you might have had something to do with it, that you were in with these people or had been bought by them. I just didn't know where to turn, what to do, who to trust."

My mind was racing: I felt like a .400 hitter who'd just been thrown a drop-dead slider. What in hell did this all mean? Mentally, I sorted out all the information while I stared blankly at Noreen who was watching me anxiously.

Taking a stab in the dark, I asked, "Does your contract have anything to do with a Superfund clean-up in Queens?"

"Yes. Todd told you?"

"Not in so many words. Do you know a government agent named Turner?"

"Name is familiar. I think I've seen him, met him; maybe it was at one of those hearings in Washington."

"Do you know what agency Todd worked for?"

She frowned. "He never said, but it must have been something to do with Superfund because that's when I first met him—when we first bid on the project."

"When was that?"

"Four months ago."

I stared at the folder in my hand, calculating. "But that doesn't make sense. The accidents started at least a year ago." I looked at her. "Did you know you were going to bid on this job that long ago?"

"Not that particular one, but we bid on another one about a year ago. Tom Berry got it."

"Tom Berry? Of Berry Enterprises?"

"Yes, do you know him?"

I shrugged. "Not personally. I've heard of his company. Why didn't he get this one, too?"

"I don't know, but I think Todd had something to do with the contract coming to us instead. He didn't like Berry for some reason."

"How do you know? Did he say something specific about Berry?"

"Not really. He asked a lot of questions about Tom. My father and Tom went into business about the same time. Berry had a powerful backer and went up fast. Dad plugged along and built his company step by step. Then, when Tom married Louise Winthrop and the Winthrops infused the business with heavy money, he became Berry Enterprises and moved his whole operation to Westchester County."

"So Berry is familiar with your operation?"

She shrugged. "I suppose so, but he's so far beyond us now, I don't know why he'd bother with us."

"Do you see him socially?" I didn't know what I was looking for so I was just tossing out questions, hoping to hit a home run.

"We're not in his social class anymore." She smiled wryly. "I guess you don't know who the Winthrops are."

I shook my head. "Not really. I've seen the name in the papers, but I don't know the family."

"If they didn't come over on the Mayflower, they came soon after. They made their money in land—the King—don't ask me which one, my ancestors were still farming in Italy at that time—gave them a huge land grant in New England. Then, they got into railroads where they increased the family fortune on the bloody backs of Irish and Italian laborers. Recent generations have been able to live off the interest and devote themselves to politics and good works. The current senior Winthrop, Tom's brother-in-law, is president of the Winthrop Cultural Foundation."

Frowning, I muttered, "Wouldn't be the first time that bloody money ended up doing good . . . or evil."

"Can you help me?"

I stood up and wandered to a window where I stared down at the yard, letting my computer run. A jet silently took off from Kennedy and headed out over Jamaica Bay, indicating just how well soundproofed this building was. Izzy's cart flashed around a row of trailers, almost skidding under the wheels of a backing tractor. I held my breath until she squirted to safety. "I think I can help you," I said as I turned to look at Noreen. "My fee is twenty-five thousand plus expenses if I don't solve it and fifty thousand if I do." I smiled. "And if I streamline your operation at the same time, that's an additional fee which you can discuss with my secretary."

"You aren't cheap, are you?"

"No, but I'm damn good at both professions. I'll give you a free sample. Come here." I pointed at some trucks moving in the yard. "If you change those roadways and your yard traffic pattern, you'll save time and fuel moving vehicles around the yard."

After watching for a few minutes she said, "I see what you mean. I've seen that scene thousands of times and never noticed." She gave me an admiring look. "You are amazing aren't you?"

I smiled modestly. "Just lazy, I guess. I'm always looking for easier ways to do things and I have a gift for seeing the whole picture and spotting the incongruities."

11

Tuesday Afternoon

As I drove out of Caledonia's gate, I tried to spot anyone who might be following me, but no suspicious vehicles lurked in the area.

"You're getting paranoid, old girl," I muttered as I decided to have a look at the accident scene.

Recalling the gaunt derelict, I stopped at a liquor store where I bought a cheap bottle of whiskey; then, I pulled into a Burger King and got a bag of hamburgers and fries. The smell of them filled the car, reminding me that I had skipped lunch again. I fished a burger out of the bag and gulped it down.

After a couple wrong turns I located the area where the truck had gone over. Sure enough, there was a sort of hobo city interspersed in the open areas underneath the overpasses of the exit and entrance ramps. Cardboard boxes, a couple of ragged, faded tents, charcoal hibachis, abandoned debris such as mattresses, refrigerators, tires and the rest of the detritus of urban litter, and a fire in a barrel. Home.

Sitting in the car, I stared at the scene. "More like Calcutta than America . . . or maybe America in the Depression," I mused aloud as I waited and watched. Curiosity finally lured some human beings into the open. I studied them as they stared at me.

I replayed the news broadcast in my mind. Yes, the man slouching towards the fire barrel and looking furtively over his shoulder at me was the man on television.

"Hey you . . . mister," I shouted as I slid out of the car. He looked startled, shifty as if he was going to run. "Wait, I have something for you."

He froze.

Waving the Burger King bag, I shouted, "Look, burgers." I waved the paper sack with the booze. "And a little something to take the chill off."

I could smell him before I got within ten feet of him, the reek of poverty and despair. His eyes were red-rimmed and crusted with dried matter, one moment challenging and hostile, the next, frightened and servile.

Never taking his eyes off the bottle, he rasped, "Who're you? What ya want?"

I smiled. "I saw you on television last night." I gestured towards the overpass across the road from us. "I work for the trucking company . . . want to ask you a couple questions." I sidled closer, extending the bags to him.

He grabbed them, took out a hamburger and tossed the bag with the rest of the burgers and fries to a woman who was edging up behind him. He swallowed the burger. He uncapped the whiskey, took a long pull, his throat working convulsively.

"Ah." he sighed, "good . . . what you want to know?" He ushered me closer to the fire like a homeowner inviting me to partake of the warmth of a fireplace.

I spread my hands above the warmth. "Ah, that feels good." I smiled. "Last night, on TV, you were staring at something off screen . . . at something that looked like it bothered you. Did you see the accident happen?"

"You a cop?" His eyes narrowed and he backed off a step.

I shook my head. "No . . . just trying to help. The driver left a wife."

I stamped my feet, wishing I had worn heavy boots. The temperature was dropping with the sun. How can these people live like this, I wondered as I glanced around. They had crept out of their boxes and tents to stand a respectful distance away, watching me. They were a pretty rough looking bunch of men and women; I should have been afraid but I wasn't.

"What's your name?" I asked, returning my attention to him.

"Don't have no name."

"What did you see last night?" I prodded.

He stared across at the overpass and the charred remains of the crushed car. The truck had been taken away. I wondered if Caledonia or the police had removed it.

He took another swig of whiskey. "I saw another truck."

"Another truck? What was it doing?"

"Chasing the first one."

"Chasing? What do you mean?"

"It crowded the first one just before the exit, forcing it off. He was goin' too fast, shot over and crushed that car."

"Can you describe the other truck?"

"Shiny silver."

"Any name?"

He pondered as he stared at the traffic passing overhead. "Something 'to deliver'. Didn't see all of it."

"Could it have been 'We aim to deliver'?"

He shrugged. "Mebbe."

"Remember anything else?"

"He stopped."

"Who?"

"The other driver." He pointed at an area beyond the exit. "Right up there. Got out, stood at the guard rail and stared down at the accident . . . then, he drove away."

"What did he look like?"

He shrugged. "White guy. Skinny. It was dark. I couldn't see him too good."

I thought about my accident. Had I seen the driver? If I had, he was gone from my mind now.

"Doesn't make sense," I muttered. I hadn't been working for Caledonia then, so why would the same truck or company be involved in forcing me off the road and destroying one of Caledonia's trucks?

"If you think of anything else, give me a call." I handed him a twenty wrapped around my card. He stuffed them in his pocket without looking at them as he glanced fearfully at the others. I realized he didn't want them to know he'd gotten any money.

I gestured at the others. "Do they know anything?"

He shook his head. "Most of them were asleep or not here. I was up taking a leak."

I nodded. "Take care of yourself."

12

Tuesday Evening

Chris had left me a stack of computer printouts topped by a note saying, "Left early to catch up on the banking before your checks start bouncing."

I punched the phone recorder to listen to my messages. I was sick of those automatic dialers who left all sorts of uplifting pleas to buy something.

Finally, a familiar voice as Jackie said, "Mother, somebody's following me. What're you involved in now? Call immediately."

Ah, back to mother again, I groused to myself. I thought we were on a nice mom and daughter relationship instead of this formal nonsense. Stress, probably. Then I grinned. Told Chris she was smart and would spot my watchdog.

I punched the automatic dialer; as soon as I heard her voice, I sternly said, "This is your *mother* . . . what can I do for you?" In my Groucho voice, I added, "Say the magic word and you win absolutely nothing."

"Oh, mother, can't you be serious. Something's going on and I'm worried. Somebody's following me. Are you working on a case?"

I visualized my beautiful California blond daughter. "Hey, Jackie, ease up. No problem. I hired someone to keep an eye on you while I'm working on a particularly strange case."

I laughed. "And I bet Chris you'd spot them right away."

"Okay, mom, isn't it possible for you to warn me about things like this. I thought he was the campus rapist."

"Jackie, I'm a little pushed for time right now; I'll call you back in a couple days and tell you all about it. How're your classes going? Need money?"

"Classes are fine. I don't need money. Oh . . . you'll appreciate this. Dad called. He has a continuing role in that new mystery series, Beach Patrol."

I giggled. "Guess he finally had to get a job . . . now that he's no longer entitled to child support for you from me. Maybe it'll make a man out of him. How about his teeny bopper girl friend?"

"He didn't mention her."

"Okay, kiddo, I've got to run. Keep in touch. Love ya."

I punched the play button again. An invitation to a Valentine party, a message from the dry cleaner warning me to pick up my suit or it would be sold, and a final mumbled message.

I replayed it, listening carefully. "Ms. Doyle, this is Turner . . . I need to talk to you . . . have info . . . Mason . . . meet me . . . lunch . . . South Street seaport . . . third . . . south end . . ."

I listened to it again but I couldn't pick out much more. I assumed the luncheon date was tomorrow. Leaning back in my chair and propping my feet up on the desktop, I closed my eyes and contemplated the voice I had just heard. What agency? Good guy or bad guy? Did he have anything to do with Todd's death? What possible danger could there be in the middle of one of New York's popular tourist attractions at high noon?

The hamburger wore off and my grumbling stomach prodded me to the kitchen where I scrambled a couple eggs and washed them down with a Molson Golden.

I called Channel Four and asked for an old college buddy who was in the news department. "Hey Sammy, Abby here. I need a favor. You know that truck accident last night . . . do you have any more footage on it? You do . . . great. Could I bring a friend later tonight to take a look at it? Fine . . . see you about nine-thirty."

Returning to the office, I scanned the screens that showed me the area around the factory. No suspicious vehicles, no menacing strangers—just well-dressed, bundled-up New Yorkers hurrying to the fancy restaurant on the river. I shivered. God, it looked cold out there. I thought about the homeless, especially the ones I'd seen under the overpass. How could they stand it? How could the richest country in the world tolerate this situation?

I punched Standish's number on the dialer and waited impatiently for her to answer. "Hey, Standish, guess who," I said as soon as she said hello.

She groaned. "Doyle, I'm out. This is a recording. At the beep, don't leave a message . . ."

"Quit clowning," I interrupted, "I have some information for you. You're still doing homicide, aren't you?"

"Nah, I've been transferred to zoo patrol. The chief said my last involvement with you was unprofessional. Actually, that was the mildest thing he said."

"Did you see that truck accident on TV last night?"

"Yeh . . . so?"

"It was no accident . . . it was murder," I said dramatically.

"Doyle, you see murder everywhere, especially when it's profitable. Don't bother me, I'm busy. This is my laundry night."

"Wait! Don't hang up. Just listen to this." I read her a summary of the Caledonia accidents for the past year. "Well, what do you think?"

"Maybe," she said reluctantly. "I'll have a look at the accident report in the morning."

"Standish, I've made arrangements for us to look at the complete video tape of the accident at NBC tonight. Meet me there at nine-thirty. Ask for Sammy."

Standish sighed. "There goes the laundry. If I don't see anything in this video, will you promise not to bother me again?"

I crossed my fingers. "You bet, Standish. I'll even buy you a pizza after the viewing."

Sammy and Standish were waiting for me. Sammy, five-three with delusions of grandeur, was flirting shamelessly with Standish who towered over him, grinning girlishly. I'd never seen this side of Standish. She was usually all business. I had to admit that what Sammy lacked in height he more than made up for with charm and good looks. A miniature Paul Newman.

I cleared my throat. "Hope I'm not interrupting anything. Remember me, Sammy . . . your buddy, Abby Doyle."

Eyes twinkling, Sammy turned to me, winked and said, "Ah yes, Ms. Doyle, I'll be with you in a minute. I just want to talk Marg . . . er . . . Detective Standish into going to Bermuda with me."

"Hey, can we get real here, guys. I don't have all night," I snapped, hating myself for acting churlish.

Standish's green eyes narrowed. "Right, let's get on with it. Let's see your show and tell, Doyle, and it better be good."

Sammy snapped a cassette into a machine. "Here you go, ladies. Call me if you need me." He winked at Standish.

"He's too short for you."

Standish raised an eyebrow. "What's this, Doyle—jealous?"

I laughed. "Sammy charms women and birds right out of the trees. Plus he's one of nature's gentlemen, a truly lovable person. Did he mention his wife and kids?"

"Yup. Also told me she's tall and models. Now, let's see this tape. I don't have all night."

We watched silently as the tape rolled. It had been filmed by one of the city's many freelancers who had been a short distance behind the truck when the accident occurred. His footage was graphic. The worse parts hadn't been shown on the news—the mangled bodies of the four women in the crushed car and the bloody head of the truck driver. I've seen lots of dead bodies but they never stop affecting me. I choked back rising bile. I glanced at Standish who was leaning forward intently, her expression bland.

"Stop it . . . back up a little bit," she ordered. "There, see it . . . another truck, someone standing beside it, just watching. I thought truck drivers helped each other. Shouldn't he be running down there, trying to pull the driver out or something?" She glanced at me. "Is that what you meant? Is that your basis for believing it was murder?"

"No. Wait." I zapped it on again. The cameraman had panned the area. I stopped the tape. "See the guy in the background? He lives in a cardboard box in that area. He was outside, as he says, 'taking a leak' when the accident happened. He watched it unfold. Says the truck you see parked up there forced the other one off the road, forced it to take that exit too fast. The law of gravity took care of the rest."

I reversed the tape and froze the image of the parked truck. The silver trailer certainly looked familiar, but then there were a lot of silver trailers on the road. "We Aim to Deliver" stood out on the side. I hadn't really gotten much of a look at the driver who had run me off the road so I couldn't tell if he was the same one driving this truck. This guy didn't show up very well—too far away. The only thing I could tell for sure was he was slim and he was white.

"See that slogan on the side of the trailer, Standish? That was on the one that tried to annihilate me in the Catskills."

Standish leaned back in her chair, never taking her eyes off the screen. "But you said you weren't working for Caledonia then, so where's the connection?"

"Do you agree that this might not have been an accident?" When she nodded, I told her about Todd's murder and what he might have been doing—his connection to Caledonia.

Standish stood up and stretched. She opened the door and called, "Hey, Sammy, we're finished." When he entered the room, she asked, "Can you get a hold of the guy who shot this?"

"Sure, he has a car phone." He dialed and handed the phone to Standish. "His name is Calvin."

"Calvin, Detective Standish, homicide. I've been looking at a tape you shot last night of that truck accident in Queens. I'd like to ask you some questions. Can you meet me . . ." she frowned at me.

"Little Rock bar, across the street," I whispered.

"A little bar across 48th Street from Rockefeller Center . . . Little Rock. Twenty minutes . . . fine. I'll be the tallest redhead in the place."

Twenty minutes later, a lanky guy wearing jeans and a sheepskin vest slouched through the door of the bar and peered through the smoke. He smiled and waved when he spotted Standish.

"Detective Standish, I presume," he drawled.

She stared at him. "Texas, right?"

After introductions were made and beers ordered, Standish got down to business. "How far behind that truck were you last night?"

"I could see the tail lights of the one that crashed and the other truck passed me going like a bat out of hell. It pulled up beside the first truck. I saw the first truck's brake lights go on, then he fishtailed, straightened the trailer out and then they ran side by side for a ways until the exit when the first truck tried to slow and get off. The other truck veered towards it. Then, bingo . . . like slow motion I saw the whole thing unfold in front of me. The tractor shot off the exit, didn't make the curve in the ramp and was airborne. One hell of a crash I can tell you. I jumped out with my camera and started filming."

"Did you notice the other truck? What did the driver do?" I asked.

"Lady, I was so busy filming the wreck, I wouldn't have noticed anything. Hey, what is this anyway? It was just an accident—wasn't it?" He looked from one to the other of us. "Is this some insurance thing?"

I smiled. "Right. I represent the company that insures Caledonia. Do you have any additional footage?"

He gave me a suspicious look. "I did have, but a guy bought it from me this morning. Caledonia's insurance agent. Hey, lady, just who the hell are you?

What's going on here?" He looked at Standish. "You got a shield, some ID?"

She dropped her shield and police card on the table. "Little late in asking, aren't you, Calvin? Did you ask the guy this morning for any identification?"

"His ID was good—five Ben Franklins."

"What'd he look like?" Standish asked.Calvin shrugged. "An ordinary man. Nothing special. Only saw him for a few minutes. Hey, I didn't do anything wrong."

"It's okay, Calvin, no problem. Probably someone else from our office." I winked at Standish. "If you think of anything else, give me a call." I extracted a phony business card with a fictitious insurance company name and my real phone number and handed it to him.

After Calvin had slouched out, Standish asked, "Does the insurance man ring a bell?"

"Nope. I doubt that he was even an insurance man. Now, do you believe me? This was no accident."

Standish unfolded herself from the chair and loomed over me. Her eyes burned into mine. "Have you told me everything, Doyle? No surprises? No little tidbits held back for your private enterprise?"

I crossed my toes. "Everything, Standish, I've told you everything. Cross my heart."

She nodded. "I'll check the report from the Accident Investigation Unit. Talk to you tomorrow."

13

Wednesday Morning

I was on my second cup of coffee when Chris arrived, dumped the mail on his desk and looked longingly at my coffee.

He blew on his hands. "You'll need a gallon of that if you're planning to go out today. Freezing. What's new?"

"Get some coffee and I'll bring you up to date."

Chris sipped his coffee and took notes while I told him about my activities of the previous day.

"By the way," I added, "Jackie called; she spotted your man right away."

"Like mother, like daughter." He flipped some pages. "How do you want this Caledonia billing set up?"

"She'll call you after she makes up her mind. If she wants her operation streamlined, bill at our usual hourly fee. Now, listen to this." I turned on the tape of the Turner call.

Chris, head tilted, fingered the knot in his tie as he listened. He glanced at me. "Going to meet him?"

I chewed my lip and gazed at the Gus Hedlund print, *Silent Wings*. I lost myself in the scene with the snowy owl hunting silently along a frozen creek, reminiscent of the Northern New York area where I grew up. The phone jerked me back to reality.

Chris picked it up and listened. "Just a moment, Detective Standish, she's right here." He hit the record button.

"Standish, how goes it?"

"I checked the accident report and talked with the first highway patrolman on the scene. He doesn't recall the other truck; he was too busy trying to free the truck driver who was still alive when he arrived."

"The driver was alive! Did he say anything?"

"Quit interrupting. He kept repeating 'flow'. Mean anything to you?"

"He might have been saying Flo, short for Florence, his wife's name. Did he say anything else . . . anything about the other truck?"

"He said, 'no axe' and died."

"No axe? Wait, Standish, what if he had been trying to say no accident?"

The silence lengthened. I could almost hear the wheels in her brain turning.

"Standish, are you still there? Share your thoughts . . . phone home, ET. Damn it, Standish, what do you think?"

"Look, I'm wrapping up a case now and I'm busy. Besides, there really isn't enough evidence to open a homicide investigation."

"Are you blind?" I sputtered. "Come on, Standish . . . you heard what the video guy said."

"I'll get back to you." She hung up on me.

"She's the most exasperating woman I've ever known. They should never have let women become cops."

Chris raised one eyebrow. "You aren't serious, are you?"

I grinned sheepishly. "Nah, she's a good cop; after all, she saved my life once. She's just the most bullheaded, stubborn person I've ever dealt with. Why can't she see it was murder? She sees it . . . she doesn't want to admit I'm right."

"Are you going to rant all morning? We have some work to take care of before you go—uh, where are you going today? Nothing on your calendar."

"I think I'm going to lunch at the Seaport. Noreen Caledonia said she thought she'd seen Turner at a hearing. Is there anything else?"

"The Berry report. Did you read it last night?"

I shook my head. "Summarize it."

"Berry Enterprises is doing well on the stock market; shares are up because of rumors of a big government contract to come their way soon." He flipped a couple pages. "Specifically the trucking arm of the company. We'll be getting his last annual stockholders' report by messenger today." He frowned. "Incidentally, he expands his trucking business by taking over companies that are having financial difficulties. He absorbed a good-sized Canadian hauler a few weeks ago. Is Caledonia in trouble?"

I shrugged. "If they don't hang onto this government contract, they could be . . . I guess. I haven't really gotten into their books or learned much beyond a few superficial details. To be honest, I'm more interested in what Todd's connection with Caledonia was and if it got him killed."

Chris wrote some notes before he said, "I have a friend in the Environmental Protection Office here; let me call him again and see if there are any new Superfund cleanups coming up in the metropolitan area."

"Is there anywhere you don't have a friend?"

He grinned at me. "That's the advantage of working as a temporary for so many years; I subbed in many different companies and government agencies, met a lot of people, learning how the system works."

"Ever think about going into business for yourself?"

"No thanks. I have enough trouble keeping your life straight and worrying about your scrapes."

"You're a gem, Chris." He was not only the best secretary-assistant that I'd ever had, but his wife was also my attorney. In fact, she had recommended Chris for the job when my longtime secretary had retired.

While Chris was on the phone, I wandered into my living room and stared out the window at the Manhattan skyline. A grim, gray day. Oh to be in sunny California. Why don't you fly out, old girl, hang out, relax, get to know your daughter better.

We had made a start on cementing a real mother-daughter relationship when she had visited in January. I had convinced her that I hadn't really abandoned her when she was a child. Her father had manipulated her and maneuvered the judge into granting him custody and child support. Devastated, I believed my child had rejected me so I kept her at a distance, spending only vacations with her. I wanted to make time for her now; I didn't want to lose any more time with her.

Chris tapped me on the shoulder. "Are you in another world? I've called you twice."

"Sorry," I smiled, "just thinking about Jackie. As soon as this is wrapped up, schedule me for a few days off so I can visit her." I followed him into the office. "What's up?"

"Ms. Caledonia doesn't remember Todd mentioning Turner; however, Turner called her a few days ago and asked for an appointment. She didn't catch his agency name either, but he said it was important—to her. She also said she was almost positive he had been at some of the Congressional hearings on the trucking industry."

"Did she meet with him?"

"No. Between the accident and Todd's death, and then your arrival, she never got back to him. My friend at EPA says the only Superfund cleanup around here is the one in Queens. A radium factory. Isn't that the one Caledonia has the contract for?"

"I think so. So that must mean Berry thinks Caledonia isn't going to be able to fulfill the contract and he'll get it by default. Interesting. What did Noreen have to say about our project?"

"She'd like you to streamline her operations. We settled on the usual rate. She'll be available all day tomorrow. I told her I'd get back to her."

I nodded. "Set it up. Today, I'm lunching with Mr. Turner to see where he'll lead me."

Chris frowned at me. "Be careful."

I smiled. "What can possibly happen in the middle of South Street Seaport at noon?"

"If anything can, it will happen to you. Stay in touch."

14

Wednesday Afternoon

South Street Seaport, a typical Rouse development on the lower east side of Manhattan, featured striking views of the East River and its bridges, Governor's Island, Brooklyn Heights, Queens, and a glimpse of the Statue of Liberty peeking over the top of the Staten Island Ferry building.

Tourists poked through the pricey boutiques and financial workers poured into the bars after work. The seaport is another of those developments devoted to that great American sport—shopping. Pier 17, the renovated shopping area that juts out into the East River next to the array of old ships that make up part of the South Street Seaport Museum. I sniffed the fishy odor from the Fulton Street Fish Market and caught the tang of salt air that reminded me the ocean wasn't far away. The area is an odd mixture of the real and surreal.

The wind blowing off the river was brutal, I shivered as I hustled across the plaza to a ground floor door. Usually, I climbed the outside stairs and admired the view from every level, but today I elected to look at the sights from inside with a hot cup of coffee in hand.

The third floor contains a number of take-out food booths and bars. I picked up a cup of coffee and headed for the east end of the building where most of the tables were still unoccupied. Selecting one near the South end entrance, I sat down, propped my feet up on a chair and stared south, watching the traffic on the river. Blue and white police patrol boats buzzed around the river and government ferries plowed back and forth from Manhattan to Governor's Island. Tug boats pushed garbage scows and fuel barges.

A sparrow landed near my coffee container and tilted his head, fixing me with a beady eye.

"Sorry, pal, I don't have a thing for you."

He flitted up to the top of one of the potted trees. A woman jumped up from her chair and held the door open, letting a blast of Arctic air in while she called the sparrow.

I smiled at her. "He's not crazy . . . it's warm in here and he has plenty to eat. Why should he want to go out there."

"How silly of me." She let the door close and returned to her table.

A large group of tourists with clicking cameras climbed the outside stairs. They burst through the door near my table, chattering and twittering like a flock of sparrows.

"This seat taken, Ms. Doyle?"

I hadn't even noticed him. Distracted by the tourists, I had stopped watching for Turner; now, he stood across the table from me, balancing a tray. About forty, sand hair graying at the temples, mild gray eyes, five-ten, slender—the kind of man you'd pass by in a crowd. When I looked closer, I imagined a hint of menace in his eyes and noted a calculating set to his thin lips. He was cataloging me as thoroughly as I was him. We eyed each other, waiting to see who would blink first.

He put the tray on the table. "I understand you like junk food." He gestured. "These are great hot dogs." He slid a paper plate across to me.

"Mr. Turner?"

"Just call me Turner."

"Fine. Call me Doyle." Two could play this game.

"I heard you were tough."

"I prefer strong . . . a nicer connotation. Why did you want to see me?"

A flash of neat, even teeth, a smile that never reached his eyes. His Sears gray suit was uncreased, unlived in, his black shoes polished to a high gloss. He reminded me of a college mate who was always perfectly turned out, always quiet and polite; one day he went home and butchered his parents and younger sister because his father said he couldn't drive the Mercedes to school.

"Could you pick me out in a line-up?" he asked.

"Pardon me?"

The flash of teeth. "You were staring at me."

I smiled. "Sorry, I was expecting somebody more menacing."

"And I look like an accountant."

"Right . . . but then, an accountant from the I.R.S. can be pretty scary."

"You've never had a problem with the I.R.S. In fact, you file model returns, you lean over backwards to be fair to the government. You were eminently fair to your ex-husband, too."

His voice droned on, reciting my life to me. At times his voice dropped to a mumble and I missed a few words. He never took his eyes off mine as if he was doing a clever party trick and waiting for applause. He stopped.

"Impressive," I managed to choke out as I picked up my hot dog.

He flashed his teeth. "You shouldn't be surprised, Doyle, in the computer age. Press a few buttons and start the chase. You use them yourself."

"Humm. Does the government have this complete a dossier on all its citizens or just the ones who are problems in one way or another?"

He shrugged and took a bite of his hot dog. "If you want to know, file under the Freedom of Information act." He shifted in his seat and looked around our area to make sure we were still relatively alone.

"What I want to know is your relationship with Todd Mason."

I smiled sweetly. "Couldn't your computer tell you that?"

"I'm asking you."

I shrugged. "We were just good friends." Forgive me Todd, I pleaded silently; I really wanted to pound my head on the table and shriek, but I couldn't.

I leaned toward Turner and stared at him. "What did Todd do in the government?"

He raised his eyebrows. "You don't know?" I shook my head. He frowned. "I don't know either. Todd is . . . was . . . a very shadowy, figure. Sort of like a trouble-shooter, not attached to any one agency. He reported to somebody in Congress—I don't know who so don't ask."

"Did you put a lid on the investigation of his murder?"

He looked startled. "A lid on the investigation . . . no, no, I didn't. I thought . . ." His voice faded as he looked over my shoulder. "I've got to go. I'll be in touch . . . be careful."

And he was gone.

I turned to look in the direction he had been staring. I saw a young couple leaning on the railing outside, hugging and kissing. Out of the corner of my eye I glimpsed a dark coat disappearing down the stairs. Was it a man or woman? Was it the one who had spooked Turner.

I pushed the half-eaten hot dog away. I still didn't know who Turner was, what part he played in this drama. Could I trust him? What had scared him? Or did he just not want to be seen with me?

I thought about what he had said about Todd reporting to somebody in Congress. Had he been with some Congressional subcommittee investigating the trucking industry or Superfund clean-ups?

"Damn it, Todd, where did you keep your files?" I muttered aloud, wondering what the mysterious key could possibly fit.

I called Chris. "Anything doing?"

"Not too much. You're set to spend tomorrow at Caledonia. Ms. Caledonia will be out for most of the morning, but she said to help yourself to anything you need, talk to anybody. She's told her staff to cooperate with you. Also, you had a very unusual call. Are you interested in doing a rush job in Chicago that could pay you a quarter of a million dollars?"

"Are you serious? Who?"

"Carlsbad Consolidated. Meat packing. They heard about you from Johnston and want a complete survey of their plant and want it yesterday; that's why they're prepared to pay such heavy money."

I put my computer in gear. I'd never heard of Carlsbad, but I had surveyed one of Johnston's plants three years ago. Drop everything and go to Chicago. I smiled. What a great way to get me out of town? Who in their right mind would turn down a quarter of a million?

"Are you still there, Abby?"

"Umm, yes. Give my regards to Carlsbad. Tell them I'd be happy to talk to them in a few days. Run a check on them . . . find out who owns them."

"Do you have an idea?"

"One guess—Berry. If I have to make a second guess I'd bet on a government connection." I described my meeting with Turner. "See if you can run him through our network. I'd like to know more about the mysterious Mr. Turner."

"When will you be back?"

I sighed. "I'm going to play hooky, Chris, clear my mind. See you tomorrow."

I walked a couple blocks to catch the A train north. The car was half empty and I slouched in a seat for three, closed my eyes and relaxed as the train raced up Manhattan.

"Columbus Circle, next stop, change for the K across the platform . . ."

the voice degenerated into static.

I was a little disoriented, trying to remember where I was going, what I was going to do. The local train was across the track and I groggily followed the rest of the people to the K train.

The American Museum of Natural History ad was above my head. Why not, I thought, it's one of my favorite places. It's quiet, it's warm. What better place to play hooky.

I traded a peek at my membership card for an admission button and headed for my favorite spot. Standing at the railing, I gazed up at the gigantic blue whale suspended from the ceiling. Then, I wandered through the Hall of Birds.

Next time Jackie visits, I'll bring her here, I resolved. I glanced at my watch. Almost five. Outside, I wandered down Amsterdam Avenue until I got to Shannon's Bar, my favorite Irish pub. Even had an Irishman behind the bar. I suspected he was one of the thousands of Irish people in the country illegally. They blended in even with their brogues because we had professional Irish who had been in this country for generations who still talked like they'd just come over from the Old Sod.

"Ah, Abby Doyle," Kelly said as he drew a Bass ale for me. "Long time no see. Have ye been to Ireland yet?"

That was our standing joke. "Not yet, Kelly, not yet."

I sipped my ale and looked around. A soccer game was on the big screen in the corner. A couple Irish cops with thick white hair and shiny black shoes argued in a back booth. The shoes gave them away every time. A tired waitress with her shoes off perched on the stool at the end of the bar, sucking at a cigarette and staring at the screen.

The joint smelled smoky, sweaty, and old like a bar should. A garlicky pea soup aroma floated from the tiny kitchen in the back.

"Not many customers, Kelly."

He swiped at the bar with a damp rag and frowned. "'Tis all Yuppies up here now. They want to drink where it's light and airy. Fern bars, ye know."

I grinned. "A fern might liven up this place a little and maybe a wee spritz of air freshener."

"Sacrilege . . . and you an Irish lass, too."

A blast of cold air on the back of my neck drew my attention to the door. A man abruptly pulled it closed. I sprinted for the door, ran outside, yelling, "Turner" as I looked up and down the avenue. Rush hour crowds filled the sidewalks. I shrugged, not even sure it had been Turner; probably just some Yuppie startled when he found out Shannon's wasn't **a** fern bar.

I returned to my ale.

"Somebody ye know, Abby?"

"Thought it was, but I guess not. I'll have a refill and a bowl of the soup before I head back to Queens."

15

Wednesday Evening

I hate subways when they're crowded. I was wedged into a corner next to the conductor's booth where some oaf was standing on my foot and another was approaching criminal intimacy from the rear. When the train lurched around a curve, I smashed my elbow into the nameless gut behind me and heard him go "oof" as he inched away from me.

The car was hot and steaming, enhancing the mingled odors of sweat, curry, garlic and cheap booze. I covered my nose with my sleeve to filter the air. I pushed my way off at my stop and inhaled the cold air.

"Never again," I swore, but I knew I'd take the subway again; it's the fastest way to get around New York.

Ambling up my street, I tried to recall everything Todd had ever told me about his work. Amazing, when I thought about it, how little he had talked about himself when we had been together. And how little we had really been together in the past couple years. Oh, Todd, where did the time go. We'd just let it all slip away from us.

I glanced up at the factory. "Ah, home sweet home," I muttered, anticipating a nice warm shower and a slightly chilled glass of red wine.

A low pitched growl stopped me. Apollo, the factory guard dog, was unhappy about something. I listened again, puzzled. You shouldn't be able to hear him through all that soundproofing, I said to myself as I headed into the alley. A side entrance door halfway down the alley was slightly ajar. I flattened myself against the wall and thought about it. Apollo had somebody cornered in there and here I was with no weapons.

I retreated to the freight elevator and took it to my apartment. I wished my monitors scanned the inside of the factory so at least I would know how many were waiting there. I loaded my gun and headed for my bedroom where I pressed the release button on the bookcase. It swung out, revealing a narrow stairway to the factory—a handy escape route when anyone was watching the front of my building.

I crept down the stairs, leaving the light off so it wouldn't show when I opened the factory door. I prayed that Apollo wouldn't give me away.

I slid through the narrow opening and crouched down behind a machine. Still in a crouched position, I sidled from machine to machine, moving closer to the area where I could hear Apollo growling.

A male voice pleaded, "Nice boy, nice boy."

Another voice snapped, "Why don't we just shoot the mutt?"

"Don't be stupid. We're not supposed to leave any signs. A dog with a bullet hole between the eyes is a sign."

I grinned to myself. At least Apollo was safe, but was I? They were obviously armed. Apollo had the situation in hand for the moment so I slid down into a sitting position to ease the pressure on my aching knees while I pondered my next move. Who were they and , what did they want? And what on earth were they doing in the factory? Were they after me or something in the factory? Very few people knew about the entrance to my bedroom through the factory.

The first voice said, "Why don't you try moving towards the door and see what the mutt does."

Second voice. "You move and *I'll* see what he does."

I stood up and aimed the gun at them. "Why don't neither of you move and I'll tell you what the mutt will do," I said pleasantly.

They exchanged frustrated looks as they slowly raised their hands.

"Hey, lady, it ain't what you think it is," the first voice said. He was burly with a military hair cut.

I smiled. "You don't know what I think it is. But I'm sure the cops can sort it out." I moved closer. "Apollo, nice dog." I whistled. The Doberman wagged his tail. "Sit, boy." Apollo eased back onto his haunches, still staring at the two men, his tongue lolling out of his mouth.

"Okay, gentlemen, remove your guns and place them on that bench. Place your wallets next to the guns and take four steps back and clasp your hands behind your necks."

They followed my orders while nervously staring at me. When they were safely out of range, I stepped forward and flipped open the first wallet. I dumped the cards on the bench and riffled through them. I glanced up at the big guy. "Well . . . who are you? Derek Smith, Roger Miller, John Cory or Mose Rogers?" He shrugged. I repeated the procedure with the second wallet and repeated the names represented there. "John Smith, Joseph Carter, Robert Jaynes, Well, do you care to claim one of these as your real name?" He stared at the floor.

"Okay, I'm easy to get along with; you don't want to talk to me, talk to the cops." I ushered them to the employees' lounge where there was a phone. "Have a seat." I gestured at two deep easy chairs so battered and softened that you couldn't get out of them in a hurry if you wanted to.

I dialed Standish. "Hey, Standish, I have a couple presents for you. Just caught two guys who broke into the factory . . . on their way to my place. Apollo cornered them."

Standish groaned. "Doyle, don't you ever rest? I'm having dinner. Call the precinct. I don't do break-ins."

"But Standish, they were after me. This isn't your run-of-the-mill burglary. They're carrying guns and they have several false ID cards."

Standish was either thinking it over or continuing her dinner. Finally, she said, "This is against my better judgement but I'll be right over."

I was glad to hear Standish at the door. "In here, Standish."

She strode through the doorway. "Evening, everybody, what do we have here?" She waved her shield at them. "Detective Standish, homicide. Name," she snapped at the big guy. He shrugged. Her eyes narrowed. "Tough guy. You . . . name." The second one continued to stare at the floor.

"I told you, Standish, there's something fishy about these guys."

She phoned for a blue and white to pick up the two men. We waited silently until two cops entered. Officers Gonzalez and Marks. I'd talked to them often in the neighborhood. We all referred to them as Cagney and Lacey.

After they'd left with their prisoners, Standish eyed me. "Do I dare ask what you've been up to today?"

I smiled. "Not much. Lunch at South Street Seaport, a visit to the American Museum of Natural History, and dinner at Shannon's pub. I took the day off." I kept my fingers crossed behind my back.

Standish looked puzzled. "Sounds innocuous enough. I'll call you after I have a chat with those two."

"Just come up and have a beer. I'm going to take a shower and have a drink. By then, I'll feel human again."

The bell rang an hour later I checked the monitor. Standish was scowling up at the camera. I buzzed her in and waited by the elevator door for her.

"Geez, I'm going to move to Miami if it gets any colder." She shed her jacket and walked into the living room where she stood at the window, staring at the Manhattan lights and brooding.

"Beer, Standish?" She grunted so I got her a Molson. "Going to tell me what happened at the precinct or do we play twenty questions?"

She rubbed the bottle between her hands for a moment before she took a long pull of the beer and sighed. "They were kicked loose ten minutes after they were there," she snapped.

"You're kidding!"

She eyed me distastefully. "I don't kid, Doyle. You have the strangest friends . . . or should I say enemies? Have you checked lately to see if the FBI is running a file on you?"

I shook my head. "But I've heard rumors. What happened?"

"Those thugs made one phone call and within minutes, two gray suits appeared . . . you know the type . . . tall white males buttoned down and buttoned up. They flashed a piece of paper at the lieutenant and presto . . . the bad guys belonged to them. Gonzalez said she saw them get into a limo, laughing, all buddies together." She slugged back some more beer. "Any ideas? Any thoughts you'd like to share with a hardworking cop?"

I poured myself another glass of wine. If this keeps up, I'll be an alcoholic, I thought.

"Todd was a government type, but I don't know what agency he worked for . . . something hush-hush." I fidgeted with my glass. "I flattered myself that it was a romantic tryst he was offering, but upon sober reflection, I think he was worried and scared of something or somebody and needed my help. In other words, he wanted my brain, not my body." I sighed. "If he had lived, he probably could have had both."

Standish looked away to give me time to brush away the tears and control my emotions.

"Okay, where do we go from here?" she asked gruffly.

Noting the "we", I didn't say anything, knowing how embarrassed Standish would be by my profuse thanks.

"Let's go back to the truck accident," I said. "What did you find out?"

She shrugged. "Inconclusive."

I jumped up. "Come on, Standish, we're going calling."

"Where ?"

"The homeless guy. Listen to him and then you'll believe it wasn't an accident."

She looked at me as if I was crazy. "Doyle, it's late, it's freezing out and I have my good clothes on. I don't—I repeat—I don't want to go prowling underneath the BQE."

Ignoring her protests, I went to my bedroom where I donned my favorite black outfit For good measure, hung the stiletto around my neck before putting on the black jacket.

"Okay, Standish, let's go. Got your car?"

She groaned. "You're like a damn steamroller. Okay I'll talk to this creep, but that's it."

16

Late Wednesday Night

We drove silently to the accident scene and Standish parked across from where the homeless were living. A barrel of burning debris faintly illuminated the area.

"So quiet," I whispered.

"This is against my better judgement. Let's get it over with."

We crossed the street and stood uncertainly at the edge of the lot.

"Anybody here?" I called, raising my voice to be heard over the whine of tires coming from the expressway. "He lived in that box." I pointed. "I'll just see if he's there."

"Great. I'll wait by the fire."

I rapped lightly on the box. "Hey . . . you in there?"

I squatted down, parted the flaps and peered into the box. "Flashlight, dummy," I muttered as I pulled it out of my pocket and pointed it inside. At first, I thought it was a pile of rags; then, the outline slowly took shape and the smell hit me—the smell of death, of all the bodily functions giving up at once.

"Standish," I yelled, "come here."

She joined me and followed the beam of light.

"Jesus!" She squatted down and gingerly touched the body. She stood up, wiped her hand on her jacket and stared into the dark.

"It never gets easier," she muttered as she turned to me. "His throat is slit." Then, she shouted, "Hey, anybody here?"

"Forget it, Standish, they're long gone. They don't want any trouble with the police."

She sighed. "Right. You stay here and I'll go call the homicide team."

"Wait . . . I don't want to stay here alone."

She smiled like a shark. "Somebody has to guard the crime scene."

"But I'm not a cop," I protested.

"But you like to play cop. Now, here's your chance to do what a real cop does . . . the messy part of the job. Don't touch anything."

Mournfully, I watched her drive away. As soon as her car disappeared, I crouched down and flashed my light into the box and around the body. I spotted a piece of white under his outflung right hand. Carefully, I edged it out; it was half of my business card. Holding my breath, I gingerly lifted his hand and found the other half. I pocketed them, silently apologizing to Standish for messing with the evidence, but I didn't want his death tied directly to me.

"Poor bastard," I muttered as I stood up. "Did you get killed because you talked to me or did one of your buddies do you in for the twenty?" I didn't have any illusions about people who lived in vacant lots. Drugs, alcohol—you name it; they'd kill their mothers for a fix or a drink.

I checked the other boxes and the ragged little tent for signs of life. Not only were they empty, but all the possessions had been removed. These people were not returning; however, I bet a new group would take up residence before the week was over.

Moving back to the barrel, I rubbed my hands together, holding them over the flames. I stared across the street at the expressway; I had a terrific view of the exit where the Caledonia truck had crashed.

"Come on, Standish . . . hurry . . . my feet are freezing." I stamped my feet nervously as I listened to the whine of the tires and the wind.

I kept looking over my shoulder. Chills ran up and down my spine and I didn't think they were from the cold. Ever notice how your senses sharpen when you're alone in a spooky situation? Well, mine were operating at peak efficiency and I felt something watching me. I peered into the dark.

"Something just moved over there," I whispered. I flashed my light. Something darted into the shadows. "Come out," I yelled, "I've got you covered."

When it moved into the light, I grinned and put my gun away. A black cat with a flash of white on its chest trotted towards me. It rubbed against my ankle, looking up hopefully at me and purring.

"I don't need a cat, but don't go away. Maybe Standish is a sucker for cats."

I looked around the field. I stared at the pillars supporting the highway. Anybody could be there. Watching me.

A break in the sound from the expressway attracted my attention. I stared up at the roadway before the exit where a dark car had pulled off the road. Its driver was standing beside the car, staring down at me. I stared back at him—or her. Skinny and white, skinny and white. A laugh floated through the night as the driver returned to the car and sped away. Too far for me to catch a plate number or even to tell what kind of car it had been. But the driver had been skinny and white.

I shuddered, feeling more alone than I had in a long time, mourning Todd, missing Jackie feeling sorry for myself because I was standing in a deserted lot with a slaughtered man fifty feet away. I was losing control of this case. Hell, I was losing control of my life!

The whooping of sirens lifted my spirits. I often wondered why police and emergency vehicles used their sirens even when there obviously was no emergency. The body wasn't going anyplace.

Standish's vehicle burped into the lot and stopped with its lights aimed at the box. She left the motor running and the lights on.

"See you found a friend," she said, nudging the cat with her toe. "Or is he a witness?" She chuckled.

"Cops have a weird sense of humor."

She shrugged. "Keeps us from crying when we have work to do."

Two black cops got out of the second car. They ambled over and looked inside at the body. One made a remark and the other laughed.

The laugher hitched up his gun belt and strolled over to Standish, "Begging your pardon, Detective, but me and my partner know the stiff. We were here earlier tonight. He had a beef with one of the other tenants." He grinned.

Standish and I exchanged looks. Her eyes narrowed. "You going to let us in on the joke or what?"

He flipped open his notebook. "Here it is. Eight-thirty, dispute. We arrived and the stiff in there was surrounded by three of his buddies. They wanted a share of some lucky money he had come into and he had a fresh bottle of whiskey. We took one of them in . . . he had a zip gun. When we left, the guy in the box and the other two were peacefully sharing the bottle." He smirked.

Standish stared thoughtfully at the box. I was grateful she hadn't said "I told you so". Yet.

"Get any names?" she asked the cop.

He studied his scratchings. "Smith, Jones, Johnson, and Weinstein."

"Weinstein?" I yelped, resigned to a string of phony names. "For real?"

He grinned. "For real . . . he's the dude we took in. He's a binger, lives with his sister most of the time until he goes off on a toot and she throws him out and he ends up living with some street people like these."

"I'll talk to him," Standish said. "Give Doyle a ride home." Turning to me, she added, "I'll call you in the morning. I'm sure one of his buddies offed him so you don't need to feel guilty. I could just see that conscience of yours oozing all over the lot when I pulled up."

I shook my head. "Later, Standish, later."

17

Thursday Morning

After I scrambled a couple of eggs, I sat at the counter and pushed them around the plate while I leaned my chin on a hand and stared into space. I replayed the scene from last night, trying to recapture the image of the person who had stopped on the expressway and laughed.

That bothered me. Was it somebody who had something to do with the case or was it just one of New York's garden variety freaks? Or just a drunk urinating on the side of the road? If he had been black. Or fat. It would mean nothing, but I was sure he, and I was sure now it was a he, had been skinny and white.

Maybe Standish believed the derelict had been killed over a bottle of whiskey, but I didn't. But then, she didn't have the advantage of finding my business card under his body. Should I tell her?

I sighed. "You'd better snap out of this funk and get to work, old girl." I glanced at my watch, noting that Chris would arrive in ten minutes. I ate the cold eggs.

When Chris entered the office, I was sitting at my desk, staring at the computer screen and making notes—the image of a hardworking, cheerful efficiency expert.

"Good morning, Chris." I smiled.

He raised one eyebrow and waved the Daily News at me.

"Is this your derelict on the front page?"

"As a matter of fact . . . yes, but it has nothing to do with us. He and a couple buddies fought earlier in the evening over a bottle of whiskey." Was I trying to reassure Chris or convince myself, I wondered.

Chris smiled. "That's a relief. We don't need any more complications in this project. Did you get my message about Jackie yesterday?"

I slapped my forehead. "I was so tired I didn't listen to the messages or check your notes. What about Jackie? Is she all right?"

He frowned. "I wasn't paying attention when you said she was being followed by a man. It hit me yesterday; I hired women to guard her. I called her and asked her about it to make sure you had heard correctly. She did say a man. I checked with our people and they've got it under control. They checked him out . . . he's legitimate . . . an operative from another company. Naturally, he won't say who hired him. What do you want to do about it?"

"I should never have had a child," I groaned. "When she lived with her father and we had very little contact, nobody paid any attention to her or were even aware that she existed. Now, she's apparently going to be a target every time I work on a special case."

I looked pleadingly at Chris. "Frankly, it scares me and I don't know what to do about it. Do you have any ideas?"

"You just have to live with it, I guess. I talked to Jackie; she's pretty level-headed and she learned her lesson after her kidnapping when you were working on the Thorne case. She said not to worry and she'd be careful. You have round the clock guards . . . I don't know what more you can do unless you want to drop the case."

"Which case?"

He looked startled. "Good question. Is it somebody connected with the government because of Todd or somebody to do with Caledonia?"

"Before I can answer that, I need more information about Turner, about Caledonia's problems, and our Mr. Berry. I have a funny feeling about Turner; he wasn't what I expected and he acted strange when I accused him of shutting down the investigation of Todd's death. I think I want to get back to the Catskills pretty soon."

"You won't be welcome up there and it could be dangerous. What makes you think you could learn anything new?"

I chewed my lip. "I'd like to return to that inn. Somebody had to know Todd was going to be there. How? And why did that truck run me off the road?" I rubbed my eyes. "We need to know why he died before we can even start looking for his murderer."

Chris stared at me. "I have a bad feeling about this case, Abby."

"Me too, Chris, me too."

The phone rang. I picked it up before Chris could and signaled him to activate the recording system. I didn't bother notifying anyone they were being taped; after all, I reasoned, the government doesn't have enough agents to bust into everybody's home looking for phone recorders.

Standish barked. "Somebody say hello. You there, Doyle?"

"Yup . . . morning, Standish." I had picked up the phone and forgotten to say anything because I had just thought about something about Turner's reaction to my news about Todd's murder investigation. The thought flew when Standish spoke.

"I didn't get a chance to speak to Weinstein," she said. "He'd been kicked loose by the time I got around to him. I called his sister. He didn't come home last night. I've put out a pick-up order on him, but don't hold your breath . . . he could be in a shelter or a vacant lot anywhere in the city."

I groaned. "Don't tell me he was saved from the law by two federal agents."

"Nah . . . no room in the inn. We kick out the minor offenders in hopes we'll have enough room for the biggies. Last night they had a gambling raid in the precinct."

"Are you going to treat the truck accident as a homicide?" I asked. When she hesitated, I knew the answer. "Standish, please, it's important. You have to believe me . . . it was no accident."

"Hey, Doyle, I believe you, but I have a boss, too, and he has other ideas about how I should spend my working hours. The Caledonia accident is not on his list. I'm sorry. If you get something more convincing, let me know."

"How about my dead body? Would that convince you?"

"I'd certainly come to your funeral, Doyle." She hung up.

I slammed the phone down. "That woman!"

Chris grinned. "I thought you said you and Standish were becoming friends."

"We were . . . when she agreed with me." I shook my head. "Must be some way I can convince her," I muttered as I started throwing papers into my briefcase. "I'll be at Caledonia if anything comes up. Maybe, I should take that quarter of a million and forget this nonsense."

"You know you couldn't do that. Be careful, Abby."

"I know . . . I know . . . don't get run over by a truck!"

With that thought in mind I returned to my bedroom and put on my knife. I might be in that area after dark, I reasoned, not wanting to face the truth that danger might await me at Caledonia Trucking.

When I checked in with the receptionist, she smiled and said, "Ms. Caledonia said to show you anything you wanted to see; she's sorry she'll miss you today but she has a meeting in the city. Mr. Caledonia will be glad to help you. He asked me to notify him when you arrived."

"Fine. I'll go up to my office now. You can tell him I'm ready for him if he has a few minutes. I might want to talk to you later, too."

"I'll be here." She rummaged through her desk drawer. "Ms. Caledonia said to give you these so you'd have access to everything anytime." She hand-ed me a set of color coded keys and explained the system.

I let myself into my temporary office, dropped my case on the table, and stood staring down at the yard.

"Ahem . . . er, Mrs. Doyle?"

I turned and studied the man who had just entered the room. He was about five nine, twenty pounds overweight with a softness around his face and a slyness in his dark eyes. A distorted picture of his sister. Where she looked strong, he appeared weak. I could guess why she had become the company president. I noted the flashy diamond ring on his little finger, the tailored suit. A dandy.

"You must be Russell Caledonia," I said as I crossed the room with my right hand extended. His fingertips brushed my fingertips. They were damp. I resisted the urge to wipe my hand off.

He glanced around the room. "If there's anything you need . . ." His voice petered out. "I mean . . . if I . . ."

Wondering if this man ever finished a sentence, I wanted to pull the words out of him.

I smiled. "Your sister said I could have access to anything and anybody. I might like to talk to you in a day or two if that's all right."

"Well . . . I'm sometimes . . . pretty . . . busy . . ."

I waited. I smiled. "Sometimes it's hard to have a stranger underfoot, pry-ing into your business, but just remember that I'm working for you to ben-efit your company by putting it into a more efficient operating mode."

He looked bewildered. Considering my convoluted sentence, I could understand why.

"Well . . . any . . . help . . ." He waved a hand and backed out the door.

I perched on the table and stared at the door, letting my mind run, filing Russell Caledonia under ineffectual, harmless. But the evasive look in his eyes bothered me. Did he resent his sister so much that he wanted to see her fail? But this company was his bread and butter, too, and you don't destroy your own livelihood—do you? I shrugged. I'd get to Russell later; now, I wanted to learn how the company worked.

I had asked Noreen for a list of her employees who worked in the office and in the yard. The list was on the table. I scanned it, noting the amount of time each one had worked for Caledonia. Most of them had been here at least a few years except for two or three. Page, the guard, had been employed for a year, the yard switch man, Stratton, for six months, and one of the dispatchers for almost six months.

"A dispatcher would know what was going on," I muttered as I contemplated the name—Elvis Potter. Fine old Southern name.

I dialed Noreen's secretary, Irene Day. "Can you tell me why Elvis Potter was hired when he was and who he replaced?"

"He replaced Maurice Bush. Maurice was crippled by a mugger last August."

"How was he hired? Did an agency send him?"

"Russell—Mr. Caledonia—brought him in. I don't know what rock he found him under."

"Excuse me? Rock?"

She laughed. "You'll see what I mean when you meet him. Anything else I can help you with, Ms. Doyle?"

"Just tell me how to find the dispatcher's office."

I followed her directions to the nerve center of the operation on the second floor of the tower. I stopped a man who was just leaving. "I'm looking for Elvis Potter."

"Over there."

I studied the man who was talking on the phone. He was about thirty and thin as a snake, all muscle. I noticed his fingernails were manicured and buffed. His shifty blue eyes passed over me, returned and winked. He was dressed like a Broadway cowboy—a plaid western shirt with pearl buttons and a string tie. His belt had a big turquoise buckle in the shape of a revolver. He was wearing snakeskin cowboy boots. A lot of men wore boots in the trucking business; considered themselves the last American cowboys I guess.

As I crossed the room, his eyes inventoried my body.

"Mr. Potter. I'm Mrs. Doyle. I think Ms. Caledonia told you about me."

He covered the mouthpiece. "Yup. Told us to tell you anything we knew, to help you in any way." He licked his lips. "She didn't mention you were a good lookin' broad." He pointed to a chair. "I'll be through here in a minute or two. Make yourself comfortable."

I remained standing. Be cool, old girl. As soon as he hung up the phone, I said in a level voice, "Mr. Potter, just pretend I'm not here and do what you usually do. If I have any questions, I'll ask them."

He shrugged. "Suit yourself."

I pulled the chair into a corner and sat down; I watched him work. He was in radio contact with a couple of drivers, one of whom was obviously a woman he addressed derisively as "Butch". I rolled my eyes, thinking what a slob this guy is. As if reading my mind, he glanced at me and winked as he lasciviously licked his lips.

I was so revolted by him that I felt almost compelled to give him a bad rating and suggest that he be fired. But in spite of all his obnoxious personal habits such as the compulsive groin scratching and suggestive leers, he seemed competent.

After an hour I flipped open my notebook. "Mind if I ask you a few questions?"

He smacked his lips. "I'm single and free for dinner."

"Wrong answers. Can you tell me how the dispatching system works?"

"Yup." Standing up, he stretched and scratched his groin before he pointed to a board with two rows of names. "This is the main board. At a glance I can tell you the drivers who are out, their truck numbers and where they're headed." He pointed. "This row tells me the drivers who are available in the order they're to be called. The radio system keeps me in touch with drivers in the Metro area. Drivers hauling hazardous materials are required to call in and report their position every five hours."

"Is that routine?"

He shrugged. "We've had some problems lately and we're being cautious . . . maybe overcautious."

"If I wanted to hijack one of those trucks, how would I do it?"

"Are you serious?"

I smiled. "Semi."

He chuckled. "I'd take the dispatcher out, wine and dine and bed him . . . then he'd tell you everything you needed to know."

Ignoring his expectant leer, I asked, "Is that the only way?"

"Does that mean you're not going to take me out?"

"You got it. Sorry, I already have a friend." I jotted down some notes. "Other ways," I prodded.

He shrugged. "Steal the route sheets from a driver's cab. Kidnap a driver's or dispatcher's family. Or wait, and follow one of the trucks from the plant. There're lots of ways." He squinted at me. "What do these questions have to do with the efficient operation of a trucking company?"

I smiled. "All information is useful. Thanks for your help." I packed my briefcase. "I might have some more questions for you tomorrow."

"I'll be waiting eagerly, Sweetie." He held the door open for me, forcing me to squeeze by him.

Ugh, I thought, he makes me feel dirty. I slung my bag into the back seat of my car. Leaning against the fender, I stared up at the dispatcher's office, feeling his eyes on me. I mulled over the information he had given me; he had seemed forthcoming and cooperative, but I had sensed an undercurrent. Was it just his macho posturing or was he hiding something?

Izzy careened up in her golf cart, skidded to a halt and greeted me with a big grin. She stuck out her hand and I shook it, keeping a straight face as I felt a piece of paper in her palm. She released the paper, grinned at me and zoomed away.

In the car I opened the note. "Meet me in the Flyway diner, Springfield Boulevard near the Belt. Flo Warren." I glanced around. Flo Warren? Oh yes, the dead trucker's widow. Why didn't she just come up to me here and talk?

I located the diner, walked in and looked around for a woman who fit my idea of a female truck driver. A good-looking middle-aged woman, sitting in a window booth, caught my eye and waved.

I stopped at the booth and smiled at her. "Flo Warren?"

"Right. Coffee or something?"

"Coffee's fine." I sat down.

"You're not what I expected," she said in a soft Southern drawl.

"Neither are you," I admitted. "How'd you get into trucking?"

"Jack . . . either share his driving or see him once a month or so. Seemed easier to learn how to drive a truck than to do without him." She sobbed. "Excuse me," she said, fumbling for a tissue.

"It's okay, it's understandable. Please accept my condolences." I sipped my coffee while I waited for her to regain control.

She was a soft-looking woman, not at all what I had expected of a woman in the macho trucking world. She must have loved him very mach to join him in wrestling one of those damn trucks around the country.

"I'm not usually the weepy type," she apologized, "but I can't seem to get a hold of myself since Jack was murdered."

"Murdered?"

She leaned forward. Intensity gleamed from her eyes. "Yes, murdered. That was no accident. Jack was too good a driver to do something that stupid. A detective called me today."

"What was his name?" I interrupted.

"Her name was Standish."

That son of a gun, I thought, she is investigating behind my back. "What did she ask you?"

"Just some general questions about Jack and truck driving." She looked at me curiously. "She also asked if you had contacted me . . . said you believed Jack was murdered, too."

I smiled. "Standish and I don't always see eye to eye, but she's a fair detective. Did she say she was investigating it as a homicide?"

"No, she said the department had no real evidence that it was anything but an accident. However, she advised me to talk to you."

"Why didn't you talk to me at the office?"

She stared out the window for a few minutes as if she was debating something with herself before she answered, "There's something wrong at Caledonia . . . a strange atmosphere . . . can't describe it, but I was afraid to talk to you there."

I nodded. "How long have you worked there?"

"Only two years."

I raised an eyebrow.

"Jack and I got married three years ago . . . second time around for both of us. I was a truckstop waitress in Virginia when I met Jack. We had both just gone through bitter divorces." She sighed. "He was the kindest, gentlest man I have ever known. Our fourth anniversary was coming up." She choked up again.

"So you decided to become a driver?"

She nodded. "I'd seen all the temptations drivers face on the road, and Jack wanted me with him. He didn't want a parttime marriage either, but he didn't want to give up driving."

"What're you going to do now?"

She stared out the window. Finally, she said, "I don't know, but I'm going to stay at Caledonia until I find out what really happened to Jack."

"Are you going to drive again?"

She nodded. "I'm scheduled to take a short run to Jesup, Maryland, in a few days."

"Maybe I'll see if I can be your partner. I'd like to experience an actual trip and a short one would fit my schedule. Would that be a problem for you?"

"Nope. You'll have to get permission from the boss, but that shouldn't be any problem for you. What about Jack?"

"Don't say anything about his accident; it would be dangerous for you to voice your suspicions to anybody at the trucking company—or anywhere else for that matter. There was a witness to the accident; he said another truck forced Jack off the exit ramp." I paused for dramatic effect. "That witness is dead . . . throat slit."

I watched her closely. Standish apparently hadn't mentioned the homeless man because Flo was surprised and looked horrified or she was a damn good actress.

"That's terrible. The detective didn't mention any witness. Who was he?"

"A homeless man who lived in a lot across the way. As a matter of fact, there was at least one other witness in a sense. He was one of those freelance video reporters who rove the city. He saw the accident and taped it. I had noticed the derelict in the background on a television newscast and tracked him down and I also talked to the cameraman. If I did it that easily, someone else did, too. The police are putting the derelict down as murdered by one of his buddies for a bottle of whiskey." I finished my coffee. "By the way, do you know a company who has 'We aim to deliver' on the side of its trailers?"

"It's a common enough slogan. One is AIM which stands for American International Motors; another one is Morcol, and then there's Canale's Freightway; and I'm sure many more. Trucking companies aren't too imaginative when it comes to slogans. Why do you want to know?"

I told her about my Catskill experience and about the slogan on the one that had forced Jack off the road. "If anything comes to mind, call me at this number." I slid a card across the table. "I'll fix it up casually to accompany you on your trip. Otherwise, treat me like everybody else does there—a nosy nuisance."

When I paid my bill. I glanced at the wall behind the cashier. It was covered with television monitors showing various places inside and outside the diner.

"You have that much crime in the neighborhood?" I asked the cashier.

She shrugged. "Armand, one of the owners, is an ex-cop and he says it's important to make people feel safe. Besides, I think inside he's still a cop . . . know what I mean?" She tapped her chest.

I watched the scan of the parking lot. A familiar face was sitting in a gray sedan parked a few spaces from mine. I motioned for Flo.

"Watch that screen. See that car?" She nodded. "Do you think you could stall your car right behind his so he can't move until I get out of here?"

She grinned. "Piece of cake. Who is he?"

"I'm not sure, but he follows me once in a while."

I watched the monitor as Flo stalled her car behind Turner's, got out, opened the hood and peered helplessly inside. Turner jumped out of his car and from his expression, was shouting at her.

I hurried to my car and drove away, pretending not to notice them. In my rear view mirror I saw Turner slam his hand on the trunk of his car as he stared futilely after mine.

18

Thursday Afternoon

"Just a moment, Mr. Turner, she just walked in," Chris said into the phone as he motioned to me to pick up mine.

"Turner?"

"That was a cute trick you pulled at the diner. I only wanted to talk to you. What in hell is wrong with you? Paranoid?" he raged.

"Okay . . . okay, Turner, slow down. Why are you following me?"

"I'm not following you; I called here earlier and your boyfriend or whatever he is told me you were on a job. I knew you were working at Caledonia so I drove there and you were just leaving, so I followed you to the diner. I was about to go in when I saw you join that woman so I decided to wait outside for you. I need to talk to you."

"Why don't you come up to my office now."

A long silence. "I . . . can't. I'm . . . I've got to hang up; I'll call you back."

"Turner," I shouted into the void. "Damn, what is he up to?"

"Boyfriend," Chris said indignantly. "Chauvinist. Hasn't he ever heard of male secretaries?"

"Well, you are kind of cute." I leered at him.

"Abby, don't be ridiculous. How'd your day go at Caledonia's?"

After I repeated my interview with the slimy Mr. Potter and Flo Warren, I added, "I think I share Flo's suspicions. There's something wrong at Caledonia, but I can't put my finger on it. I haven't been there long enough. I suspect it's something that goes back into the past. Caledonia senior was killed in a car accident in the Catskills and I was run off the road in the Catskills, does that suggest anything to you?"

"Don't vacation in the Catskills."

"Cute. Serious ideas?"

"Why don't you meet this Turner and see what he has to say."

"I don't know if I can trust him; I don't even know who he's working for. He's apparently some kind of government agent but he's scared stiff of something or somebody in his own government. Are they after him because he killed Todd or does he know something about Todd's death? I just can't read the man. He seems so innocuous until you look into his eyes . . . they're deadly. I don't mind admitting he scares me a little." I sighed. "But I guess you're right . . . I'm going to have to meet him. If he calls again, set something up . . . in a public place, please."

"That Chicago job . . . I think you were right. When I called and said you wouldn't be available for a few days, they said forget it."

"I wonder what the next offer will be. Get Standish on the phone."

"Detective Standish? Ms. Doyle to speak to you."

"Doyle, I told you I'd call when I had something—I don't have anything."

"Slow down, Standish, you'll have a heart attack. Flo Warren tells me you talked to her. Are you investigating the accident or not?"

A prolonged silence and a sigh. "Doyle, can you stay out of police business and do whatever it is you do for big bucks. Let us poor unwashed civil servants do our thing. I have nothing to say to you. Don't call me anymore."

I was puzzled. "Standish, is this you? Is somebody applying some pressure? Is somebody listening to your end of the conversation?"

"You got it, Doyle. Don't bother me. I'm busy, investigating real murders." She hung up the phone.

I leaned back in my chair and brooded. "What did that sound like to you, Chris?"

"Coercion. Somebody is trying to stop this investigation on all sides. Todd's death in the Catskills, Warren's accident and death, the homeless man. Somebody is desperately trying to put a lid on the whole kettle of fish."

"But why?"

Chris smiled. "Beats me. You're the detective. What do you think?"

Before I could answer, the phone rang and Chris picked it up. "Excuse me . . . would you repeat that? One moment please." He frowned at me as he covered the mouthpiece. "You have a reservation at Babbling Brook Inn tomorrow night. This is a call to confirm." I nodded. "Yes, that's correct. Thank you." He hung up and stared at me. "Did you make a reservation?"

" I didn't, but I'm willing to bet Turner did."

"And you're going?"

 "You bet."

"It could be dangerous."

"Not only could be, probably will be, but this time, I'll be prepared. It may be my only chance to find out what he's up to."

"Do you want me to cancel Caledonia tomorrow?"

"No. I'll work a half day and leave directly from there. Don't tell anyone where I've gone." I stood up. "When you finish those reports, you can leave."

I went to my bedroom where I sat on the end of my bed and hugged myself. Babbling Brook Inn. I repeated the name several times, trying to convince myself it was just another place.

But why did he pick the inn as a meeting place? Maybe, he's just a sadistic bastard, old girl, or maybe there's something important there. I sighed. Would tomorrow ever come?

19

Friday Morning

Page opened the gate and signaled me to follow Izzy who flashed ahead in her cart to the main office front door area where she skidded to a halt. She pointed to a freshly painted parking sign. DOYLE. Impressive.

I pulled my briefcase out of the car, turned to Izzy and asked, "How come the sign?"

Grinning hugely, she thumped herself on the chest.

I patted her shoulder. "Thanks, Izzy, I appreciate it. See you later."

After I let myself in, I nodded to the guard who indicated the sign-in sheet. "Has Ms. Caledonia come in yet?" I asked.

"I'm not sure. She didn't come in this way, but that doesn't mean she couldn't have come down the passage."

"Passage?"

"Yeh. Runs underground from the garage to here and to the loading docks. Sometimes, when she's having her car serviced or something, she comes through there so she doesn't pass this guard station."

"Does she pass any guard station?"

"Nope. The passage comes out in the area of a back stairwell and she goes up that."

"So someone could come and go with no one being the wiser. Right?"

"Yes ma'am . . . if we didn't see them on the video monitors."

"Could you show me this passage?"

"Just a moment. Hey, Nicky, watch the desk; I'll be right back."

I followed the guard to the other side of the building to an unmarked door. He opened the door and pointed down a dimly lit passageway. "This is it. Go down about a hundred feet and you come to a right hand turn . . . that leads you to the garage area. Go straight and you end up at the loading dock office."

"This door isn't kept locked?"

"Nope."

"With all the other security you have, isn't that odd?"

"No ma'am, the assumption is if you know where that passage is and where it goes, then you work here."

"I see. How would I get to Ms. Caledonia's office from here?"

He opened the door across the hall. "These stairs lead up to each floor. Go as high as you can and you'll be there. Exit on the third floor and you'll be near your office."

I thanked him. As I climbed the stairs, I pondered this flaw in Caledonia's security system. How many outsiders knew about the passageway? When I reached the third floor, I pushed the door open and peered into the hall. Three offices radiated out from the core on my floor: my temporary office, a large filing area with workstations, and the comptroller's office.

I entered my office and glanced around. Why did I have the feeling that someone had been there recently? I sniffed. A faint odor of cigarette smoke lingered in the air. I shrugged. Probably a cleaning person. I pushed the button for Noreen.

"Noreen, Abby Doyle. Are you free? . . . I'd like to come up and talk to you."

Noreen was seated on the couch, pouring coffee when I entered. She waved me to the chair across from her. She seemed morose.

"Is something wrong?" I asked.

"It's Russell. He thinks I shouldn't have hired you to investigate the accidents. He's being difficult." She sighed. "We had a big argument this morning."

"That's strange . . . he seemed all right yesterday when I talked to him . . . a little vague."

"He's always a little vague. That's why the board made me president; they weren't sure Russell could handle the position, and he's acted strangely ever since."

I let the silence deepen, my favorite ploy to elicit more information. Sometimes it worked and sometimes it didn't. This seemed to be one of those latter times as Noreen just sat there, sipping her coffee and gazing into space. I couldn't stand it any longer.

"What have you decided to do?" She looked at me blankly. "About me," I added. "Are you going on with the investigation or am I being fired and you don't know how to break it to me?"

"Russell doesn't think there's anything sinister about our accidents; he thinks we're just having a string of bad luck. After all, trucking can be a dangerous business."

"What do you think?"

"Someone is trying to destroy my company," she whispered. She lifted her head and the fire was back in those black eyes. "And I want you to find out who."

"Good. Don't lose your nerve. Now, I'd like to take a short trip with one of your drivers just to see what it's like. Can you arrange that?"

"Let me see." She went to her desk and dialed a number. I couldn't hear what she was saying but I had my fingers crossed that it would work out the way I anticipated. She turned and asked, "Jesup . . . Maryland . . . an overnight?"

"When?"

"Sunday morning to Monday morning."

Perfect, I thought, it would give me a day's leeway in my Catskill trip. "Sunday's fine . . . who's the driver?"

She hung up the phone, made a note on a pad and returned to the couch. "Widow of the driver who was killed . . . Flo Warren. It's her first trip alone so it's probably just as well she'll have some company. A female driver might be more forthcoming to you."

"Fine. I'm looking forward to it. Now, I want to discuss the government contract, the Superfund clean-up. Exactly what will your trucks be carrying and how?"

"Radium-226."

I raised my eyebrows. "Isn't that dangerous?"

"You bet! Radium-226 is intensely radioactive. It was once used in treating cancer. The radiation level inside this factory is so high that the factory will have to be demolished, sealed into lead-lined containers and shipped off for burial in a nuclear waste dump in Nevada. Even the soil and sewer pipes will have to be removed."

"If this stuff is so dangerous, how do you move it?"

She stared out the window. "Carefully. We start with flat bed trucks and an odd-looking metal canister the size of a dining room table. This canister contains a cluster of fifty-five gallon drums containing more layers of lead, concrete and steel. We're only talking about four ounces of the stuff. We take twelve thousand radium filled needles. Each one has a tiny flake of radium . . . about the size of your little finger nail." She paused for effect. "We can only move one flake at a time!"

"Wow . . . you're kidding." But I knew from the expression on her face that she wasn't. "Then, what happens to these things?"

She shuddered. "Radium's half-life is 1,620 years so it has to be buried in areas so arid that there is no possibility it will leach into water supplies someday. The only nuclear waste dump in the country licensed to take radium waste is in Nevada."

"What would happen if somebody hijacked one of these trucks? How could they use this stuff?"

"I don't even want to think about that."

"Why do you want this contract?"

"Money."

We sat silently, each lost in our own thoughts. I was thinking of Jackie and possible grandchildren. How could we mess up the world as much as we had? Love Canal, Three Mile Island, Chernobyl, Alaska oil spill, destruction of the wetlands . . . the list rolled on and on in my head.

I sighed. "When do you start this operation?"

"That's the catch," Noreen said bitterly. "We were supposed to start it as soon as possible, but now we're being held up while they inspect our current accident rate. Seems someone reported that we'd had a number of recent mishaps and insinuated that it was the incompetent way I ran the company; that these weren't simple accidents but incidents caused by neglect and mismanagement." She dropped the file onto the table and glared at me.

"Of course, I can't blame them . . . an accident carrying this stuff could be disastrous." She looked at me appealingly. "Abby, I need help and I need it fast. Russell is wrong. These aren't just accidents. I know someone is destroying this company and I won't let it happen. My father worked too long and too hard to build it; I won't preside over its demise." She inhaled sharply to bring her breathing under control. "I'm sorry, I didn't mean to raise my voice. I promised myself I'd remain calm and stoical through this whole situation."

I smiled. "You don't want to appear to be the hysterical woman . . . right?"

She smiled wryly. "Right. Especially since that's the stereotype of the Italian mama."

"It's okay to cry, to get angry; in fact, I'd wonder about you if you didn't. I have a theory—crying relieves stress." I grinned. "And if crying doesn't work, try a hot fudge sundae."

She smiled. "You're irrepressible, aren't you? Doesn't anything faze you?"

"Lots of things. Some days . . . everything. But I keep plugging along. I have a simple philosophy: will it matter a hundred years from now? There's also a Jesuit principle I like: no one is bound to do that which would be useless." I refilled my cup. "Let's get to work. I have to leave early today to meet somebody in the Catskills tonight."

She glanced out the window. "Better check the weather forecast. Snow was mentioned this morning."

"Just what I need," I grumbled. "Can I show your accident files to a friend of mine, a homicide detective who helps me out once in awhile?" I smiled to myself, imagining Standish's face if she heard my last statement.

"I guess so. What can she do for us?"

"She can confirm some of my thinking. She's a smart gal. Now, can you find out what someone could do with this radium if they got their hands on it?"

"I guess I can contact someone in the Department of the Army."

"Don't mention to anyone here what you're doing. In fact, don't even tell your brother. If he bothers you anymore about the investigation, tell him you agree with him and that I'm only streamlining the operations."

She shook her head. "I don't think Russell is that dumb. Russell is not as vague as he seems. He talks like that, I think, in rebellion against our father. Dad used to talk like a machine gun—ideas and words tumbling out simultaneously, and he was very impatient with Russell. You know the Italians . . . they want their sons to be number one. I'm like my father, quick-witted and quick-tongued."

Then, it dawned on me. "You and Russell are twins, aren't you?"

Nodding, she said, "Yes, but please don't mention it to Russell. He doesn't admit it, discuss it or refer to it in any way; he doesn't want anybody to know we're twins. I don't think anybody outside of the family and a couple close friends, former classmates, that sort know about it."

"Do you trust your brother?"

She gave me a shocked look. "What do you mean? Of course, I trust Russell."

I smiled. "Ever hear of sibling rivalry? Happens all the time. Brothers are jealous of brothers, especially if they're better athletes or handier with the ladies. Sisters are jealous of sisters who are more beautiful, marry better. Sisters are jealous of brothers who seem to get all of dad's attention. Brothers are jealous of sisters who become president of the family company."

I watched her as she thought about what I had just said. I didn't know what I was getting at exactly, but I hoped she could point me in the right direction.

Noreen paced around the room. She stopped and glared at me. "No. N0. Russell doesn't have anything to do with the accidents. It's his company, too. He'd be crazy to destroy it. Besides, he's my brother . . . my twin for God's sake, and I'd know if he was doing anything like that. We're close, very close . . ." her voice faded.

"Okay, forget it. It was just a thought." I tried to make my voice casual. "But for now, could we leave everybody outside of the information loop except you? I'll report to you, but just keep the data to yourself for the time being."

20

Friday Afternoon

As I plowed my way through the stack of files Noreen had left me, I glanced out the window and worried about the increasing velocity of the snowfall. At noon it had been spitting a few flakes. An hour later it was snowing lightly but steadily and patches were sticking on the roadways below. I was getting anxious to start for the Catskills and careless in my reading.

Sighing, I gathered up the folders and locked them in a file cabinet drawer. "Later, old girl. You'll miss something important if your mind isn't on it." I picked up the phone and called Noreen. "Noreen, the weather is worrying me so I'm heading out now. I locked up everything. Tell Mrs. Warren I'm looking forward to our trip together."

"Drive carefully, Abby. Some of the drivers have been calling in . . . roads are getting a little slippery. We haven't had our February blizzard yet."

"You're a real comfort, Noreen. See you Monday after I get back from Maryland."

When it snows in New York, they should close the city. Most of the drivers are reduced to motor morons at the sight of a snowflake. I picked my way along the Van Wyck expressway, dodging out-of-control cars and getting my windshield splattered by trucks and buses. This too will pass, I thought, as I squeezed by a fishtailing trailer. It took me twenty minutes to get across the Triborough Bridge. At last, I was winging my way upstate on the Thruway—if you can call fifty miles per hour winging it.

By the time I hit the Poughkeepsie area, I was having second thoughts about the trip. It was snowing and blowing harder and visibility was difficult. Lefty had neglected to tell me that his gem's heater was sporadic at best and the defroster struggled to keep two portholes clear.

I settled into a driving rhythm after traffic thinned out. I liked driving alone, thinking, isolated from all outside distractions. Why would anyone want a car phone?

Todd was uppermost in my mind as I recalled how excited and happy I had been on that previous trip to the inn. Was it only a week ago that my world had been shattered. So many things had happened.

The miles whizzed by unseen as I let my mind range over the interviews I had conducted, searching for a common thread. The one common ingredient was Caledonia Trucking.

"Solve Noreen's problems, old girl, and you'll find Todd's killer," I muttered as I peered through my steamy windshield, searching for the Kingston exit.

I paid my toll and drove to the nearest motel. After a quick trip to the bathroom, I headed for the phones.

"Is Trooper Caleb Smith there?" I asked. I heard the sergeant shout, "Hey, Cal . . . phone . . . woman . . . sexy voice." Thanks, Sarge, I thought to myself.

"Hello, Trooper Smith."

"Trooper Smith, this is Abby Doyle . . ."

He interrupted, "Where are you?" I told him. "Stay there. I'll be with you in ten minutes . . . in the bar."

I settled down at a table and ordered a Molson Golden. I stared at the door. I almost didn't recognize him in civilian clothes.

He stood over the table, looking down at me with a solemn look on his face. "What are you doing here?" he asked.

"I'm fine, how are you, pleased to see you again. Really, Trooper Smith, is that any way to greet a taxpayer?" I smiled at him. "Sit . . . I'll buy you a beer or is that bribery?"

He shook himself. "I'm sorry Mrs. Doyle, you just surprised me. I thought you were safely in New York."

"Hundreds of miles away, you mean," I finished for him. "Actually, I've been invited back to Babbling Brook Inn." I paused, surprised at the horrified expression on his face. "Is something wrong, Trooper?"

"Call me, Cal." He shook his head in disbelief. "I didn't think you'd ever return there after what happened. Are you crazy? Why are you going? What's going on?"

"Whoa, Cal, I'm the one with the questions. You're supposed to be the one with answers."

"I'm sorry." He glanced up at the waitress. "A Bud, please." He watched her leave before he said, "I don't have any answers. I shouldn't even be meeting you. You, lady, are strictly off limits to all of us."

I studied his face; he had aged in the past few days. His long fingers fiddled with the ashtray as he waited for his beer. After the waitress plunked the bottle down on the table along with a bowl of stale popcorn. Cal glanced at me.

"Okay, let's start again. Why are you going to the inn?"

I told him about my mysterious invitation. "So you see, I may get some answers from this Turner."

"Or you may end up in the creek with your head bashed in."

I winced. "Cheerful thought. Did you ever see the autopsy report?"

He shrugged. "There wasn't one."

"Impossible!"

"They took the body away from Doc Farris before he could finish the autopsy."

"They? Who in hell are *They*?"

He shrugged.

"I want to talk to Farris. How can I get a hold of him?"

Cal smiled wryly. "Try Bermuda."

"Bermuda!"

"Yup . . . he won some kind of trip to Bermuda and it had to be taken right away. He'll be there a couple weeks. What's that expression mean?"

I laughed. "I was offered a lot of money to do a rush job in Chicago and Farris wins a trip to Bermuda. What about you?"

"I'm just a lowly trooper."

"Your boss—what's his name?"

"Investigator Mickens." That fleeting grin again. "He's been transferred to Buffalo."

"Game, set and match," I muttered. "What about the files on the investigation?"

"I looked before I left the barracks. Gone."

"What do you think about all of this, Cal? Your honest opinion."

He shifted uneasily in his chair, looking around the room, looking everywhere but at me. He crammed a handful of popcorn into his mouth and chewed slowly. I waited patiently, staring at him.

Reluctantly, he looked at me and whispered, "I think something funny is going on and I don't mind telling you, it worries me."

"Did you talk to Mickens or Farris about this?"

"I didn't see Doc before he left, but I did see Mickens for about two minutes. He said to me . . . if you want a career in the State Police, concentrate on traffic patrol."

I raised an eyebrow. "What was that supposed to mean?"

"A warning. Mickens is an okay guy, but he's nearing retirement so he didn't dare make any waves and he was telling me if I want to succeed, I'd better forget your friend's death, too."

I wanted to scream at him—remind him it was his sworn duty to serve and protect the people of the state of New York and he wasn't doing a very good job. I wanted to remind him about ethics, conscience, and all those righteous things, but the words died in my throat as I gazed into his strickened eyes. I knew then that I didn't need to remind Caleb Smith about his duty because he knew it and was severely troubled.

I patted his hand. "I'm sorry, Cal . . . I guess I am being unreasonable. I didn't mean to insinuate you were derelict in your duty and I have no right to ask you to endanger your career and possibly your life. Are you married? Children?"

He smiled. "Yeh . . . my wife, Kathy, is a nurse. We have a son, Caleb, Junior, five years old and hell on wheels." He took a deep breath. "How can I help you?"

I chewed my lip. "I'm nervous about this meeting. Hell, I'm more than nervous, I'm scared. What I'd like is to be able to count on you as backup, if I need it. A phone number where I could reach you anytime. I don't want to compromise your career or anything, but I don't know anybody else up here to ask for help."

He wrote down two numbers on a napkin and slid it across the table. "The top one is my home, the second one is the barracks. If you call the barracks, tell them you're my Aunt Jean and if you need me in a hurry at the inn, tell them the package is ready."

I glanced at my watch. "I'd better get going. I don't want to keep our friend waiting. What's the weather forecast for up here?"

"Snow and more snow. You could end up snowbound."

"Great. I can't imagine anything worse than being snowed in with

Turner—if it's Turner who shows up."

"Be careful, Mrs. Doyle, real careful."

"You bet I'll be careful." I patted the back of my neck for reassurance. Of course, Cal didn't know about my hidden stiletto. Or the .38 in my glove compartment.

He walked me out to my car and glanced up at the sky. It was snowing harder.

"Looks like an all nighter," he said. "You may have a little fun on that road to the inn, but this old tank looks like it can handle it. Where do you get these cars anyway?"

Laughing, I told him about my banishment from the major car rental firms. "And if anything happens to this one, I'll probably be banned from Lefty's too." I winked at him. "Take care of yourself, Trooper Smith, I'll be in touch."

21

Friday Evening

After what seemed like hours, I skidded into the turnoff to the inn, noting there were no car tracks in the fresh snow so either I was the first to arrive or my host had arrived much earlier.

Dark had settled in early because the snow blotted out the sky. My headlights picked up bare bushes lining the road. The pine trees lining the road turned it into a tunnel.

I was uneasy as I drove along the road, dreading my first sight of the scene of Todd's death—a far cry from the sense of anticipation I had felt last Friday night when Trooper Smith had delivered me to the inn.

I sensed the opening before I actually saw it. The inn looked deserted. I pulled up until the bumper nudged the front steps. I turned off the engine. The silence was overpowering.

"Should I blow the horn?" I wondered aloud. A faint light glowed in the front window.

I rested my head on the steering wheel as I suddenly felt dizzy. Was I coming down with the flu? Or was this a reaction to returning to the death scene? Where is the cool, unflappable Abby Doyle who mouthed all those platitudes to Noreen, I sneered at myself.

The car was cooling off fast. I shivered. I just wanted to get inside and crawl into bed. I honked the horn. The door opened and a sliver of light knifed across the porch. The figure outlined in the doorway was too short to be Jack Heims. Why should that surprise me; I was sure there was a logical reason for his disappearance, too.

Stepping out of the car, I called, "I'm Abigail Doyle; I have a reservation."

A deep voice responded, "Yes, Mrs. Doyle, we're expecting you. Do you have luggage?"

"An overnight bag. What should I do with my car?"

"Leave it there . . . nobody else is coming."

Just as I thought. That meant Turner or whoever was already here. I shrugged. I knew what I was getting into before I came. Ducking back into the car, I pulled out the .38 and dropped it into my blazer pocket.

I slipped and slid around the car and onto the front porch where I paused to scrutinize the man holding the door. About twenty-five, I guessed. Even though he was wearing a plaid wool shirt and jeans, he was no mountain boy. He had big city written all over him. I could picture him better in a suit and tie.

"Where's Jack?" I asked as I walked into the hall.

A pause. "I'm Benny Fields, Jack's cousin."

Likely story, I thought.

He added, "Jack's in the hospital . . . fell . . . broke his hip."

"His sister?"

"In town . . . she wanted to be near Jack."

I waited for him to offer me the registration book, but he didn't. Instead, he started down the hall, saying over his shoulder, "Your friend is already here. He's in the dining room . . . waiting for you."

My heart leaped—my friend—then I remembered: my friend was dead. I shook my head to clear it.

"Take me to my room first. I'd like to change clothes. Tell my friend, I'll join him in half an hour."

He glanced at the dining room door before he said, "As you wish. Let me show you up."

I followed him upstairs. "Anybody else here?"

"No . . . just the three of us."

"Looks like a blizzard brewing."

"The forecast said tapering off before midnight, but right now it doesn't look too good."

"Does that mean we'll be completely isolated?"

"I don't know."

"You don't know?"

"What I mean is we'd have to wait for a plow to come in. No problem." He paused at the door to the room I had been in last week. "Here's your room."

I steeled myself before I entered, but it was just a room, I thought, as I looked around. No wine and cheese waiting in front of the fireplace. No fire. Just an empty room.

Whatever Benny might be, I thought, he's no innkeeper. Surely, there should have been wine and flowers and a fire waiting as there had been the last time. This was like walking into a Holiday Inn room.

"I'll be down later," I said as I herded him out the door and closed it behind him. I shrugged out of my parka and draped it over a chair near the door.

I crossed the room to the door that led to Todd's room. When I opened the door, I don't know what I expected to see, but it was just an empty, dusty room. In my mind's eye I saw his clothes draped over the chair and papers scattered on the nightstand.

"Oh, Todd, you idiot, why didn't you tell me you needed help," I said into the silence.

I returned to my bedroom; it was dusty and untouched. I crossed the room to the window that overlooked the creek. I peeked out but it was pitch black. Shuddering, I saw again Todd's body sprawled on the ice. I leaned my forehead against the cold glass. Steady, old girl, steady.

I hung my blazer on the chair and the gun clunked. I stuck the gun in the nightstand drawer. After I pulled off my boots, I sprawled on the bed, hands behind my head, and stared at the ceiling. I wanted nothing more than to sleep, but I had to get up soon and face whoever was waiting in that dining room.

I dozed off for fifteen minutes, awoke feeling sharper and ready to face my enemy, but I had a few preparations to make first. I changed my clothes and pulled on the boots again. Then, I fastened an ornate western belt that hid a recording device around my waist. I hooked my holstered gun to the back of the belt so the gun was nestled in the small of my back. I smiled wryly—that'll make me sit up straight. The knife was in its usual spot, hanging down my back. I felt mild embarrassment at so much armament, but I wasn't going to underestimate the situation again.

I glanced around the room. Well, I'm as ready as I'll ever be.

"Wish me luck, Todd, wherever you are," I whispered, glancing up at the ceiling. I frowned. I wonder why people always look skyward when they talk to the dead?

I tiptoed down the stairs, pausing at the bottom steps, wondering where

Benny was before I crossed the hall to the front door. I tried it. Locked. I tip-toed back to the stairs and up three steps before I clumped down, making a lot of noise.

Benny immediately appeared from the rear of the inn. He smiled. "Dinner's almost ready. Follow me."

The dining room was small, almost filled with an oak round table that was set for two people. Turner slumped in one chair. He barely glanced at me when I slid into the chair next to him.

"Good evening, Turner," I said urbanely as I draped the cloth napkin over my lap and turned to Benny. "Do you have any wine? Beaujolais?"

He looked nonplused. "Oh . . . of course. I'll be right back."

I nudged Turner and whispered, "What's going on?"

His eyes glittered. "Later," he whispered. When Benny returned with a bottle of wine in hand, Turner slurred, "I'll have another Scotch and soda."

I raised an eyebrow at Benny and said sarcastically, "Charming. How many has he had already?"

Benny shrugged. "Is this wine all right?"

I read the label. Can't go wrong with George DuBoeuf. "Fine. You'd better serve dinner now. I'm starved. I missed lunch."

I watched with amusement as he struggled to uncork the wine; obviously a man more used to screw caps than corks. "Some of them can be difficult," I said sweetly. He grunted.

He finally wrestled the cork out of the bottle and filled my glass before he plunked the bottle down in front of me. I sipped it. "Fine," I called to his retreating back.

"What's going on, Turner?" I hissed. "Why this drunken charade? Who's this Fields? What do you want with me?" I heard footsteps. "So, Mr. Turner, to what do I owe the pleasure of your company?" I asked brightly as Benny entered bearing a platter of fried chicken that probably came from the frozen food section of the local supermarket.

Turner grunted.

The only place I eat fried chicken is Mrs. Wilkes Boarding House in Savannah. I prodded a piece with my fork. Just as I suspected, it was sodden with grease.

"Could I just have a salad?" I asked Benny.

He glared meaningfully at Turner before he headed back to the kitchen.

I kicked Turner's ankle. "Damn it . . . give me some answers."

"Later," he muttered. "Trust me." He leaned over and poured most of his drink into a wilted, potted fern. "Another Scotch, my good man," he said as Benny returned with a couple of nuked potatoes and a plate of burned brown and serve rolls.

"I don't have any salad."

"Cereal will be fine. I'm not very hungry," I mumbled. I was starving.

I winced as Turner grabbed a piece of chicken and cheerfully crunched it. "Better eat something," he said. "Long time till breakfast."

"I can wait . . . where on earth did they get this guy? And why don't they have a chef? This is supposed to be a very exclusive inn, not some highway greasy spoon."

Benny entered as if on cue with a bowl of Cheerios and a quart of milk. "The chef is snowed in and can't make it tonight. I'm doing the best I can." The cry of put-upon men everywhere, I thought.

"Look, Turner, let's get to hell out of here before we're snowed in. We can go to that nice motel in town, have a decent dinner and discuss whatever it is that you want to discuss. If we stay here, we're apt to be snowed in for days . . . we could starve to death." I pushed my chair back as if to get up.

"Stop." I looked across the table at Benny who was glaring at me. "You're staying right here; it's not Turner who wants to talk with you . . . it's me."

I raised an eyebrow. "Really?"

He sneered at Turner. "Go to bed, Turner; I'll deal with you later." He sat down across from me and watched as Turner slowly shoved his chair back and struggled to his feet. He stood there, swaying, looking from one to the other of us, trying to signal me with his eyes.

Turner mumbled, "Night. I'll just take this with me," and picked up his drink before he lurched out of the room.

❧

I chewed my lip as Benny and I eyed each other. Who was he? Turner's boss? A government agent? A friend of Todd's? An enemy? I sipped the wine. Your move, pal, I thought as I eased back in the chair, comforted by the hard nudge of the gun against my spine.

"Mrs. Doyle, we can do this the easy way or we can do it the hard way. It's up to you."

I smirked at him. "Sounds like the beginning of a bad B movie *Agent Fields*." I gave a sarcastic twist to agent. "I don't know what you want.

Suppose you tell me precisely who you are and what you want and then we'll go from there."

I was aware of the silence outside and inside. I couldn't hear Turner upstairs and the snow muffled all outside noises. The room was warm and I felt sweat standing out on my forehead, but I resisted the urge to wipe it off: never let them see you sweat.

Benny tried a smile, but it didn't reach his eyes. "Todd and I were good friends. You were probably the last one to talk to him."

"Except for his killer," I reminded him.

He ignored the interruption. "When Todd came to meet you, he had some papers he had accidentally taken from the office, and I need them back. I think you have them. Could I have them . . . please."

I smiled. "Really, Agent Fields, do you take me for a fool? Do you have any identification to show who you are, what agency you're from?"

"The same as Todd."

I shook my head. "Not good enough . . . you see, I don't know who Todd was working for. We didn't have any conversation before he was killed."

A floorboard creaked above our heads. Benny looked upward, a frown on his face. When there was no further sound he relaxed and looked at me. "We don't seem to be getting anyplace, Mrs. Doyle."

I shook my, head. "There's just no place to get to, Agent Fields, until you level with me. I can't function in the dark." I pushed my chair back. "Shall we call it a night?"

"You don't work for the Government at all, do you?" I played a wild card.

Benny looked startled, his eyes narrowed. "I don't think you need to know where I work. All you need to know is that I can cause you a lot of trouble if you don't cooperate. I can cause your family trouble, your friends, your business associates. You name it . . . I can make your life a living hell. Do we understand each other?" He glared into my eyes. "I . . . want those . . . papers."

My stomach was churning but I kept my expression bland. I needed those papers as badly as Fields did; they were obviously the key to Todd's death.

"I'm afraid you're wasting your time threatening me . . . I don't have the papers, I've never seen the papers . . . and at this point, I hope I never do. I'm getting tired of this case. Nobody is paying me and it isn't worth the aggravation."

I sighed. "It was a personal quest to find out who killed Todd, but obviously he was mixed up in something that I can't even comprehend." I forced tears to well up into my eyes. "I'm just so tired . . . I don't feel good," I whimpered. "I just want to go to bed."

I looked him in the eye and said, "I'll leave in the morning and we can all forget this night ever happened. You can assure your boss that I'll mind my own business from now on. I just want out."

The cat and mouse game continued as we stared at each other. I noticed beads of perspiration on his forehead, too. He was apparently used to people doing what he wanted without having to reason with them. A strong-arm boy. But whose strong arm was he? And why was Turner subservient to him? You would think if they were government agents that Turner would be the superior officer, not this young thug.

He said something.

"Excuse me, I didn't hear you."

"I said . . . go to bed, we'll finish this in the morning."

He needed instructions. I had thrown him a curve ball and he wasn't sure whether or not to swing at it. If only I could overhear his conversation, I thought, as I tried to remember something about the inn's phone system. Switchboard? Phones in the rooms? Damn, I couldn't remember.

I stood up. "That's the most sensible thing you've said. I would be delighted to go to bed." Don't overdo it, old girl. "Maybe, in the morning we'll both make more sense."

I glanced around the room. No phone. I suspected the only phone was in the hall registration area or the kitchen. People came to places like this to get away from phones and television and all the cares of modern life.

"I'll show you to your room," he said, breaking into my thoughts.

I smiled. "Don't bother . . . I remember where it is."

I felt his eyes boring into my back as I left the room. I wondered if the outline of my gun showed. I resisted the impulse to look back at him. I walked upstairs, making lots of noise like my feet were too heavy to pick up because I was exhausted. I didn't have to do much acting since I was nearing the end of my rope. It had been a long day, emotionally and physically.

After I opened and closed my door without entering the room, I pressed against the wall next to the door and listened for noise from below.

He moved quietly from the dining room to the foot of the stairs where he paused. Listening for me, I thought, as I pressed harder against the wall, hoping he couldn't hear the thumping of my heart. I prayed he wasn't going to come up and tuck me in. I exhaled when I heard the scuff of his shoes as he headed for the kitchen.

I crept down the stairs, pausing at the halfway mark, slumping down on the step to listen. I counted the tiny beeps of the buttons on a touch tone phone. Long distance. After easing down the last few steps, I slipped down the hall until I was just outside the kitchen door where I could hear the murmur of his voice.

"She says she doesn't know . . . anything . . . the papers. Yeh, I believe . . . her. Turner will cooperate . . . I'll take care . . . everything. Don't worry . . . I know what . . . I'm doing . . . tomorrow . . ."

I didn't wait to hear the rest. I scooted silently halfway up the stairs, reversed my direction and repeated my noisy descent trick. He stuck his head out the kitchen door.

"I thought you went to bed," he said suspiciously.

"I did, but I got a craving for hot chocolate. Do you have any?"

"I . . . uh . . . have to look. I'll bring it up."

"Fine, just set it on the table in the sitting room. I'm going to take a long, hot shower."

I turned on the shower before I returned to the hall and glanced over the railing. He was still puttering around in the kitchen. I left my door ajar as an invitation for him to bring the hot chocolate inside, hoping he would assume I was in the shower.

Meanwhile, I tried hall doors until I found Turner's room. I tapped lightly and pressed my ear against the door. I heard a faint snore. I turned the knob as I glanced nervously over my shoulder towards the stairs. The door opened and I slipped inside.

The set up was the same as my suite and Turner was in the bedroom. I could see his feet on the end of the bed.

"Turner," I whispered. "Turner, wake up." I shook him hard. "Turner, wake up . . . I need to talk to you." I shook him harder. "Damn. you're dead to the world. Why'd you get drunk?"

I glanced around the room. Nothing much to see. A carry-on bag, a parka hanging in the closet, miscellaneous change and keys on the dresser top, and a paperback with a half-naked woman on the cover on the bed where it looked like it had just dropped from his hand.

I picked up his glass and sniffed. No odor, but I noticed a trace of powder in the bottom. Since when do you powder a Scotch and soda, I wondered. I checked his pulse. Slow and steady. I thumbed up one of his eyelids.

"He's not asleep, he's out like a light," I muttered. How could you be so dumb, Turner, I wondered as I pulled the cover over him.

I stared at him. "Who are you?" I muttered. I glanced at the dresser again. No wallet. I went through his parka and found it in an inside zipper pocket.

I riffled through the wallet. Not much. No personal pictures. Seventy-two dollars in cash, three different credit cards, an Audubon membership card. I raised my eyebrows—Turner, a bird watcher.

I studied his driver's license. It told me he was thirty-nine, weighed 145 pounds, was five feet ten inches tall, had gray eyes and blond hair, and lived in Bridgeport, Connecticut. I dropped his license into my jacket pocket.

I chewed my lip. Government people carry official identification cards with their pictures and other pertinent data on the cards. Where was Turner's card? Or was I wrong again and he had nothing to do with the government? I was sure Chris could track him down with his driver's license.

I listened for sounds from the hall before I left Turner's room. I eased the door open; the hall was empty. I returned to my room. The hot chocolate was standing on a tray on the table in front of the fireplace. I felt the cup; it was cool.

After I turned off the shower, I returned and looked longingly at the chocolate. "Don't be an idiot. You know it's drugged, too," I muttered as I carried it to the bathroom and poured it down the drain.

I turned one of the chairs near the fireplace so it faced the door; I placed the other one in front of it with its back to the door so it formed a protective wall. After I turned out the lights, I groped my way to the first chair and sat down, squirming into a semi-comfortable position after I moved my holster to the side.

I stared at the door and waited, wondering how long it would take Benny to come and check on his handiwork. Not long, I hoped, yawning and suppressing an urge to fall asleep.

22

Late Friday Night

My chin thumped on my chest, jerking my neck painfully and waking me up. I rubbed my eyes, wondering what time it was and what was I doing freezing to death in this uncomfortable chair. Then, I remembered where I was and why.

A strange sound, an undefined roaring puzzled me. I sniffed. Smoke! I leaped up from the chair and tried to turn on the light. "Damn," I yelled. No power. The storm must have knocked down the lines. I groped my way towards the hall door, wondering about the smoky smell. I noticed a glow coming underneath the door from the hall. Strange, I thought, the hall light is still on.

As I started to open the door, a voice in my mind shrieked, "Abby, stop." I realized I'd yelled out loud. The door was hot. My befuddled mind suddenly cleared and I realized that wasn't a light in the hall, but the glow of flames. Smoke was curling in under the door. I quelled rising feelings of panic and forced myself to stand still while I considered the possibilities: they weren't too many nor too good.

Every fiber of my being wanted to open that door and look, but my brain knew better. Turner! Was he still in his room? Unconscious? Benny? Where was the mysterious Mr. Fields?

The sound was horrifying, a train-like roaring, inexorably moving closer to my room. The smoke was filling the room. Think, Abby, think. Remember all those television instructions after all those hotel fires a few years ago. I had to do something. I groped my way to the bedroom where I got my flashlight, and then to the bathroom where I soaked a towel to wedge under the door to buy me some time.

The reporter had emphasized, "panic kills", so I moved slowly but deliberately as I wedged the wet towel underneath my bedroom door. I sat down on my bed to think about the situation.

I blocked all thoughts of Turner out of my mind; I couldn't get to his room and I didn't even know if he was still there.

This is save yourself time, old girl. Get dressed. I added another heavy sweater, took off my pants and put on my pajama bottoms before pulling on the pants again. Layers and layers of clothing—that's the ticket, old girl. Extra socks. Boots. I put on my parka, zipped my wallet into an inside pocket along with the car keys. I pulled the hood up over my head and tied it securely.

I perched on the edge of my bed listening to the fire. It seemed to be moving along the outside walls now and I knew I didn't have much time. I'm not ordinarily a praying person, but I prayed then. And I thought about Jackie, mentally saying good-bye, wishing everything had gone better between us. I even had a random thought for my ex-husband, that handsome ex-beachboy. Well, I thought, we'd both been young, and he did give me Jackie so the relationship hadn't been a total loss.

I thought of Todd. I felt close to him, almost as if he was in the room, guiding me, saying in his reasonable voice, "Come on, Abby, it's time to go. Follow me."

I glanced towards the window and took a deep breath.

"Now or never, old girl." I tried to push up the window. "Strange," I muttered, "it went up easily the last time I was here." I flashed the light along the edge of the frame. Nailed shut.

Gritting my teeth, I drew my left hand into the sleeve and shielding my eyes with my right arm, I smashed my left arm into the window.

"Ouch, damn it." The window was intact, but my arm hurt like hell. I picked up my briefcase, averted my head and swung the case at the window. The window shattered. After I brushed away the broken glass, I leaned out the window and tossed the case as far as I could.

I brushed snow out of my eyes and looked at the fire. I could see that the whole kitchen end of the house was ablaze and the fire was racing along the wall in my direction. As I looked out the window, I could hear the fire break through the hall door into my sitting roam.

I leaned further out and looked towards Turner's room but I couldn't discern anything except that the fire hadn't reached there yet. I looked down. The snow obscured the view. What's down there, old girl? Bushes? Lots and lots of snow, I hope.

As a kid, I was always jumping out of the hay mow into the piles of hay below. One day, I had jumped and missed the hay, landing on the wooden floor on my back. Gasping for air, I had been sure I was going to die. My Uncle Henry had snatched me up, slapped me on the back and set me on my feet like it was no big deal so I had no fear of heights.

"Well, here goes nothing." I swung my leg over the sill, turned so I could get both hands on the sill and eased my body down until I was dangling full length.

"Okay, let go into a nice soft snow bank." Muttering a quick prayer, I released my grip. A branch slashed at my cheek and then I was on the ground, rolling like a parachutist. Half buried in the snow, I tried to catch my breath. Suddenly, I realized it was as light as day and the heat was intense. My cheeks felt sunburned. I scrabbled through the snow on my hands and knees, putting some distance between the house and me. I was almost to the creek before I collapsed in the snow.

I hate fires. Once when I was a young reporter, I had covered a fire on New Year's Eve, an apartment building where two children had burned to death while the firemen, spectators, the family, and I had stood, looking on, powerless to help. I can still hear those children screaming. I had consumed a lot of liquor that night, hoping for unconsciousness, but I had stayed alert and sober.

My heart pounded from the exertion and the fear as I stared at the house. The walls were crumbling. The shape of a chair or a couch here and there flared into flames and disintegrated into ashes before my eyes.

I should get help, I thought. I shrugged. What for? There was no help for anyone still in that house. Only God could help them now.

Sweat poured down my face. I had to get out of here, but where could I go? The car. I groaned. Oh no, was it still next to the steps? I floundered through the snow, keeping my distance from the flames. I rounded the corner and stared at the front area. The old Chevy was limned in flames, giving off a stench of charred plastics.

"Lefty will never believe this," I groaned.

I cocked my head, listening intently. Had someone screamed? As I started towards the house, the rest of the building collapsed with a crash. The only thing left, a stone fireplace chimney, loomed up at one end of the building. An eerie sentinel standing guard over the follies of man. The pine trees near the house were now ablaze, snapping and cracking.

I stopped. "Could have been anything, the wind in the trees," I muttered. "No one is alive in there."

23

Midnight

I trudged in a wide circle around the house to avoid flying debris and ashes and the heat. I found no signs of life. I said a prayer for Fields and Turner as I wondered what to do next. If I didn't find some kind of shelter soon, I'd freeze to death.

An idea nibbled at the back of my mind. Something Heims had said on that first visit: the inn was for total privacy. He and his sister lived in a near-by cabin. Where in hell was that cabin? If it weren't for the snow, I could find that path. I worked my way back to the creek, guessing I was near where we had found Todd's body.

The fire was dying down, but still illuminated the area. I turned my back on the brook and stared back at the shell of the house. The path to the cabin had gone off from the kitchen area.

"There has to be some kind of opening," I said as I did jumping jacks to keep warm. Maybe, I could huddle near the fire and wait for help. Certainly someone had seen the flames, but then it was pretty late and probably no one had been out in this snowstorm.

I floundered through the snow, gasping for breath. I tripped and fell, sink-ing into the soft snow, wanting to stay there. Forever.

"I'm so tired, so tired . . . God . . . I can't go . . . any further. Tired." I let my face sink into the snow and tasted the cold flakes. Is this how it ends, old girl? "No, no . . ." I yelled, struggling to a sitting position. Not yet—some-one is going to pay for Todd's death.

I crawled to my knees and glanced sideways at the house area; the flames were low and smoldering. I stood up. I shivered and swung my arms back and forth to force my blood to circulate. I stumbled a few more steps.

"That's curious." I pulled out my flashlight and shone it on the snow. Among the scuff marks I had made were faint tracks. I straightened up and stared in the direction they seemed to be heading. The cabin is that way and I bet my friend Benny is going to be there.

A real city person would have missed the trail, but I had spent a lot of time with my father, roaming through the woods, hunting deer, and fishing. I hadn't used my tracking skills in some time. They were a little rusty, but still good as I slowly followed the tiny marks left in the snow.

Instinct stopped me on the edge of a clearing. I turned off my flashlight to let my night vision return as I listened and looked. Finally, the outline of a building emerged about fifty yards from where I was standing. Every one of my senses was operating at peak efficiency. My ears strained to hear. All I heard was the sighing of the wind and the swishing sound made by falling snow.

I stared at the cabin, not really seeing it, but more a sense of a hole in the curtain of snow. No lights. No sign of life. No movement. I sniffed. A faint smell lingered n the air. "A car," I muttered. "A car's exhaust."

"Well . . . old girl, you can stand out here and freeze to death or you can go to that cabin and get shot . . . maybe." I smiled. Some choice. Thinking about the exhaust smell, I figured the cabin was empty. In fact, I was willing to bet my life as I placed one foot in front of another and shuffled across the opening, ready to dive into the snow if necessary.

"This is absolutely the last time I get involved in a criminal case," I swore. No more. I'm getting too old for this nonsense. I could be home in bed without a care in the world.

When I reached the steps. I paused and listened as I flashed the light on the porch. Footsteps were still discernible in the sheltered area and where the door had been recently opened, there was a semi-circle of pushed-back snow.

I knocked and yelled, "Anyone home?", feeling foolish. Number one, if there is anyone here, he's going to blow my head off, and two, I'm just whistling in the wind. I pulled the storm door open and tried the inside door. It opened.

I stepped inside, remembering at the last second that I had a gun in my pocket. Fat lot of use it was there, I thought, as I called, "Anybody here?" I found a light switch. Nothing happened. Probably the cabin was on the same electrical line as the inn.

Flashing the light around the room, I looked for a phone. I spotted one sitting on the counter between the living room and a small kitchen. I crossed the room and picked it up. No dial tone. Optimist, I chided myself.

I slumped down on the couch and closed my eyes. I wanted to go to sleep but my mind kept ticking away, sorting through my options. Doesn't take too long to consider two options—go or stay.

My body voted stay and so did my mind. I struggled to my feet and stayed awake long enough to build a fire in the fireplace. I found a comforter in the bedroom and carried it out to the living room where I curled up on the couch.

24

Saturday Morning

The sun woke me up. I stared at the fireplace, trying to remember where I was and why. The horror of the night before hit me and I began to shake. I raced to the bathroom where I had the dry heaves. Leaning my head against the cold tile on the wall, I pondered my options. Coffee was first on my list.

The kitchen was small but well equipped; unfortunately, everything was electric. Didn't these people believe in roughing it? Oh well, I shrugged, I wouldn't have to clean up the mess. I soaped the coffee pot with dish washing liquid before I filled it with water and coffee grounds. After I breathed new life into the fire, I placed the pot in among the hot coals and cooked the coffee.

"Ah, best coffee I've ever had." I sipped the coffee and wondered what to do next.

The door burst open and I was looking down the barrels of three nasty looking guns carried by three men, one bearded.

"Freeze," yelled the one in plainclothes.

I raised one hand. "Careful, fellows. I'm Abigail Doyle . . . Trooper Smith knows me." I nodded at the bearded one. "Right, Trooper?"

He smiled in relief. "That's right, I know Mrs. Doyle." He indicated the man in the suit. "This is Investigator Hurley. He replaced Investigator Mickens . . . this is Trooper Bunkowsky. We've just come from the inn." He inhaled and his voice came out a little ragged. "I thought you were dead."

I smiled. "I thought I was too, Trooper Smith. It was a close call. How did you find out about the fire?"

"Someone called it in . . . about two hours ago," Hurley replied with a warning look at Smith. "They said we could find the torch holed up in this cabin. Care to tell us what's going on?"

I studied Hurley; he was one of those men who's born mature. Even though I guessed his age at no more than the mid-thirties, he had the quiet steadiness of a much older man. He was watchful, alert, patient. He was a homely man with a craggy face and eyes set too close together.

"Have you been informed about what happened at the inn last weekend?" I asked. He glanced at Smith before nodding. "Did you find a body in the ruins?"

"Yes."

"Where?"

Trooper Smith answered, "In the rear right corner as you're facing the front door. Do you know who it was?" I hesitated too long. "You do don't you," he prodded.

I frowned. "I might but I'm not sure and I only know what he told me. I didn't know him personally. He called himself Turner." My hand closed around the driver's license in my pocket. I suppressed my conscience as I left it there.

"He hinted that he was some kind of government agent. He invited me here to discuss Todd's death or should I say Todd's life, but we never got the opportunity. We were going to talk today. We were both exhausted last night and the snow storm was depressing and I felt like I was coming down with the flu and . . ." I knew I was rambling, but I couldn't stop and suddenly I began to shake again.

Cal wrapped a blanket around me and held me close. Looking over my head at Hurley, he said gruffly. "She's had enough. Shouldn't we get her to a hospital, get her checked over?"

I peeked at Hurley who was staring indecisively at the fireplace. "I don't know . . . there's something she isn't telling us." He moved closer and looked me in the eye. "Did you set the fire?"

"No," I whispered. "I could never do that . . . never . . . never. I saw two little kids die that way. Horrible . . . I'll never forget it . . . never." I closed my eyes. "And I'll never forget this either . . . please take me away from here."

I paused in the doorway and looked directly at Hurley. "You'll never know how I felt last night, knowing I couldn't save that man, couldn't do anything to help him. I barely saved myself. I was trapped in my room with the fire raging closer and closer. I jumped out of that second-story window." I touched the dried blood on my cheek. "I was lucky; the snow cushioned my fall. I watched that inn burn . . . I thought I heard a man scream . . . I wanted to die. I laid down in that snow and almost died but something pulled me back to life.

"And God help me, the only thing I could think of was I was glad . . . glad it wasn't me in that building. I have a life to live. That poor, poor man . . ."

"Enough, Mrs. Doyle, you can talk to me later." He nodded to Trooper Smith. "Take her to the hospital. Wait there with her until I come. I'm sorry, Mrs. Doyle . . . can you walk back down that path to the inn? We can't get our car into here."

I glanced around the clearing, surprised that there were no car tracks; I had smelled the car exhaust just a few hours before or had I imagined it? A four-wheel drive could get through this snow.

I nodded. "I can walk."

Trooper Smith walked beside me, his arm around my shoulder. He chatted about inconsequential things like what his son had done last night, where he and his wife would like to go on vacation. I knew he was trying to distract me, to soften the blow of my first view of that building.

Last night the path to the cabin had seemed long, but in the daylight and walking in the tramped down path, I realized it was just on the other side of a small grove of conifers from the inn.

I stared at the scene before me.

Two state police cars, an ambulance, a fire truck and an unmarked car were parked in the churned-up snow of the driveway and parking area. Men leaned against the fire truck, staring wearily at the remains of the inn. Two men were loading a body bag into the ambulance. I glanced away until I heard the slam of the double doors.

The inn was a blackened ruin, the second floor collapsed onto the first floor. There was the frame of Lefty's car. I could make out the shape of a couch near the front. The stone fireplace and chimney were blackened but still standing. I imagined someday they would probably rebuild the inn, leaving the fireplace as an integral part of the new structure. Right now, it looked like a monument to death.

I forced myself to look at the ruins as I tried to recall the sequence of the previous night's events.

Hurley asked, "Can you tell us exactly where you think the fire started?"

He flashed Smith a warning look.

I pointed towards the end nearest us. "Right here . . . in the kitchen. It moved fast. First, I smelled smoke, then I heard that roaring noise a fire makes when it's consuming everything in its path. I'll never forget that noise."

He walked to the area I had indicated and asked, "Here?" I nodded. He yelled, "Hey, Greene, check this area for a fire accelerator." One of the firemen wearily detached himself from the group and joined Hurley. They talked quietly for a couple minutes.

Hurley returned to us. "Take her away, Smith. I'll see you in a little while."

Another fireman intercepted us as we were headed for Cal's car. "Excuse me, ma'am, is this yours by any chance?"

I looked blankly at the attaché case before I recalled I had thrown it out the window last night.

"Yes . . . yes, it's mine. Thank you."

Before I could take it, Trooper Smith took it from the man and glanced at me. "Sorry, but I'll have to look in here."

I smiled. "It's okay . . . just business papers. I used the case to break the window. It had been nailed shut. Then I threw it as far as I could. I forgot all about it."

After he glanced through it, he tossed it on the back seat of the car. "Now you get to meet my wife, Kathy; she's on duty today in the emergency room."

I sighed. "Seems every time I come up here, you end up taking me to the hospital. You must think I'm a jinx."

He eyed me curiously, "I don't think you're a jinx, but I certainly think you're in an odd business for a nice lady like you. Why do you do it?"

"I wish I knew, Cal, I wish I knew." I smiled. "Other people do crossword puzzles or play golf for recreation,, I solve problems for the wealthy . . . unfortunately, they usually involve crimes. My friend, Detective Standish says I'm a nosy do-gooder who does good and makes a lot of money at the same time. I'm not sure which she resents most . . . my doing good or making money."

Cal laughed. "Cops do good too, but we don't make a lot of money doing it, so she probably resents the money."

I shrugged. "I don't do it just for the money. Sometimes, a private citizen can do things that cops can't."

I leaned my head back against the headrest. "I think I like your Investigator Hurley. He's a nice improvement over Mickens."

"Don't underestimate Hurley because he's so soft-spoken," he warned me. "He's a tenacious and thorough investigator. I almost think someone slipped him into this situation to combat the hush-up. Don't try to lie to him or fool him. He doesn't say much, but he notices everything and he remembers. You have leveled with him, haven't you?"

I smiled. "I hope he's also sly. If they, whoever they are, realize how good he is, they'll transfer him to Fort Covington. I'll tell him everything I know when I see him later." I crossed my fingers. I hated to lie to Cal, but if Hurley was such a paragon, he could be somebody sent by these elusive people. I couldn't trust anybody. My weakness was passing and my mind was beginning to function again. A little voice inside warned, "Careful, Trooper Smith may not be what he seems to be either. Why wasn't he transferred, too?"

"When did it stop snowing?" I asked idly.

"About two this morning."

"They certainly clear the roads in a hurry."

He laughed. "You mean it's not like New York City. Well, we have real snowplows, not garbage trucks in disguise."

The hospital visit was routine. A female Indian doctor poked and prodded, pronounced me fit, and stuck a Band-Aid on my cheek. I figured the Band-Aid would cost my insurance company at least two hundred dollars as I gratefully sipped the coffee Cal had brought me, and chatted with his wife. I suspected she had been assigned to keep a discreet eye on me while he made some phone calls.

"Your husband is a nice man."

She laughed. "He has his moments." She looked across the room at his back. "Sometimes, I worry about him when he's on duty. Then, I worry that he'll get transferred. I like this area and my job."

"You mean because of last week . . . like they transferred Mickens?"

She lowered her voice. "I shouldn't tell you this, but I have to trust someone . . . please don't say anything to Cal. Someone called me at the hospital Wednesday and warned me."

"Warned you! How? What did he say?"

"Told me to make sure my husband minded his own business. Mentioned my child by name."

"Why don't you tell Cal?"

"Tell me what?" We hadn't heard him slip up behind us.

Kathy laughed. "Nothing . . . girl talk." She warned me with her eyes.

"Are you pregnant again?" He asked with a gleam in his eye.

"Oh Cal, don't be silly. Now, you may not have any work to do, but I do. Nice meeting you, Mrs. Doyle. Take care of yourself."

"I will . . . and don't worry, I don't plan to visit the Catskills . . . ever again!" I gave her a reassuring look.

I walked beside Cal towards the exit, stopped abruptly and exclaimed, "Darn, I left my watch. Be right back." Before he could offer to go, I darted back to the emergency room where I caught his wife.

"The person who called—male or female?"

"Male, I think. Muffled voice, slow talking, scary."

I chewed my lip. "Look, you can't take any risks with your son. Tell Cal so he can take precautions."

"Tell me what?" he asked. "I wondered what was keeping you." He looked suspiciously from one to the other of us. "What's going on?"

"Ask her," I said.

"Nothing much, Cal . . . just a phone call. Probably means nothing."

"Let me be the judge of that."

She told him about the threat.

His eyes were bleak as he stared at the wall. He turned to me. "What's it all about, Mrs. Doyle? What are you really mixed up in? Who are these people? Why would they threaten my kid?" He held out his palms helplessly, a scared look in his eyes.

Before I could answer, Hurley strode into the room, nodded at Kathy, and motioned to Cal to follow him. Kathy and I stared at each other. I had an uneasy feeling.

"If I don't get some more coffee, I'm going to fall asleep," I complained.

"I can handle that." Kathy left and returned with a steaming cup of coffee.

As I sipped the coffee, I stared at the door, wondering what Hurley was up to, how I would get back to New York, and if this nightmare would ever end.

Hurley returned. "I'm taking you to headquarters. I have some questions and there are forms to be filled out." He asked Kathy, "Is Mrs. Doyle physically all right?"

Kathy glanced at me and I nodded. "She's fine except for being exhausted. She had a horrible experience, Investigator Hurley . . . couldn't your questions wait until tomorrow?"

"'Fraid not. Come along, Mrs. Doyle, I'll even buy you breakfast first."

25

Saturday Morning

Hurley and I faced each other across his desk. We had eaten breakfast silently, lost in our own thoughts. My feelings about him were mixed. Should I trust him? Should I tell him anything? Everything?

"Mrs. Doyle?"

I smiled. "Sorry . . . sometimes I drift off. You were saying?"

"On two successive weekends you visit the Catskills—the Babbling Brook Inn to be specific—and on two successive weekends, we find a murdered male there. Now, as a police officer, wouldn't you be a little curious about the woman who is the common denominator in each crime?"

If I was facing Standish across that desk, I'd probably have a flip answer, but with this man, I wasn't sure that would be too bright. I riffled through possible responses, discarding all of them. I shrugged.

He raised his eyebrows. "A shrug? That's your answer? I had hoped this wasn't going to be an adversary proceeding. I know you've been through a lot. You're exhausted . . . emotionally drained and you just want to go home, but I need some answers before I can let you go." He leaned back in his chair and stared at me.

I rubbed my eyes. "Investigator Hurley, I don't know what I can add to last week's files." I watched his eyes. "And I can't tell you much about last night, because outside of the fire, not much else transpired."

"Shall we quit sparring, Mrs. Doyle? You know as well as I do that the files concerning Todd Mason's death have disappeared . . . and you're the only one who knows what happened last night."

I held up a hand. "Whoa, Investigator Hurley,, just back up a little there.

What do you mean I'm the only one who knows what happened last night? What about the killer? What about Benny Fields . . . have you tried to find him? Have you talked to Jack Heims? Is this Fields really his cousin? Did he see him? How did he break his hip? Was it really an accident? Did anybody in town see this Fields? Did he shop anywhere? Buy groceries? Gas? Rent a car? Did anyone notice any strangers in town? Other than skiers, I mean. Are you sure you've covered every avenue of investigation?" I leaned back, exhausted.

"Fields? I thought you said this guy's name was Turner? Who in hell is Fields? What about Jack Heims? What're you trying to pull, lady? Detective Standish was right—you are one devious son of a gun." He scowled at me.

I closed my eyes. You idiot. Your runaway tongue has done it again. I opened my eyes and smiled at him. "Damn, I'm tired. Cant we do this later? I'd like to go to a motel or even one of your cells and sleep for awhile. I'm just not making sense."

"You have the right to . . ."

"Wait. You don' t have to do that. I haven't committed any crime. I just hadn't gotten around to telling you about Fields."

"You're not a fool, Mrs. Doyle, and you know about police investigations so let's get down to serious business. Now—from the beginning—Mason's murder."

"You've seen the files on that . . ."

"Spare me, Mrs. Doyle, you know as well as I do that they're missing, but I had access to most of the information. Trooper Smith has an excellent memory and I convinced him it would be to his advantage to trust me. Can't I do the same to you? Detective Standish said you can be exasperating but you are smart."

"Standish? That's the second time you've mentioned her. How did you get her name? When did you talk to her?"

"This morning. She's on her way here. Trooper Smith said you used her as a reference last week."

I sighed. Usually, I wasn't that thrilled to see Standish, but I prayed she'd arrive soon and get me out of this mess. Police types seemed to get along better with each other than they did with me.

"Could I have more coffee, please?"

While Hurley was out of the room. I mentally sorted through the information on Todd's death. I decided not to mention Todd's connection to

Caledonia Trucking. I would stick to the facts that had been in the file. As for Turner, I would give him the minimum there. Fields? What should I do about him, I wondered. The police could probably find him easier, but I needed to find him first. Oh, if only I could get to a phone and get Chris started on a paper chase. He could track down practically anyone using the telephone and all of his contacts he had made in his years as a temporary employee.

I passed Hurley in the doorway. "Gotta go to the bathroom . . . be right back."

When I walked by the desk sergeant, I smiled and waved a quarter. "Got my one phone call." From the pay phone in the hall, I called Chris at home.

As soon as Chris answered, I said, "Haven't got time to explain, just listen and act. Run a check on a Benny Fields, and Turner." I read the information from Turner's license.

"Turner is dead. Call in any favors you have to but I need everything about these two guys. I'm at the state police barracks in Kingston and Standish is on her way to rescue me. Glancing over my shoulder, I saw Hurley bearing down on me and he wasn't smiling. "Oh, oh, Chris, gotta run."

"Had to call my insurance agent," I said.

Hands on hips, he glared at me for a minute before he jerked his head indicating I should return to his office. Fast.

We resumed our places in his office.

"Is your husband still alive, Mrs. Doyle?"

"If you can call living in California being alive, he's still alive. We're divorced. Are you asking for social reasons?"

He blushed. "No, my wife is alive and well and at home. I was just curious if there was someone you drove crazy on a fulltime basis."

I laughed. "I'm sorry. Investigator Hurley, I think we've just gotten off on the wrong foot. I have a tendency to irritate people, especially police officers. I guess I should stick to dealing with inanimate objects. Now, how can I help you?"

"That's better. Let me tell you what I know about last weekend; then, you can fill in the gaps for me."

I chewed my lip as I listened to his recitation of the basic facts concerning Todd's death. I envisioned the body sprawled on the ice. I shuddered.

"Wait . . . what did you say?" I interrupted.

"It's typical of some of the mob hits we've been seeing in the trucking industry—kill by injecting lithane, and then as an added fillip, do something bizarre with the body. I read about one where they hung the victim upside down from a rafter in his horse barn. Mason died from the injection. He was dead when they bashed his head against the ice." He looked at me. "A message perhaps . . . that it's not too wise to use your head, to ask questions . . . do you have any ideas? Was he working on anything to do with the trucking industry?"

I shrugged. "Wish I knew. As I told Mickens, I didn't talk to Todd because it was late and I had a mild concussion. We exchanged greetings and went to bed . . . separately. That was the last time I saw him—alive." I choked down the lump in my throat. "Now, which mob are we talking about?"

"Somebody is trying to control all of the hazardous waste shipping in this country from the looks of it. It's a lucrative racket. I asked the area FBI agent about it, but he fobbed me off with that need to know nonsense." Hurley's lips tightened.

"Was Turner an FBI agent?"

"Mrs. Doyle, I'm going to level with you. I don't know if we should have a free exchange of information or not because I don't know who you work for . . . who you really are. In other words, I don't quite trust you."

"But Standish . . ."

"Cops have been bought before and there's a lot of money at stake here."

I smiled. "I'd like you to say that to Standish's face when she gets here . . . and then, duck! She won't even take a cup of coffee."

I suspected that Hurley had been playing on my emotions by going over last weekend's events, hoping to trick me into revealing something he didn't know. You gotta be cool, old girl. Trust nobody.

"You were run off the road by a truck, weren't you?" he asked.

I shrugged. "As Trooper Smith said—you scrape up their leavings all the time. Coincidence . . . accident."

A trooper stuck his head in the door. "There's a New York detective out here." He rolled his eyes. "She's a big'un."

"That's right, Trooper, now step aside," Standish growled as she nudged him aside and stalked into the room.

"Investigator Hurley? I'm Detective Margaret Standish. I believe you have one of my constituents here." She glanced at me. "Ms. Doyle, you've done it again, I see."

The two cops eyed each other. I hid a grin as Standish towered over him and engulfed his hand in one of her big ones. He nodded to himself.

Standish sat down in a chair beside me. She flipped a pad open. "I ran a check on that Turner as you requested." She glanced at me. "You want to talk in front of her?"

He grinned. "It will save her having to pump you on the way back to the city."

I was beginning to like Hurley; he was realistic and had a sense of humor. I wished I could trust him and I wondered how I could warn Standish to be cautious.

"Investigator Hurley thinks New York cops are soft touches, easy marks . . . corrupt." I smiled sweetly at Hurley who was gritting his teeth.

Standish looked startled. Then, she grinned and shook her head. "You never give up, do you, Doyle? She's always knocking cops. If she had her way, there'd be no police except traffic cops; crimes would be solved by people like her for big bucks. These private cops give me a royal pain in the rectum. Sure you don't want to kick her out?"

Hurley shook his head, a faint smile playing around his lips.

Standish gave me a triumphant look before she continued, "Okay, Mr. Turner is from Bridgeport, Connecticut. He works for a Congressman who gets a lot of bucks from trucking companies. All apparently legal contributions . . . but this guy has never met a piece of pro-trucking legislation he didn't like, if you get my drift." She frowned. "Now, things get funny. Bickers—that's the Congressman—had a heart attack about three weeks ago and Turner fell in love. Bickers is pretty well incapacitated, and Turner has sort of been wandering around on his own. That's all I had time to run down before I left for here."

Hurley doodled on the pad in front of him. I stared at my feet. Standish sat quietly. The steam hissed in the pipes. Somewhere in another room a phone rang. Time stood still as we all pondered the implications of Standish's report.

Why hadn't I trusted Turner? He was ready to turn. Love . . . no less . . . and I had treated him like a leper. So much for woman's intuition, I scoffed. Wonder who he was in love with? If I could find her, she might have papers or information.

Hurley cleared his throat. "Ah, er, Mrs. Doyle has added another name to our list since I talked to you earlier. Benny Fields. Ever heard of him? She claims he was in the inn last night, that he probably torched it." He gave me a skeptical look.

Standish jotted the name on her pad. I glanced at the pad and kept a straight face. She had also written in capital letters: KEEP YOUR MOUTH SHUT.

She shook her head. "Doesn't ring any bells with me. I'll run it on our computers when I get home. Now, can I take Doyle off your hands? I'd like to get back to the city. I get nervous out here in the wilderness."

Hurley laughed. "I used to feel like that. I grew up in lower Manhattan. My first assignment with the State Police was in the Lake Placid area. For the first six months I was sure there was a bear behind every tree. Had a hard time getting used to the silence. Now, I wouldn't live in the city if you paid me." He looked at me. "Well Mrs. Doyle, do we have anything else to discuss?"

I smiled. "I don't think so. I'm so tired I can't think straight. If I remember anything else, I'll call you." I stood up and extended my right hand across his desk. "Thanks for everything, I wish we had met under more pleasant circumstances."

26

Saturday Morning – Early. Afternoon

I followed Standish out to the parking lot where she headed for a familiar looking limousine and opened the door with a flourish. "Your car, Madam."

I recognized Johnson from Michael's Limos; he drove me frequently. I nodded to him and then looked at Standish,

"What's this all about?"

"I know you always use Michael's, so I called and charged it to you." She gave me a surprised look. "You didn't expect me to drive all the way up here, did you? I only drive in the city. I wouldn't even know how to find Kingston . . . I'm not some fancy world traveler. I thought you'd be pleased by my ingenuity."

I grinned. "Surprised and thrilled, Standish. Luxury is just the ticket after the night I've had." I climbed in and said, "Home, Johnson." Home—has a nice ring, I thought.

The limo purred down the Thruway while I napped. When we reached the Tappan Zee bridge, I woke up and peered through the mist at the faint outline of the Manhattan skyline way down the Hudson River.

I glanced at my watch. Since it was after twelve, I opened the bar, poured some red wine out of the carafe, knowing that Michael's would have filled it with DuBoeuf's Beaujolais Villages.

I nudged Standish. "What'll you have?"

Opening one eye, she grunted. Then, she sat up and peered into the bar. "Do you have beer?"

"Molson." I poured her beer into a glass mug and passed it to her. "To crime," I toasted her.

She took a drink. "Geez, why don't you travel like this all the time instead of driving around in those old junkers?"

"Wouldn't this be a little conspicuous? Besides. I'm not one of those Wall Street millionaires." I giggled. "I hope Hurley didn't see your limo after I'd just assured him you were the most honest cop in the world. He might wonder how you could afford a limo on a cop's salary."

"I'm sure he could figure out that you were paying for the limo. Why do you think all cops are idiots?"

"Hey, Standish . . . don't get huffy. I don't think cops are idiots . . . just misguided. Sometimes you don t see the big picture because you're only working on one small part of the investigation. When a crime crosses municipal lines or even departmental lines, you don't have all the information or else you have to stop pursuing the case just when you're getting close to a solution. Follow me?"

"Yeh, you're saying you hotshot private eyes can go anywhere, do anything, and get damn well paid for it. Well, I got news for you, Tootsie, most crimes are solved by hard working cops . . . plain old public servants . . . not by some mythical Sam Spade."

"Whoa, peace, truce . . . have another beer. It's your day off."

She shook her head. "You're weird, Doyle. Two weekends in a row, someone has tried to off you and you act like Pollyanna. Wake up. Someone wants you dead. Probably they'd like to exterminate all your friends and family, too." She raised her eyebrows. "Whose toes have you been stepping on?"

Her mention of family sobered me. Jackie. If Hurley was right about mob involvement, they'd stop at nothing to prevent me from solving the case.

I rubbed my forehead. "I'm sorry, Standish, sometimes I'm just too cute for my own good. You're right. This is serious business and we'd better get down to it. Why did you write that note in Hurley's office?"

She shrugged. "I wish I knew. A funny feeling, you know, a premonition. Hurley was smooth. I don't trust smooth cops. Most of us are a little ragged around the edges—know what I mean?"

I nodded. "But your experience is mostly with city cops; maybe they're different in the country, more laid back. I was impressed by him and my trooper friend says he's good." I chewed my lip. "But there was something about him . . . I wish I knew more about him, if I could trust him." I faced Standish. "Could they transfer someone in that fast? Legitimately?"

"I don't know how the State Police work, but I suppose they could.

Somebody had a lot of clout to move everybody out, to close down that investigation. Remember when we first met—the dead general—well, when I started nosing around the Pentagon, someone wanted me shipped to Staten Island, but it didn't happen. Now, if somebody had a lot of political clout, maybe they could arrange it, but it would take some time. This deal in the Catskills was almost instantaneous. That says to me that someone pretty high up in Government is interested. Your friend, Todd, must have been important or he had something on somebody important. Until you know what he had, you're spinning your wheels."

I brooded as the limo rolled along the Major Deegan over the Triborough Bridge in Queens several blocks from where I lived. "Where would you like to be dropped?" I asked Standish.

"Your place."

"But this is your day off, Standish."

"I've got nothing better to do. Let's see what your boy has found."

I shook my head. "Really, Standish, you're such a chauvinist. Chris is my assistant, not my boy." I picked up the speaker. "Johnson, home, but go once around the block slowly before you let us out."

The neighborhood was quiet. The factory was closed on Saturday.

"Will you be wanting me any more today, Ms. Doyle?" Johnson asked as he opened my door.

"No thanks, Johnson, but I appreciate your coming up to get me."

As I watched the limo pull away, I remembered how much Jackie had enjoyed riding in it when she was home in January. I sighed. I missed her; after this was over, I'd definitely fly to San Francisco to visit her for a few days.

Fingers snapped. "Hey, I'm freezing out here."

"Sorry, Standish, I was daydreaming about Jackie. I'd better check on her first thing."

Chris was on the phone when we entered the office. He lifted an eyebrow and wagged a finger at us as he continued, "Uh huh, yes . . . I understand." He rolled his eyes. "Sure, I wouldn't have it any other way. You can count on me. Great . . . Thanks a lot."

Sighing, he hung up the phone. "I used to work for this woman when she was just starting out in government. She's gone a long way since then and I had to assure her that I wouldn't tell anyone where I got the information."

"Well." I prompted.

"You're not going to believe this, but Turner worked for Todd."

I sat down. "You're right, I don't believe it." I glanced at Standish who was sprawled on the couch, gazing at the ceiling. "But Standish told me Turner worked for a Congressman Bickers. How could he work for Todd?" I looked to Standish for an answer.

She shrugged. "Self-interest?"

"Meaning?"

"Meaning—Todd turned him or Todd put him into the job with Bickers in the first place. Anyone know how long Turner worked for Bickers? That wasn't in our files."

Chris grinned. "As a matter of fact, Detective Standish, I do know. Eight months."

I slammed my hand on the desktop. "Damn, why didn't that idiot tell me he worked for Todd?"

"How'd he know he could trust you? Obviously, Todd didn't tell him much about you," Standish drawled.

I stared at Standish for a moment before I turned to Chris. "What else have you dug up?"

"Saturday is not a good day for digging; everything is closed. Do you know how many Benny, Benjamin, Ben Fields there are in America? A lot. I've weeded out the too old, the too young, and the black, leaving me with a dozen or more in his age range here in the metropolitan area. Do you remember any distinguishing marks?"

I closed my eyes and visualized Fields moving around the dinner table. "He's right handed and plays golf."

"How do you know?" Standish asked.

I opened one eye, "He had a slight tan, and I remembered thinking he'd either come up from the South or been on a vacation there. Now, I recall his left hand wasn't tan from the wrist down. Ergo . . . golf glove. So he plays golf and he's right handed. Notice I resisted the urge to say 'Elementary, my dear Watson'."

"I noticed. You were going to check on Jackie."

"Right." I nodded at Chris who put the call through, listened for a few minutes and then shook his head.

"She's gone for the weekend. Her roommate isn't sure where she went." He frowned. "Maybe to visit her father?"

I chewed my lip. "I doubt it . . . they're on the outs right now. Ask her roommate what she took with her . . . clothes." The word "mob" reverberated through my mind. Jackie, I thought, if you're just off on an innocent weekend, I'll kill you myself.

Chris looked puzzled. "I thought you were an only child."

"I am. What's that got to do with anything?"

"She went to visit her aunt. Her roommate just remembered she mentioned an aunt."

"She has no aunts . . . on either side. Get that agency. See what they know." I glanced at Standish who was now sitting up, leaning forward, elbows on knees, an intense look on her face.

I sighed. "I feel like this is a repeat of that January nightmare when Farnsworth kidnapped Jackie. She can't be dumb enough to allow herself to be kidnapped twice in two months . . . can she?"

"Maybe she takes after her mother—too cocky by half," Standish snapped. "Didn't you warn her you were working on a tricky case?"

"Yes. I even hired a bodyguard service for her. I took every precaution or so I thought, but I didn't dream there was any mob connection to this case."

Chris laughed as he hung up the phone. "'You have an aunt.'"

"Oh God . . . of course, Aunt Lizzy. She must be close to ninety. She lives in Napa Valley. Is that where Jackie went?"

"Yup . . . seems it's your aunt's birthday and Jackie gathered up her bodyguard and took her there for the weekend."

"Maybe, it's lucky you didn't have this kid through her teen years; you'd never have survived it," Standish said.

I sighed. "You're probably right. At least, I would never have gotten into this sideline. This may be my last case. I'm not sure I can cope with the added pressure of worrying about Jackie every time I get involved in a criminal case." I nodded to Chris. "Aunt Lizzy is in the automatic dialer. Let's give her a call and make sure everything is under control; then, we'll get back to work."

Aunt Lizzy was delighted to hear from me; she was really enjoying her surprise visit from Jackie and her nice young friend. However, she wondered a little about the friend and she whispered into the phone, "She carries a gun. Do all young ladies do that today?"

I assured her that Jackie's friend was very nice and well-brought up, and that they should all enjoy the weekend. I resisted the urge to say, "Don't allow any strangers in the house."

Jackie came on the line. "Checking up on me again—mom?"

I laughed. "So I'm a neurotic mother . . . what can I say? Now that I have you, I don't want to lose you. Remember our little discussion last month about the dangers in my business . . . well, I seem to have stumbled into another of those convoluted cases. For my sake, you have to be extra careful. Now, the alternative," I said in my Groucho voice, "is a convent in Switzerland."

"Oh, mother, can't you ever be serious."

"Damn it, Jackie, I am serious. I need you to follow my orders in this matter without question. No cute tricks. If you go away again, call Chris and tell him. Stay in touch. If I spend all my time worrying about you, I'll get careless."

After what seemed an hour of silence. Jackie sighed and said, "Okay, I get the message. I seem to have gained a mother and lost a life. Can we discuss this after your case is over?"

"Oh, Jackie, I know how you feel. I realize walking around with a body-guard isn't normal . . . unless you're the President's daughter. We'll talk about it in a few days. If necessary . . . I'll have to retire. Bye."

"Funny, isn't it," Standish said, "men go out there, doing dangerous jobs, putting their children in peril, and consider it part of the cost of doing busi-ness. When women do it, they agonize over it to the point of withdrawing to a safe haven." She looked pointedly at me. "Your daughter could learn to make some accommodations to your work."

I raised an eyebrow. "Gee, Standish. I thought you'd be happy to see me retire from detecting—especially in your territory."

"I'd be happy to see you retire because you wanted to, not because you were forced to. Now, let's get to work."

"Were you ever married, Standish?"

"No. Cops shouldn't have families," she snapped. "Okay, are we through with the Brady Bunch syndrome?"

Chris asked me, "Speaking of work, do you have anything from your meeting at Caledonia yesterday?"

"Right. Let me get my attaché case. Fortunately, I saved it, threw it out the window. Actually, it probably saved me since I used it to smash out a nailed-down window." My hand froze in mid-air as I reached for the case and I turned to Standish, "They were trying to kill me. That window wasn't nailed shut last weekend. I always sleep with my window open, I remember opening it."

"If I were you, I'd be extra careful," Standish emphasized.

I opened the case, dropped the Caledonia notes on Chris's desk and then pawed through the case. There were some extra papers, papers I had never seen before. CLASSIFIED stamped in red on top of each sheet flashed at me. I slammed the case shut. "Guess that's it, Chris."

"Well, I have a couple little things to add," Standish said as she flipped open her notebook. "The Caledonia trucker . . . I agree, I think he was murdered, but I can't prove it yet. As far as the derelict is concerned, he was probably killed for his booze. Happens everyday."

"What convinced you about the trucker?" I asked.

"His wife. She came to see me yesterday afternoon. She's positive her husband could never have made such a basic truck driving error and he didn't drink or take drugs. However, don't get your hopes up; my boss still considers it an accident, so no official investigation."

"Damn, that reminds me. I'm taking a truck trip tomorrow."

Standish raised an eyebrow.

I grinned. "I'm going to be a lady trucker. I'm riding with Flo Warren to Jesup, Maryland, her first solo trip. I'm going along to get an idea how the business works and lend her moral support. This has nothing to do with the murders; this is to improve the Caledonia operations."

"Don't you think you might better spend the day in bed?" Chris asked.

"I'd like to, but time is running out on the Caledonia assignment. They need help in a hurry because of that government contract. As soon as we're through here, I'll take a nice long shower and a long nap. Anything else?"

Standish stood up and stretched. "Gee, I wish I could go on that truck trip. When I was a little girl, I used to play with toy trucks."

I grinned. "That surprises me, Standish."

Her eyes narrowed. "I bet you thought I played with dolls."

"Nope, I thought you played with guns!"

Chris laughed. "I played with dolls."

"You did," we said together.

"I had six sisters."

"That explains why you ended up a secretary," Standish said.

"Hey, hey, Detective Standish, I can be as macho as you two."

I shook my head. "Do you believe this? We sound like three little kids. I'll call you when I get home Monday, Standish, and tell you all about my truck ride. Maybe, I can even fix up a short trip for you one of these days."

After Chris let Standish out, he returned to the office and leaned against the door jamb. "Okay, boss, what're you hiding?" I gave him an innocent look. "I saw the way you slammed that cover down, like a rattlesnake was about to pop out."

"I'm not sure what I have, Chris, but I found papers that I've never seen before and they're marked Classified." I rubbed my forehead as I tried to recall the night before. "Turner must have put them in there when he went upstairs. I'm going to take a shower and fix myself a snack. I'll read them and then we'll discuss our next move."

I dropped my smoky clothes in a heap, deciding I would just throw them away. I picked up the fancy belt, ejected the cassette. It was a sodden mess. Snow, I cursed to myself.

Oh well, old girl, nothing that important on it anyway. I stepped into the shower and let the water sluice away the smoke—the smell of death.

27

Saturday Afternoon

The ham sandwich tasted like cardboard. I reread the papers, trying to digest the contents and make sense of the information. Todd had scribbled notes on several pages. Another note clipped to one page must have been from Turner, written the night of his death.

It said: "I hope I can trust you. They're on to me. After you read these, come to my room and I'll tell you the rest. Beware of Fields. He works for both sides."

I studied the section about Caledonia Trucking, an analysis of its ability to handle the Queens Superfund contract. In the margin of one page, Todd had scribbled: Noreen doesn't know her company has been infiltrated by organized crime. She's on the verge of losing the company.

Then in parenthesis, he had written, "Appt. with Jr. Tell Abby?"

Junior? Russell Caledonia? Tell Abby what?

I poured myself another glass of wine and leaned against the counter, staring at the refrigerator and letting my computer run. The mind is a wonderful thing if you'll just get out of its way and let it work. However, my mind was seriously fatigued; it refused to spit out any marvelous insights.

"What do you do now, old girl? Todd is dead. Turner is dead. Congressman Bickers is in serious condition. Fields is missing. Whom do you talk to?" Certainly not the refrigerator.

I ambled back into the office and dropped the papers on Chris's desk.

"Handle with care." I smiled. "When you're through reading them, lock them in the safe." I glanced at the clock. Almost three-thirty. I dialed Caledonia and was told that Noreen didn't work on Saturdays.

"Is Mr. Caledonia there?" I asked. Same answer. Seems to me if my company was in that much trouble, I'd be working weekends . . . but then, they had me to pull their irons out of the fire.

Chris shook his fingers like the papers had scorched them. "Whew, heavy stuff. What's your next move?"

"I'd be happier if those Government reports weren't so vague and named more names. If Todd and I had talked, maybe I'd know what to do. Right now everything is such a muddle. I'm tired—emotionally and physically, but I have to do something, even if it's wrong. I'm going to Caledonia while nobody is there."

"So much for your nap. What do you want me to do?"

"Call Standish. See if she can get any info out of the department's organized crime unit. See if Berry's name comes up . . . or Caledonia's. Oh, call me a cab. Renting cars is too expensive. By the way, what did Lefty say?"

Chris laughed. "After a string of four-letter words, he suggested that you take your business to his competitor down the street and put him out of business. The car was insured, but not for its full value and you can pay the difference. Fair enough?"

"More than I deserve. I'm just not lucky with cars. By the way, thanks for coming in today."

"No problem. Maria is in Atlanta on a case and I was bored anyway."

❧

Page greeted me at the gate and within minutes Izzy arrived in her golf cart. She grinned at me. I itched to scrub all that garish make up off her face to see the sweet person underneath. But I suppose to Izzy it was all beautiful and made her one of the girls.

I checked my office. Everything seemed untouched. I stood idly at the window for a while, watching the movements of the trucks in the yard. Organized chaos. I jotted down a note and sketched a pattern.

I went to the dispatcher's office, hoping someone besides Potter would be working, but I wasn't that lucky.

He leered at me. "Thought you wouldn't be in today."

I forced a smile. "Must have missed you, Potter." I glanced at the board. "Do you work Saturday and Sunday?"

"Change your mind about that date?"

"No."

"Shucks. As a matter of fact, I work every other Saturday. Anything special you want to know or just idle curiosity?"

Interesting, I thought, his good ole boy accent slipped.

"I was reading an article about a computer-satellite communication system used in trucking to dispatch and keep track of the trucks and loads. In-truck computers feed current information on whereabouts and load status back to the main office computer so trucks can be easily rerouted or utilized to the most efficient advantage. Would that work for Caledonia?"

He scratched his head. That was a switch, I thought, he usually scratches his groin.

"I ain't heard much about that. Sure sounds like it'd put people like me out of work. I don't think most drivers would be too crazy about it either; the company could pile more work on them."

"What do you mean?"

"Under the present system a driver has to stop every so often to let us know where he is, what he's carrying, if he needs orders for a new load . . . whatever. With this system he wouldn't ever have to get out of the truck except to piss and eat. He'd never have any time where he'd just be somewhere, hanging around for new orders. I can see where it might be great for independents, allow them to get the most use out of their rigs. How much does this thing cost?"

I shrugged. "Can't give you a definite figure, but I'd guess the initial cost for a business this size would be substantial." I glanced up at the board. "What's doing this weekend? Anything special?"

"Well, Flo baby's takin' her first trip without good old Jack. I offered to ride with her but she turned me down."

"That was nice of you."

He leered. "It's an overnight." He licked his lips. "And you know how widows are . . . especially new widows." I clenched my fist to keep from smashing it into the center of his shiny grin. "Were you born a slimeball or did it take years for you to get this way?"

He studied me blandly, but the tightening of the corners of his lips gave him away before he grinned. "Hey, lady, don't knock it if you haven't tried it. You change your mind about our date, just let old Elvis know and I'll be ready in a New York minute."

"Don't hold your breath." Trying for a dignified exit, I banged my shin against the desk. I suppressed several unladylike curses. I would not descend to this creature's level.

Potter just doesn't fit, I thought as I limped down the hall. Underneath that bad old boy exterior is a shrewd operator. Nobody could be that repulsive in reality; he's playing a role—his idea of an ignorant truck dispatcher. By grossing me out, he avoids giving me any meaningful information, I thought.

"Boy, he's sure succeeding at that," I muttered as I looked over my shoulder. He was leaning against the door jamb, watching me. When I turned, he gave me a suggestive waggle of his fingers and stepped back inside.

When I entered my office, Flo stood up. "I was wondering where you were," she said, holding out her hand. "I've been waiting for you. Are we still on for tomorrow?"

"You bet. I'm looking forward to it. What time and where?"

"Meet me in the yard at six."

"A.M., I bet."

"'Fraid so . . . is that a problem?"

"No. I'll catch up on my lost sleep next week. How're things going with you?"

She shrugged. "Like living in a nightmare you never wake up from. I wake up in the middle of the night, pace the floor for a couple hours. I keep expecting Jack to walk through the door . . . then I remember." She stared at the floor, one hand shading her eyes. "We can't even have a funeral; they're still holding his body. Nobody tells me anything." She looked up at me. "Do you know what's happening?"

"I'm not sure . . . I do know you convinced Detective Standish that he didn't accidentally drive off that ramp. However she can't convince her boss, so any investigation has to be done on her own." I gave her a searching look.

"Have you had any strange calls? Anyone following you? Anything out of the ordinary?"

"Nothing . . . unless you count Potter. He made his hot-breathed pass the day after Jack died, but then, he made passes at me before. I detest that man. I avoid his office whenever possible."

"Do you remember when he first came here? What did you think about him then?"

She shrugged. "I didn't give him much thought. Jack dealt with him most of the time." She hesitated. "Jack didn't like him . . . said he was a phony. Didn't like his cousin either."

"Cousin? Does he work here?"

"He's a trucker, but I don't know where. He brings Potter to work. He and Jack had a run-in one day, he wouldn't move his car out of the way of Jack's rig. Jack called him an ignorant yokel."

"What did Jack mean, calling Potter a phony?"

"I don't know. I don't remember exactly what Jack said at the time, but it was something to the effect that Potter wasn't like any dispatcher he'd ever known. He suspected Potter was a spy for the boss . . . trying to catch the truckers doing something wrong,"

"Interesting . . . we'll talk some more tomorrow. I'm sure you'd like to get home."

She sighed. "Not much to rush home for these days. See you tomorrow."

28

Late Saturday Afternoon

I finished my notes and leaned back in the chair, suddenly aware that the building felt empty. Even in a soundproof room, you can feel the lack of people. Stretching, I walked to the window and scanned the employee parking lot. It was empty except for the section where the drivers left their vehicles when they were away on trips. I dialed Noreen's office, and then, Russell's. No answers.

Flipping the keys in my hand, I climbed the stairs to the fourth floor where I glanced up at the security camera to make sure I wasn't visible when I entered Russell's office.

I sat down at his desk. The top was bare except for the picture of a short blond woman clutching the hand of a small boy. Well, well, . . . Russell married and a father. Surprise. Somehow, I had pictured him as the perpetual bachelor.

Either he didn't do much work or he was very neat. I opened the top drawer—a few pens, a key, an appointment book. I pulled out the appointment book and thumbed back through February and January. The name leaped out at me. January 5—Bickers.

"My, my, I didn't think I'd find you here."

Startled, I flipped the book closed and glared at Potter who was standing in the doorway, holding a stack of papers.

"What're you doing here?" I snapped.

He waved the papers. "Mr. Caledonia likes me to leave the day's runs on his desk before I go home."

"I was just checking his appointment book to see when he was free."

Damn, why am I explaining anything to this creep. "Do you have a key to this office?" I asked to change the subject.

"This master key . . . pick it up from the guard."

"I see. Well, drop the papers and run along. I'm busy."

He leered and with a flourish dropped the papers in front of me. "Have a nice weekend." He even made that sound dirty.

I watched from the window for fifteen minutes before I saw Potter emerge and flag Izzy. So that's why I didn't see a car in the lot; he didn't drive. I looked towards the gate where a car waited.

I couldn't see the driver. Probably, the cousin Flo mentioned, I thought, as I turned my attention to the master keys. How many and who had access to them?

"Better cover your rear, old girl," I muttered as I returned to Russell's desk. I was sure Potter would say something to him about my being in his office so I left a note on his desk: Russell. I need to talk to you. Half an hour would be fine. See you have nothing on your calendar for Tuesday morning. How about nine? I signed my name, hoping the note would cover me if Potter mentioned my visit.

Noreen's office was a real contrast to Russell's. Papers covered her desk. I sat down and riffled through them—routine contracts and correspondence.

I looked through her appointment book. She hadn't met with Bickers or at least she hadn't entered his name in her book. Todd's name was in two times in January. Out of frustration, I paged forward in the book, stopping at March. The first Monday in March had an interesting entry. Congressional hearing—9 a.m.

Leaning back in the chair, I closed my eyes. Was this the committee Todd had worked for? Was it Bickers' committee?

Sighing, I pulled the phone towards me and dialed my office. "Chris, see if you can get a list of congressional hearings scheduled for the first Monday in March at 9 a.m. Look for any that deal with trucking or Superfund cleanups. Noreen has one listed on her calendar. Also, Russell met with Bickers in January. I don't know what it means."

"Difficult to track anything down in Washington on a weekend, but I'll try. When are you coming back here?"

I thought a minute. "I'm going out to dinner and then I'm returning . . . to bed. The truck leaves at six a.m. We're staying overnight, returning sometime Monday afternoon. If I miss you then, I'll see you Tuesday morning."

"Be careful."

I laughed. "Do you know something I don't?"

"No . . . but trucks can be dangerous. Do you really have to take this trip or is it just for fun?"

"To make suggestions to improve the business, I have to know what happens on routine trips. Besides, Flo may have useful information that she doesn't even know she has and it will be easier to get it out of her in an informal, normal situation." Ah, I thought, there I go again with one of those jawbreakers. I giggled, "And yes, I've always wanted to ride in one of those big trucks . . . satisfied?"

Chris laughed. "You're too much. In spite of all the bad stuff this week, you're like a kid anticipating a big adventure. You still have your sense of humor."

"That's me, good old Abby. I'll probably still be laughing when they close the lid down on me. Actually, Chris, I'm so damn tired and sick at heart that if I didn't laugh, I'd start crying and never stop. When this is over, I'm going to get away for awhile."

"Promise?"

"Promise." I hung up the phone.

❧

"What are you doing . . ."

The familiar voice petered out. Startled, I looked up to find Russell hesitating in the doorway, peering suspiciously at me.

I smiled. "I didn't hear you come in."

"Well I . . . walk . . ." He frowned. "Elvis . . . said . . . you were snooping . . . you know . . ."

"Actually, I was hoping to find you here today and I left a note for an appointment on Tuesday, but this is even better. Now, I'll be able to ask you all these questions—if you have a minute." I smiled and waited expectantly as Russell looked panicky, ready to flee. I wondered why he had come to the office. Was he afraid I'd find something? But what? How'd he get here so fast? Where did he live? Did Potter call him?

"I . . . just came . . . to see if you needed anything."

"Yea! He finished a sentence. "As a matter of fact, I do have a couple questions. Do you know a Congressman Bickers?"

Russell waved vaguely. I figured out that meant "follow me" as he went to his office. He looked around like he was confused before he settled into his chair and reached out to straighten the picture of his family. I sat down across from him.

"Bickers," I prodded him.

"He . . . yes . . . trucking committees . . . nice man . . ." He frowned. "He's very sick, I . . ."

"Has his committee been investigating Caledonia?"

"Sort of . . . because we bid . . . on Superfund . . . contract . . . nothing."

I couldn't wait. "They found nothing wrong with your company? They weren't concerned about all the accidents you've had in the past year? You aren't concerned about them? You think they're really accidents? Warren's death? Doesn't any of this bother you, Mr. Caledonia?" I paused. "'It seems to worry your sister."

"Noreen . . . a woman . . . emotional . . . since father's death . . ."

"She didn't strike me as being very emotional. In fact, I found her to be intelligent and sensible." I stared at him. "Do you resent the fact that she's president of this company?"

He flushed. "No . . . I could have been . . . I don't think I like you . . . I don't want . . . to talk." He stood up, indicating our interview was over. His face had a closed, resentful expression. "I think . . . you . . . should go now."

I retreated to the door. "By the way, Turner's dead." I watched him closely. His expression never changed, but his hands clenched.

"I don't . . . know . . . any . . . Turner."

But he didn't ask me who Turner was. I smiled. "Goodnight, Mr. Caledonia. We can continue this conversation next week." I slipped out of the door and darted into Noreen's office.

Junior gave me the creeps. I leaned against the door, listening. Why didn't he leave? What was he doing? Too bad the soundproofing is so efficient, I thought, wondering if he was phoning someone.

I opened the door. He was standing in the hall staring at me.

I smiled. "Haven't left yet?" I asked brightly.

"Time . . . to close up . . . I'll walk you out." His tone was firm.

I glanced at my watch. "Right, it's pretty late. I have to make a quick phone call." I dialed Standish. "How would you like me to buy you a great Italian dinner? Meet me at Blu Adriatico on Northern Boulevard in half an hour." Standish grumbled but consented to join me.

Russell was still in the same place when I rejoined him. "I'm really looking forward to that truck trip tomorrow with Flo Warren. I've never been in one of those big trucks before. Probably be real interesting . . . exciting," I babbled as we went downstairs.

He stopped dead in mid-step. "What trip?"

"Er . . . uh, you didn't know? I'm going with Flo to Maryland tomorrow. Noreen thought it might make Flo feel better to have someone along on her first trip without Jack. And it would enable me to get a feel for trucking."

"Noreen . . . didn't mention it . . . insurance . . . maybe you . . . shouldn't go."

"But it's all set."

He shrugged. "I guess . . . if Noreen . . . says . . . it's all right . . ."

It was dark outside. Russell headed for his car without offering me a ride, as if he couldn't stand another moment in my presence. Izzy appeared from nowhere, gestured me to jump in; she took off while I was only half in the cart, jolting me back into the seat. She raced to the gate.

I patted her arm. "Thanks, Izzy. See you Tuesday."

Page was no longer on duty, but the new guard called a cab for me.

29

Saturday Night

Even though the Blu Adriatico was bustling as usual on a Saturday night, the owner found a table for me. We exchanged pleasantries about the weather and he brought me a bottle of Italian red wine. I munched on some Italian bread while I waited for Standish. Being on time was not one of her virtues.

"Hope you saved some of that bread for me," Standish said as she sat down and looked around. "Nice place. I've never been here."

"Do you eat out often?"

"Burger Kings and diners. I hate to go to nice places alone."

"Why not? You should treat yourself well, too. I eat in some of these places so often that they think I'm a member of their families. Great veal marsala and shrimp scampi here."

We made small talk throughout the meal.

Standish leaned back. "If I ate here every night, I'd need a new wardrobe. Okay, what do you want?"

"Want, Standish? Can't I buy you a dinner for rescuing me this morning from the clutches of the State Police?"

She frowned at me. "You seem pretty chipper for someone who survived the ordeal you did last night."

I shrugged. "Why not . . . I'm well-fed, mellowed out from good wine and I'm alive. What more could I ask for?" I leaned forward. "Actually, I wanted to discuss a couple things with you."

"Let me guess—what did I find out from the organized crime squad? Right?" I nodded. "Garbage."

"Excuse me? Garbage? What in hell are you talking about, Standish?"

She laughed. "Garbage. What started out as an investigation into mob influence in the carting industry has moved into hauling hazardous waste, nuclear waste—you name it. The tentacles reach not only all around America but into foreign countries, too. Now, you probably want to know if there are any familiar names involved." I nodded again.

She took a sip of her wine. "Berry Enterprises has bought out or taken over at least five trucking companies in the past three years. The investigation of Mr. Berry has been very circumspect because of his connection to the Winthrops. Caledonia Trucking is also mentioned, only briefly at this time. Suspicions center around the number of accidents they've been having. And the reason we're not investigating Warren's death, I have cleverly deduced, is because the organized crime unit has said 'hands off'."

"Don't you resent the invasion of your turf?"

She shook her head. "Really, Doyle, you're too much. You're always trying to promote dissension in police ranks. We're all working together."

"Give me a break, Standish . . . if you're all working together, how come you don't know more about what's going on?"

She glared at me. "What's that supposed to mean?"

"Well, for instance, who were those guys who broke into the factory?"

"Why don't you ask your buddy—the owner?"

"Mr. Granbeck? What does he have to do with this?"

"He refused to press charges. Says you made a mistake . . . they had his permission to be in the factory."

I chewed my lip. "Berry, I bet. He must do business with Berry Enterprises and can't afford to alienate him."

"How well do you know Granbeck?"

"Not that well. He was very grateful to me for redesigning his business and solving a personal problem for him so he made that apartment for me on top of his factory. I haven't seen him in a couple years; he's practically retired. Gee, I hope he isn't mixed up in this business. He's a nice old guy."

"Why do you keep looking around?"

"It's funny . . . I keep expecting to see Turner lurking around; then, I remember he's dead."

Her eyes narrowed. "How do you know he's dead? They found a charred body."

"You mean it could be Fields?" I shook my head. "Nah, the body was found in the area where Turner's room was. Turner was unconscious a couple hours when I saw him before the fire started. He has to be dead. But where is Fields? Who is Fields?" I shuddered. "And why do I feel like I'm being followed." I looked around the room. "But everybody in here, I've seen before."

"Anybody would be paranoid after what you've been through. Why don't you drop this case and take a nice, long vacation? Let us do our work."

I waited until the waiter who refilled our coffee cups moved away before I said, "Why do I feel like you're up to something? It's out of character for you to be so solicitous about my health—mental or otherwise. Give, Standish."

She sighed. "If I level with you, will you drop this case?"

"I can't promise that. I have a contract with Caledonia to streamline their operations so I just can't walk away from this whole situation. And there's Todd's mother—what on earth could I tell her—that I don't care who killed Todd, that I wash my hands of the whole matter? Boy, if you knew Electra . . ."

"You could tell her the police have the situation well in hand."

"Do they, Standish, do they? Are they even investigating his murder? How can you seriously expect me to believe that when the investigator has been transferred, the doctor is in Bermuda, and nobody knows anything. Who got to you?"

She drummed her fingertips on the table and glared at me, a dangerous glint in her eyes. "I'll forget that last remark because you're under a lot of stress. Nobody got to me as you so quaintly put it. I just think you're in over your head this time. These aren't all genteel rich people you're dealing with. Remember those two thugs who almost did you in last January—well these guys are ten times more dangerous. Besides, I'm not always going to be available to pull your irons out of the fire."

"Gee, Standish, hard to believe I've survived all these years without you." I pushed my chair back angrily and stood up. "I bet I can solve this case before you and all your special units because I have personal reasons for solving it, Standish. This isn't a case of money—this is personal."

Blushing, I looked around. Everyone was staring at our table. I realized I'd been shouting. I grinned and bowed, "Sorry, Antonio—you know how the Irish love to argue. Everything was wonderful as usual. I'll take the check."

I sat down. "I'm sorry, Standish. I'm tired. Maybe, you're right; I'm too personally involved in this one. I'll leave the investigation to the minions of the law. But I do have to take that truck trip tomorrow; I can't pass up the fee for straightening out the trucking company."

Standish looked at me suspiciously. "I wish I could believe you."

"I'll call you when I get back Monday. Oh, one more question, the newswriter . . . anything new on her murder?"

"Street mugging. Happens everyday in New York. She was in the wrong place at the wrong time."

"You bet." I muttered to myself.

"Want a ride home?" Standish asked when we stepped outside.

I glanced up at the clearing sky. "Nah, it's about a twenty minute walk to the subway station and I need some exercise. Talk to you Monday."

30

Sunday Morning—Valentine's Day

Turning off the alarm, I burrowed under the covers, postponing the start of the day but not for long. I crawled out of bed, showered and headed for the kitchen and my pre-cooked coffee. Ah, the miracles of modern living, I mused as I sipped coffee and waited for the English muffin to toast. After breakfast I packed a gym bag with an extra pair of slacks, sweatshirt, underwear, a notebook, and my .38. I wore a turtleneck sweater which nicely concealed my knife.

The television monitor scanned an empty street. Still dark, old girl, I thought to myself as I watched a cab cruise around the corner and stop under the streetlight at the end of my alley.

The cab dropped me at Caledonia's gate where a guard pointed to a large black tractor pulling a silver refrigeration van which I had learned is called a reefer in the trade.

"Mrs. Warren is waiting for you," he said, yawning.

I walked towards the tractor, calling, "Mrs. Warren, I'm here."

She rounded the end of the rig, waved at me and called, "Just making a last minute check. Ever been in one of these babies before?"

"No and I'm looking forward to it."

She patted the nose of the black truck. A silver streak ran from its nose back to the door where Caledonia Trucking was lettered in black on the silver streak. The truck looked menacing, gleaming in the early morning light.

Flo announced proudly, "This is your basic Peterbilt long nose. It has a sixty-three inch stand-up sleeper box—that extension behind the cab. I'll sleep there tonight; we'll get you a room in the motel." Turning away from me, she sniffed and blew her nose. I knew she had just thought about her late husband.

"What're we carrying?" I asked to distract her.

"Sorry, bad day." She glanced at the reefer. "It's empty. We're picking up a load of oranges at the Maryland market in Jesup. I'll swap this empty one for a full one coming up from Florida. We're short of drivers right now so that's why we're doing all this juggling around. We'll bring the oranges into Hunt's Point market. If all goes well, we'll be back here by noon tomorrow." She indicated my gym bag. "Stow that in the sleeping compartment. Do you want to take a nap?"

"No way. I want to see everything. This is pretty exciting . . . my first trip."

The sweet cloying aroma of roses hit me as I opened the passenger door. A bouquet of red roses was on the front seat.

"My anniversary," Flo said softly. "We have to make a little side trip."

We went from the Van Wyck to the Long Island Expressway to the Brooklyn-Queens Expressway where Flo turned towards LaGuardia Airport instead of Brooklyn. I recognized the exit where Jack had crashed.

She pulled the truck off to the side, left on the flashers, picked up the roses and got out. As I watched her, she stood on the bank, staring down at the charred area where Jack's truck had landed. I saw her lips moving. Then, she tossed the bouquet of roses off the overpass. I watched the roses separating, swirling in the breeze, floating to the ground below.

"Red roses for a dead trucker," I muttered as I watched her returning to the truck. What a great title for a country western song.

Then, I noticed that the hobo village was gone. I wondered where the people had gone, if they'd come back.

Flo got in, put the truck in gear and carefully pulled back on the road. "We'll get off at the next exit and reverse direction."

A few minutes later, she said, "Jack picked Valentine's Day for our wedding because he had such a bad memory for dates. That way, he said, he would have lots of reminders to buy me candy, roses . . . you name it. He was such a romantic. An idealist." She glanced sidewise at me. "I guess you don't think of truck drivers in those terms, do you?"

"To be honest . . . until I took this job, I didn't think about truckers much at all, except to curse them when they almost blew me off the road. Are you going to continue with Caledonia?"

"I don't know. The money's good. I feel close to Jack in a truck. We shared that. Maybe another company . . ."

As we approached the Verranzano Bridge, I looked back at the fairyland that is Manhattan from a distance rising out of the morning mist. The harbor was dotted with freighters. I said a silent farewell to the Statue of Liberty.

We chatted as we tooled along the New Jersey Turnpike. Gas tanks, chemical factories, new office buildings, shopping centers and garbage dumps went by in a blur.

I loved the views. Sitting eight to ten feet above the road, I could look down into the cars that passed us. I frowned, not sure I had just seen what I thought I had seen.

Flo laughed. "That's nothing."

"Nothing!" I yelped. "That woman had no blouse on and that man had more in his hands than the steering wheel."

"You're apt to see almost anything from up here. Some stuff is funny, but we see some scary things, too. Jack and I were near D.C. late one afternoon when this car pulled up beside us and honked to get our attention. We looked down. The guy was naked! That wasn't so bad, but he was waving a pistol at us, signaling us to pull off to the side." She shook her head. "I don't mind telling you that my heart was in my throat, but Jack . . . Jack was so cool. He slowed down as if he was going to pull over, then he floored that rig and shot off an upcoming exit. The driver of the car couldn't react in time. Jack called the troopers on the CB. They picked up the bozo a few miles down the road. His wife had run off with a truck driver, his mind had snapped and he had been looking for a driver with a woman in his truck so he could kidnap the woman."

"We live in a sick world," I said. How well I know that, I thought, recalling the past two weekends. "When do we make a pit stop?"

"Next turnpike area."

It felt good to get out of the truck and move around.

"Have breakfast?" Flo asked as she studied the menu.

"Muffin."

"Better fuel up." She ordered eggs, bacon and toast. I asked for an English muffin.

I watched the people coming and going, pausing for take-out coffee, playing the video machines, gulping breakfast, studying maps—just a typical group in a turnpike stop. No suspicious characters lurked.

"You seem jumpy," Flo said as she popped the last of her toast into her mouth. "Is there something I should know?"

I shrugged. "I had a little run-in with Junior yesterday. He didn't want me to take this trip with you. I guess Noreen had forgotten to tell him."

Flo snorted. "Noreen forgets to tell Junior lots of things. Jack once said Noreen would be smart if she paid Junior to stay home or bought him another business. Sometimes, in family businesses, the good ones get saddled by the poor ones. Know what I mean?"

I nodded. "What was the senior Caledonia like?"

"Tough. And honest. Jack said he was too honest for this business. Whenever anyone tried to buy the company, Mr. Caledonia would laugh and put an outrageous price on it." Her forehead wrinkled in thought, Flo added, "Jack heard him having an argument with Mr. Berry . . ."

"Tom Berry of Berry Enterprises? When?"

"Yes . . . that Berry. I think it was a month or two before Mr. Caledonia was killed. Jack said he heard Mr. Caledonia say . . . 'over my dead body' . . . and it wasn't but a few weeks and he was dead in that accident. Junior wanted to sell real bad, but Noreen stood fast and the board backed her."

"Who's on the board?"

"Mostly relatives and a couple outsiders—vice president of one of the Flushing banks and a woman who's high up in the telephone company. She and Mr. Caledonia went to high school together and kept in touch all these years."

"Was the vote close between Noreen and Junior?"

"There were rumors . . . that the relatives true to the Italian tradition thought the male should be president, but this woman convinced them that Noreen was the best choice."

"How'd Junior take that?"

"He sulked, but then he sulked when his father was alive. Junior is a world-class stinker. He used to annoy Jack . . ." Her eyes sort of glazed as she stared at the coffee urn. "I just remembered something."

"What?"

"Jack had an argument with Junior a few weeks ago. The drivers who work the Superfund clean-up are going to get a large amount of extra pay. Jack asked Junior if he could be one of them. Junior said no. Junior didn't like Jack. He preferred the drivers who pretended he was more important than he is. When Jack came home, he was furious; called Junior a vindictive little pipsqueak."

"Last week . . . was Jack scheduled to move that tractor or was that a last minute assignment?"

Flo fiddled with her coffee cup. "Jack was working overtime that Monday because he wanted to take tomorrow off. We were gong to have a long weekend in Atlantic City to celebrate our anniversary." She sniffled and blew her nose. "Sorry . . . anyway, Jack called me from the yard, said he'd be late for dinner. Said just as he was leaving, Junior had asked him if he'd mind dropping that rig off . . ."

"Junior! Would Junior normally be working that late?"

"He . . . you're right . . . he doesn't usually work late or on weekends. Junior puts in as few hours at the office as he can get away with. But I'm sure Jack said Junior had asked him. The dispatcher would know."

She rubbed her forehead. "I almost forgot . . . something else funny . . . Jack was elated, said we might get in on the Superfund assignment after all . . . he said Junior had had a change of heart, wanted to use only the best drivers. Jack's record was spotless."

I didn't know if Flo's information helped me or not. It made Jack's presence in that tractor too much a matter of chance. If he hadn't been at the yard late, if Junior hadn't been working . . . if, if and more ifs. What did it mean?

"We'd better get moving," Flo said as she picked up the check.

"Right." I took a last careful look around the restaurant. No familiar faces and no unfamiliar faces that seemed to have an unusual interest in us.

I followed Flo to the truck where she walked around it making a visual inspection of the connections, the tires, and the rig in general.

"Looking for anything in particular?" I asked.

"Routine. Always check your rig when you stop. You might catch a small problem before it becomes a major one on the road."

Flo wasn't very talkative when she was driving. She seemed to have withdrawn into herself. Once in awhile, she muttered a mild curse when some nut cut in front of her or drove fifty in the passing lane.

I slouched in my seat, letting my computer run while I watched the passing scenery. We passed into and out of Delaware in minutes.

Flo slowed when we hit the Maryland line. "They're tough on speeders here," she muttered as she maneuvered into the I-95 lanes to Baltimore.

I noted some of the common truck names I saw—J.B. Hunt, Ploof, Allied, CF.

"What does Berry call his trucking division?" I asked.

"Berry Transport. Fire engine red tractors with a black scrolled BT."

"Does he have a slogan like "we aim to deliver'? Did I ask you that before?"

She nodded. "I told you a few companies use that slogan, but you have to remember a Berry tractor could be towing some other company's trailer." She frowned. "You think one of his trucks forced Jack off the road?"

I shrugged. "Maybe. I just don't know. The one that shoved me off in the Catskills had that slogan. The trailer at the scene of Jack's accident could have had that slogan."

"The slogan was on the trailer . . . right? Not the tractor? Did you see anything written on the tractor? Words? Emblems?"

I visualized my accident. My only impression of the tractor was that it was dark and at night any color except white or silver might appear dark.

"I don't remember much about the tractor. Dark color. I don't recall any lettering, but then I didn't see much of it. I was too busy trying to save my neck."

Flo shrugged. "I'm sure one of Berry's rigs will be in Jesup. You can see if it rings any bells."

Traffic was light in the Baltimore area and we whizzed through the tunnel. A short time later, we exited at Jesup and Flo stopped at a traffic light.

"Want to stay at the Holiday Inn or the trucker's motel?"

"Where do you usually stay?"

"The truckstop, but then I'm going to sleep in the truck. The rooms aren't as fancy as the Holiday Inn . . ."

"But I'd hear real truck driving talk . . ."

"Right . . . and meet real truck drivers and eat real truck driver food . . ." Flo laughed. "Jack and I used to go on like this all the time. I'm glad you came with me. You've helped." She looked thoughtful. "They say when you lose someone you love, it gets easier with every passing day. Somebody told me that in six months, I wouldn't be able to remember what he looked like."

"That person sounds like an insensitive clod." I snapped. "Todd and I were very dear friends . . . lovers once. We didn't see each other often, but he hasn't been out of my mind once since he died."

Flo glanced at me curiously. "You think Jack's death and your friend's are connected, don't you?"

"I think Caledonia has a cancer and I'd like to keep it from spreading."

Flo parked the truck. "Wait here for me. I'll check in the office and see if they have any word on our Florida truck."

While I waited, I watched the activity around the Maryland Produce Market. Trailers were backed up to loading bays. On the other side of the road, fast food places, gas stations, and the huge truckstop competed for truckers' business.

Flo returned. "He was delayed leaving Florida. I'll unhook this trailer and we'll check you into the motel."

She backed into an empty space. I watched her as she disconnected the hoses and wires between the tractor and the trailer. Then, she cranked up the support legs on the trailer. After a final check, she got in and drove the tractor away from the trailer.

"I'm impressed," I said. "Wonder what men think when they see delicate little ladies doing all this hard work."

She laughed. "Some of them think we're crazy. Others really resent us. We've taken the macho out of trucking or so they think. Ready for something to eat?"

"You bet . . . trucking makes me hungry."

We killed time the truck driver way—eating, talking, playing video games. After dinner we went to my room and read the Sunday papers.

About nine, Flo asked, "Mind if I use your shower? Then, I'll head out to my bunk."

"You know it's pretty silly for you to sleep in the truck, when I have two perfectly good beds here."

She smiled. "I guess you're right. I only said I was going to sleep in the truck in case we couldn't stand each other."

"Well, I can stand you if you don't snore."

"Jack never mentioned it so I guess I don't. I'll get my stuff and make sure the truck is all right."

31

Sunday Night

I showered and stretched out on the bed. I dozed. I woke up half an hour later. The other bed was empty. No noise came from the bathroom.

"Flo?" Why wasn't she back, I wondered as I dressed quickly, slipping the gun in my jacket pocket.

I checked the restaurant, the bar and the video room before I went outside. I shivered. The temperature had dropped considerably and it was spitting snow. I trudged out back to where she had parked the tractor, relieved to see it still sitting there.

As I took a step towards the truck, a hand reached out, grabbed nay arm, and dragged me behind a dumpster before I could react. I started to scream.

"It's me," she hissed.

"Standish! What in hell are you doing here?"

"Following you . . . to make sure you don't get into any more trouble."

"What's going on?" I whispered. "Flo went out to the truck over a half hour ago to get her stuff. I'm worried about her. Did you see her?"

"She's in that truck. I saw her, followed her out and I figured she was going to sleep in the truck. Hmmm, the inside light is still on."

I chewed my lip. "She decided to share my room; she should have been back by now. Something's wrong."

"Got a gun?"

"Well . . . uh . . ."

"Come on, you got your gun or not?"

"Yeh. I know it's illegal for me to have it here, but . . . "

"Relax, I don't have any standing in Maryland either. You take the passenger door, I'll take the driver's side. Be careful."

I grabbed her arm. "Wait. Have you been watching the truck all the time since she came out?"

"Are you kidding! It's freezing out here. I saw her head towards the truck and I went back into the lobby where I've been waiting for you to appear. When I spotted you, I ducked out here to see what you were up to."

"I don't like it, Standish," I whispered. "Do you think someone is in there with her?"

"We won't find out by standing here. Let's do it."

We pulled open the doors and stared across the seat at each other.

"My God," I breathed. I leaned in and touched Flo's arm.

She was slumped between the front seats, blood streaming from an ugly gash on her forehead, running between her eyes and down the bridge of her nose. Her nose was twisted and blackened—broken. Her breathing had a rasping quality, but at least she was still breathing. A few bills and some change were scattered on the driver's seat where her wallet had fallen.

"I'll get help," Standish muttered.

Just as she turned to go, four police cars with sirens and red lights flashing roared into the parking lot and pinned Standish in the glare of the spotlights. She stuffed her gun into her pocket and raised her hands, yelling, "Police officer."

Suddenly, we were surrounded by cops. Following Standish's example, I shoved my gun into my pocket. "It's okay, Flo, help is here."

❧

An hour later, Standish and I sat outside the emergency room, listening to a burly State Police sergeant explain what had happened to Flo.

"We're always getting escapees from the prison down the road from the truckstop; they head there to rob somebody, steal a car for a getaway. Unfortunately, she met up with one of our real vicious punks. You've got 'em in New York . . . right, Detective Standish?"

"That's for sure. What did the doctor say?"

"Concussion, broken nose. He'd like to keep her here for a couple days. We'll get the punk." He hitched up his gun belt for emphasis. "By the way, Mrs. Doyle, she'd like to speak to you before you leave."

Flo looked pathetic with a big bandage wrapped around her head. She peered at me through blackened eyes, reminding me of a raccoon.

"Gee, Flo . . . I'm so sorry . . . if I hadn't fallen asleep, I might have been able to help you."

"Don't worry," she said in a weak, raspy voice. "You wouldn't have had a chance. He was hiding near the truck; he was on top of me as soon as I opened the door. I shouldn't have tried to argue with him. I forgot about the prison near here."

"Anything I can do for you? Standish and I are going back tonight. We're both too wired to sleep."

"See that the truck is secured and leave the keys with the desk clerk. Also, leave a message for our driver coming from Florida. Could you also call Ms. Caledonia and tell her what happened." Her voice faded; she was obviously in a lot of pain.

"Flo, are you sure it was this escaped prisoner, that it had nothing to do with . . . you know . . . all the stuff going on?"

Her hands clenched, gripping the table side and she stared at the floor. "That woman with you—I heard you call her Standish—the detective?"

"Yeh, she's been following us."

"Get her in here."

I stuck my head out the door and waved to Standish. She entered the room, closed the door and leaned against it while she stared at Flo.

"You looked better without the black eyes," Standish said. "You have something to tell me?"

Flo's voice was low and we strained to hear her. "That was no prisoner who attacked me. He said, 'tell Noreen Baby to sell while she still has something to sell,' then he bashed me and took my money." Standish and I exchanged looks. "Should I tell the troopers?" Flo asked.

"I'll tell the sergeant," Standish said. "Can you describe this guy?"

"Skinny . . . white. I didn't really get a good look at him. It happened so fast."

"What did his voice sound like? Any accent?" I asked.

"He sounded mean . . . maybe a drawl . . . I don't know. Bad breath . . . he had bad breath . . . garlic."

"Not much to go on," Standish muttered as she left the room.

I patted Flo's hand. "You did the best you could. Besides, the derelict told me he saw a slim white man standing on the road, watching the accident scene, and he thought he was the driver of the truck that forced Jack off the overpass." I thought a minute. "Did you notice any familiar trucks when you went out to the parking lot?"

"You mean Berry trucks?"

"Or anything with 'we aim to deliver' on it."

"I never thought I'd be spending my anniversary in a hospital . . . Jack dead . . ." She sobbed. She started shaking violently.

Alarmed, I stuck me head out the door and yelled for the doctor. As he ran by me, I told him what she'd been through in the past week.

"A little sedative and then bed will help," he said. He waved me out of the room.

32

Early Monday Morning

When Standish pulled into my alley, I glanced at my watch. Almost six. Another night without sleep.

"Breakfast?" I yawned.

"No thanks. I'm going to catch a nap before I go to work."

I smiled. "See, Standish, you can drive in the country."

"Yeh, but I hated every minute of it and for all the good I did, I might as well have stayed home. That poor woman."

"Why did you follow us?"

"I thought someone would make another attempt on your life."

"Gee, Standish, I didn't think you cared."

"I don't," she snapped, "but your daughter loves you." She glanced at me. "What're you doing for the rest of the day?"

"Routine business. I still have a trucking company to analyze unless this latest episode persuades Noreen to sell the business." I started to close the door. "Wait, Standish—one more thing—if you get anything on this Fields, call me or leave a message with Chris."

She scowled at me. "If it's not classified."

I almost laughed before I realized she was serious. "Classified? You know something?"

"Damn little, but there's a government connection." She sighed. "Life would be simpler if you'd had that conversation with your boyfriend."

"Yes . . . he might still be alive." I bit my lip to suppress my anguish. "Later, Standish."

I left a note for Chris to wake me when he came to work. It seemed like I had barely fallen asleep when Chris called me on the intercom. "Abby, wake up!"

"I'm awake—I think."

"Electra Mason is calling from London. She insists on speaking to you—NOW."

I groaned. "I'll take it in here. Switch her over and bring me some coffee, please."

"Abby, I tried to call you all day yesterday." Her tone was accusatory.

"Sorry, Electra, I was working. How are you doing?"

I listened to her complaints about the London weather—damp and cold; Lady Ursula's party—boring; the food—dull, and the conversations—insipid.

Finally, she got to the point. "What have you found out about Todd's death?"

I sighed. "He was probably killed because of something he was working on. Unfortunately, his papers are missing and nobody seems to know exactly what he was doing." I described the key to her. "Any ideas?"

"This may sound silly, but Todd had an old toy box that had a key like that."

"Do you know where the box is?"

"I saw it at the apartment once. In fact, I commented on it and Todd said it held his new toys and gave me that crooked grin of his."

"Can you describe the box?"

"Oak . . . beat up, probably eighteen inches or so by three feet."

"Where was it?"

"The foot of his bed."

"The best place to hide something is in plain sight," I muttered.

"Oh, Electra, before you hang up . . . do you know the Winthrops in Connecticut? Their daughter? Her husband—Tom Berry?" After she said yes to all three, I asked, "What do you think of Berry?"

"Diamond in the rough . . . sort of scary under that veneer of polish."

"Did Todd ever mention him to you?"

"I don't remember." Her voice rose. "Does Tom Berry have anything to do with Todd's death? I've heard he has a shady past."

Oh, oh, I thought, I'd better head Electra off at the pass. "No, I met him and I was just curious about him. By the way, Electra, I think this will soon be over and you'll be able to come home."

A long pause. "Nothing can bring Todd back . . . but I'd like to be able to come home. I want to bury Todd . . . beside his father."

I envisioned the Mason family plot with the impressive monuments. The family had been among the early settlers of Boston.

"Have they released his—Todd's body?" I asked.

"Not yet. My lawyer contacted the coroner up there or his representative. Got the run around. But if you're near a solution . . ."

"Be patient. I'll be in touch soon."

I glanced at Chris who was hesitating in the doorway holding a cup of coffee. Indicating the nightstand, I scribbled some notes.

"I was surprised to get your note," he said. "I thought you wouldn't be back until late today."

"The trip was a fiasco. Sit and I'll tell you about it." I smiled. "Not used to doing business in my bedroom, Chris? Relax." I told him about the attack on Flo and the message for Noreen.

When I finished, Chris stood up. "Where do you want to start?"

"I think I should pass the message on to Noreen—and Junior." I frowned. "Why do you suppose Junior wasn't mentioned in the message?"

"Because she's the company president."

"Maybe, but then, Junior may be willing to sell, so he doesn't need to be threatened. Oh well, let me get dressed and we'll get started. Call Noreen . . . tell her I'll be there in forty-five minutes."

"Where are you going from there?"

"The Mason apartment to see if that toy box is still there."

I wanted to deliver the message to Noreen in person so I could see her reaction.

When I arrived at her office, she looked puzzled. "I thought you were in Maryland with Flo Warren."

"I was, but we had a problem. Flo is in the hospital with multiple injuries she received from some thug."

"She was mugged!"

"Not exactly. That's what it was supposed to look like, but he had a message for you—sell or else." I watched her eyes. I don't know what I expected, but it wasn't the look of abject despair she gave me.

"I guess it's time to admit I'm beaten," she said. "Too many lives are being affected. Russell is right—we can't risk our drivers' lives any longer."

"When did you last talk to Jun . . . er, Russell?"

"Saturday. He was angry that you were going with Flo. He thought it might cause a problem on our insurance."

I bet, I thought. "Who else knew about our trip?"

"The dispatcher, my secretary. Why?"

"I didn't spot anybody following us, so he had to be waiting for us." Then, I remembered I hadn't noticed Standish either and she was hard to miss. Maybe my skills were eroding.

"I'll want to talk to them in a few minutes. May I use your phone?" I called Standish. "Did you follow us to Jesup?"

"Nah, I drove to Jesup, spotted the truck and checked at the motel. What's your problem?"

"How did you know where we were going?"

"You losing your memory, Doyle—you mentioned it. I checked with the dispatcher for the time. Now, if you don't mind, I have work to do." She hung up.

I stared at Noreen. "No one had to follow us. Seems everybody in the world knew where and when we were going."

She shrugged. "A fruit run isn't exactly classified information."

I wanted somebody to blame for Flo's injuries, someone besides myself. I had been careless.

I chewed my lip. "If you sold the company who would you sell to?"

"I guess Tom Berry. He's made several offers since Dad died." She stared out the window. "I hate to be defeated. My father worked so hard to build this company, to give us a good life."

"Are the offers fair?"

"They're a little low, but he knows we're in trouble and nobody else has offered to buy, so I suppose they're fair. What are you thinking about?"

"Call Berry and tell him you're considering selling. Put on an act . . . how weary you are about all your problems, how you'd like to just take the money and travel. But you do require a position for Jun—er, Russell, if he wants it, with Berry Enterprises. Tell him you're sending an emissary to meet personally with him tonight."

She looked confused. "I don't understand. What good will that do?"

"I'm the emissary and I hope, in a face to face meeting to determine if Berry is at the base of your problems, and if so, how I can stop him." I smiled at her. "You could run a trucking company that only had normal problems, couldn't you?"

"Of course. Dad trained me." Her eyes lit up, the fire returned. "Do you think you can help me keep the company?"

I smiled. "I hope so—with a little bit of luck and if Todd's toy box is still in his apartment and contains what I think it does."

I called Chris. "I'm headed for the Mason apartment. Has Standish called?"

"Not yet. How'd the meeting with Ms. Caledonia go?"

"Fine. We're going to continue. She's setting up a meeting with Berry and will let you know where and when. I'll call you later. If Standish calls, tell her where I've gone."

33

Late Monday Morning

The cab dropped me at the corner of First Avenue and 48th Street. As I peered up 48th, I still found it hard to believe that the shooting of Marti Carr was a routine mugging gone wrong, but anything was possible in New York.

The doorman remembered me. Or my twenty.

"Has anybody tried to get into the Mason apartment?" I asked.

"Not on my shift." His eyes evaded mine and I wondered why.

"Don't you usually work nights? You were here the night the ABC gal got killed."

He fidgeted with his lapel. "I switched to the day shift right after that."

I pushed the elevator button. Why was he so nervous? Did he see something that night that he hadn't told the cops? Maybe, I should have Standish lean on him. I smiled at the image of tall Standish leaning on this shrimp.

Only in New York would the floors from the 44th to 50th be designated penthouse apartments. I got off on the 50th floor and opened the door to the Mason apartment.

After a cursory inspection I headed for Todd's bedroom. The box was still there. The top was open, mocking me. The box was empty.

"Damn . . . damn, what an idiot I've been."

I took the elevator down and as soon as the door opened, I strode across the lobby, spun the doorman around and slammed him up against the wall.

"Who'd you let into that apartment?" I snarled.

"A cop . . . a cop . . . he said he was a cop . . ." he babbled.

I loosened my grip. "Describe him." Just as I suspected, he described

Fields, but how had Fields found out about the box. I didn't know about it until I talked with Electra and the only one I had told was Noreen.

"When was he here?"

"Just a few minutes before you came . . . you . . . you just missed him. I'm sorry . . . I didn't know."

I brushed off the front of his coat and smiled at him as I tucked another twenty into his pocket. "Let's just forget this little meeting, shall we? But don't let anyone else into that apartment or you'll be unemployed. Do you understand me?"

"Yes ma'am," he mumbled as he backed away from me.

I walked outside, glanced at the stationary police post across the street where the cop inside was staring at me, and then I walked towards Second Avenue. I scanned the street. No sign of Fields. What did he get out of that damn box? Where was he now? I wondered if he had been on my tail all the time and I had been so preoccupied by Turner that I hadn't noticed him. Had Turner just been the beard?

I walked to the Citicorp Center where I bought a cup of coffee and sat down at a table in the atrium and brooded. Oblivious to the bustle of people all around me, I let my mind go blank. Sometimes when I didn't try, the answers came unbidden.

"Mind if I join you? "

Startled, I kicked out the chair I had been resting my feet on. "Standish! What're you doing here. How'd you find me?"

She sneered. "I am a detective. When the doorman said you'd left there, I asked myself—where would I go on a cold day? Coffee. Then, I said an upscale lady like Doyle wouldn't just pop into a sleazy hole in the wall; she'd go somewhere with ambiance—I like that word, Doyle—your class must be rubbing off on me."

"Get to the point, Standish."

"So, I was standing on the corner and I looked up and lo, there was the slant roof of Citicorp. Perfect. And here you are." She sat down, loosened her coat and glanced around. "Nice that all these people have so much free time. Doesn't anybody in New York work anymore?"

"Before you ask—I didn't find anything. Somebody beat me to it. I'm back to square one."

"Ah yes, Benjamin Joseph Fields." She smiled that shark's smile of hers. "I've put an APB out on him. He won't be running around much longer. If we're lucky, he'll still have whatever he took from the Mason apartment on him when we catch him."

"Give, Standish. What did you find out about him?"

"Well, good old-fashioned police work. Mr. Fields is not a government agent as such; he works for Congressman Bickers in a number of ways—driver, bodyguard, gofer, pimp—you name it and Mr. Fields does it."

"Including murder," I muttered.

"Probably. Anyway, I found a secretary in the congressman's office who dislikes Mr. Fields. She said he had a strange relationship with the congressman. Incidentally, people are willing to talk a little more now because they don't think the congressman will be returning to Washington even if he lives. She sort of described Fields as Bickers' tame dog who turned into a pit bull a few months ago. What does that indicate to you?"

I smiled. "Blackmail. Fields had something on the congressman that put him in the driver's seat and he's gone out of control." I didn't mention the pictures I had found. "Fields probably isn't big on brains but thinks he is. He impressed me that night as someone who was operating beyond his depth, and all the more scary because he was stupid and didn't know he was stupid. They're the most dangerous people of all because they have no inkling of the consequences of their actions."

Standish nodded. "He may not be overly bright but he's cunning. I've just been talking with Hurley. Now, something interesting—no lid on the Turner investigation. Does that tell you anything?"

I shrugged. "I'm not sure. Turner covered up Todd's death and there's nobody to cover up his? Bickers is too ill to manage another cover up? Fields is too busy or doesn't care anymore?" I watched for an expression with each of my answers, but Standish just stared at me. "Well, give me a hint," I said irritably.

She sighed. "I don't have a crystal ball, but I guess it's logical that the congressman sponsored the cover up in the first place. If we can get our hands on Fields, we'll get the answers."

I glanced up at the floors above me, scanning the faces that were looking down into the atrium. I shuddered. Fields could be up there, watching us, aiming a gun at us.

"Did you talk to the doorman about his so-called cop?" I asked.

"Yeh. Fields fits that description. He could be watching us right now." Standish looked up at the floors above. Then, she glared at me. "If he is, we're sitting ducks. Let's get to hell out of here. These places give me the creeps. I like smoky little coffee shops and waiters named Moe who insult you and slop the coffee into the saucer."

"You're a Neanderthal, Standish."

"Come on, I'll give you a lift," Standish said as she led me to her car parked in a no standing zone. She flipped the police parking card onto the seat and asked, "Where to?"

"Home, I guess. I have some real work to do."

As we drove over the 59th Street Bridge, Standish said, "Incidentally, I called the hospital and found out Mrs. Warren will be released in a couple days. Also, I talked to the sergeant down there. They got their escapee. He'd gone directly to Baltimore. What did Caledonia have to say about her warning?"

"She's scared. Wants to get out of the business." I almost told Standish about my prospective meeting with Berry, but I didn't want her interfering.

She looked at me slyly. "Seems to me I remember someone else who was scared and wanted to get out of her business. Still feel that way?"

"Let's just say I'm ambivalent. I'm not sure I can handle it when Jackie is inadvertently put into danger by my actions, but I've thought about it quite a bit lately. My father was a construction worker—not exactly the world's safest profession. His friends got killed and he was badly injured a couple times, but my mother and I never thought of asking him to do something else. I think Jackie and I are going to have to come to terms with the dangers inherent in some of my investigations."

I smiled. "After all she shares in the rewards from those ventures, and I suspect she's beginning to find the life exciting."

"And you find it exciting," Standish said with a sidewise look.

I threw up my hands. "Lord knows, I do. Life would be pretty dull if all I did was streamline business operations. Maybe, in a different time, I would have become a cop like you."

She laughed. "Not enough money for you. Besides, police work—real police work—is eight hours of boredom and drudgery and eight seconds of sheer terror."

"Nobody's ever satisfied. Well, here we are. Want to come up for a sandwich?"

"No thanks. I've got work to do. Keep in touch."

Chris met me at the door. "I'm glad you're back. You have a message."

I perched on the edge of his desk. He pushed the play button.

"You have something I need and I have something you want. Let's deal. I'll call back at one." Fields' voice was confident.

34

Monday Afternoon

Chris and I alternated looking at the phone and the clock.

The phone rang, but the voice wasn't what I expected; it was a woman's. "Hello? I have a message for Ms. Doyle from a friend."

"This is Doyle. Go ahead." I nodded at Chris who had activated the recorder.

"My friend says to bring what he wants to the boat basin on Flushing Bay at two. He'll be waiting for you. Come alone. No tricks."

"I'll be there."

Chris raised an eyebrow. "Slick. That place will be deserted on a cold February afternoon."

"Right and he has access to several escape routes—the Van Wyck, Whitestone Expressway Northern Boulevard, Grand Central Parkway. It's almost impossible to stake out that area on this short notice. He'd spot a police car in a minute."

"Let me go with you."

"No way, you're needed here. If I don't get back by four, call Standish. Call me a cab and I'll be on my way." I gathered up a few of the obscene photographs, hoping that was what Fields wanted because they were all I had.

The cab driver dropped me at the corner of 126th Street and 34th Avenue so I could approach the boat basin on foot by walking underneath the Northern Boulevard overpass. The tide was out and the bay was pungent. A couple winos huddled around a barrel fire under the overpass. They eyed me hopefully, but I gave them a hard look as I passed them.

I scanned the parking area. One car that still had all its wheels and four others in various states of stripping were scattered around the lot.

As I headed for the intact car, a man got out and placed his hands on the roof of the car, leaving the car door open. He called to me. "Place your hands up on the other side and we'll talk."

I recognized Fields. His face was pinched from the cold and his eyes were red. He looked exhausted and frightened. Gone was the bullying attitude of the other night. I did as he said.

"Well, Mr. Fields, so we meet again. Are you aware that every cop in the city is looking for you?"

He looked puzzled. "You called the cops?"

I shook my head. "They want you for Turner's murder. He burned to death in that fire you set. I was lucky to escape."

He shook his head vehemently. "No . . . no, I didn't set any fire. Hey, lady, I haven't killed anybody. I just do errands for the boss. The other night the boss's secretary called and told me to get out of there, to forget it . . . it didn't matter any more, he wouldn't be returning to Washington."

I was confused. "Tell me exactly what you did that night."

He wrinkled his forehead. "Turner said you wouldn't deal because you were angry about your boyfriend being killed. I had him set up the meeting at the inn because I thought it would be easier to break you down there. Then, Turner got drunk and was acting strange so I drugged his last drink to keep him out of the way when you and I had our little chat."

"If you were going to talk to me, why did you drug my hot chocolate?"

"I didn't. I made it like you asked and left it in your room. When I came downstairs, the boss's secretary called again, told me to come back in a hurry . . . the congressman was worse."

"But how did you get out of there in all that snow?"

"I drove. I had a four-wheel drive."

"Your vehicle was at the cabin?"

"What cabin? I was parked beside the house."

"Was anybody else at the inn?"

"Not that I know of. Turner and I arrived that afternoon. Turner was acting funny. He and I didn't get along very well to begin with. He thought he was above me."

"Who'd Turner work for?"

He looked surprised. "Why I thought you knew—for your boyfriend. Turner was his bird dog."

I flexed my freezing fingers. "Could we finish this conversation in the car before we get frost bite?" He nodded and we got in the car and closed the doors. "And you worked for the Congressman," I continued, "so how did you and Turner get together?"

While we had been talking, the wind had switched and now the jets were taking off from LaGuardia right directly over the car, making conversation impossible for minutes at a time.

As soon as it was quiet again, Fields said, "Mason was investigating the Superfund clean-ups, particularly the trucking companies involved. Congressman Bickers was very close to several trucking companies since he was influential on a couple subcommittees that dealt with regulating the industry. They wanted Mason stopped. Mason wasn't bribable or blackmailable. God knows we tried. Even discovered your affair with him." He gave me a sly sidewise look and I shrugged. "So we started to look at his staff. Turner was the weakest link."

"Money?"

He laughed. "Nah . . . a dame. He fell in love at a hearing no less. That Caledonia woman and she didn't even know he was alive. So we made him an offer he couldn't refuse. If he didn't cooperate with us, we'd destroy her. He was our pipeline into Mason's investigation. After Mason was killed Turner started acting strange, erratic . . . know what I mean?" He stared at a jet as it swept off the runway.

When the sound died, I prodded, "What happened then?"

"The congressman's condition got worse and everything started to unravel."

"What was in that box in Todd's apartment?"

He looked surprised. "It was empty. Did you get the pictures?"

"These?" I dropped a couple photos on the seat between us.

He picked one up. "Stupid," he muttered. "The congressman was set up. Usually, I traveled with him, but before last Christmas he went to the Bahamas—alone. I had the flu and his wife was busy at her shop with the pre-Christmas rush. She runs an exclusive dress shop in Greenwich."

He blew on his hands. "He cut his trip short and came home. He was changed—scared, nervous, didn't want to talk to me. I knew something bad had happened, but I didn't know what until one night in January he showed me one of the pictures he'd received in the mail. Someone had threatened to send them to his wife. The congressman is a lot of things, but he loves his wife. Then, he had the heart attack . . ."

Fields leaned his forehead against the steering wheel. "I suppose you're going to blackmail him now. What do you want?" he asked in a muffled voice.

"I just want Todd's killer. I'm no blackmailer, After this is over, I'll destroy the pictures, but that's useless unless you know who took them in the first place. The negatives are still floating around. Why did he go to the Bahamas?"

"A trucking industry outing. He was the guest of Berry Enterprises."

"Berry again," I mused. "What changed during the course of Todd's investigation?" I asked myself. I stared out the window, letting my mind rove. "The Queens Superfund clean-up was given to Caledonia," I muttered.

"What?"

I smiled. "That was what changed. The Queens job was given to Caledonia. Previously, Berry had gotten most of the Superfund jobs. Now, Todd comes along and interferes somehow and the job goes to Caledonia."

"I don't understand. Why blackmail my boss? He'd always been cooperative with the trucking companies."

"I don't know . . . something is still missing. Todd had written me a letter or had some other written information for me and it still hasn't turned up. When I arrived at the apartment, the box was open and empty. How about when you got there?"

"Open and empty."

We looked at each other. Fields was no longer the arrogant young man with a powerful boss. He was scared and uncertain. I believed him.

"Have you ever noticed a slim white man at these hearings or anywhere in the vicinity of the congressman?" I asked.

"That's not much of a description."

I shrugged. "Best I can do. Nobody has really gotten much of a look at him. Slim and white describes the truck driver who forced Warren off the road and the guy who mugged Mrs. Warren. Oh yes—smelled of garlic."

"A truck driver? Italian?"

"People other than Italians eat garlic, but yes, a truck driver. He could have been the one who ran me off the road too."

He glanced at his watch. "I've got to get back."

"Have you forgotten? Every cop is looking for you."

He looked hounded. "What'll I do?"

"Give yourself up. I can arrange for you to surrender to my friend,

Detective Standish and you can tell her what you've just told me."

He shook his head. "I can't do that. Then, all this garbage about the congressman would get out. His wife would be destroyed. He's dying. What would be accomplished?"

"There's a killer running loose," I reminded him. "If I could guarantee you that these photos would not come out, would you turn yourself in?"

"I can't . . . I can't . . . don't you understand. Get out of the car." He pulled his gun and waved it at me. "Get out, get out before you make me do something I don't want to do."

"Okay, okay, stay cool." I made a reassuring gesture with my left hand as I groped for the door handle with the other one. "I'm getting out. Take it easy. Call me later. Give me a chance to sort this out before you do anything rash."

I took a deep breath after I left the car. He spun the wheels as he roared away. "Damn, at least he could have given me a ride home," I groused as I headed across the Shea stadium parking lot for the Willet's Point station.

35

Monday Evening

I trudged into my office.

Chris glanced at the clock. "You just made it; I was about to call Standish. You look like something the cat wouldn't bother dragging in."

I slumped into my chair and unzipped my parka. "I feel worse than I look. Fields isn't a killer. He may do everything short of killing for that congressman boss of his, but I'm sure he didn't set that fire and kill Turner." I stared at the top of my desk. "What am I missing, Chris?"

"Maybe you aren't missing anything; maybe, you're looking for too much." He glanced at the clock again. "You'd better shower and get dressed up. Mr. Berry is sending a car for you at four-thirty. He'll meet you at the Charpan Club."

I raised an eyebrow. "Charpan Club?"

"I made a couple phone calls. It's one of those private businessmen's clubs where they serve drinks and light foods. It's on Fifth Avenue. The chauffeur will see that you get to the right place."

I grinned. "Does he have to smuggle me in through the kitchen? I've read about those clubs; most of them are men only. I'm looking forward to meeting the elusive Mr. Berry. What else did Noreen have to say?"

"She didn't call—Berry's secretary called."

I raised an eyebrow. "Odd. Call Noreen."

Chris dialed and asked for Noreen. He covered the mouthpiece. "She left twenty minutes ago. Her secretary doesn't know where she went."

"How about Junior?"

"Junior hasn't been there for awhile either."

"Elvis Potter?"

Chris frowned. "He didn't show up for work and his phone doesn't answer. Anybody else?"

I shook my head. "Call Sarnoff . . . have them send somebody to Potter's apartment. If he's there, sit on him until I get back to them. If he's out, search the place. You can tell them what to look for. Call Jackie . . ."

"Oh, I almost forgot—Jackie called here. She said go for it; she'll be fine."

I smiled. "That's my girl. I'd better get ready for my date with Mr. Berry." I flipped through some routine stuff on my desk.

"Say . . . why don't you wrap up here and ride into Manhattan in style. Surprise Maria by getting home early for a change."

Chris looked doubtful. "I had planned on waiting here until you were safely home again."

I laughed. "Don't be an Irish mama, Chris. After I meet Berry, I'll probably go out to dinner. I feel better now that I know I don't have to keep looking over my shoulder for Fields."

❧

As the limo glided through rush hour traffic, I eyed the chauffeur, relieved that he was a tall black man—not a skinny white one. Chris sat up straight beside me, staring pensively out the window.

I squeezed his hand. "Relax. Where do you want to be dropped?"

"Madison and 42nd is fine. I called Maria, we're going out to dinner."

I told the chauffeur who turned left onto 42nd Street and found an empty space in front of the Grand Hyatt.

Chris said, "We'll be at Ibiza if you need us."

Ah, my favorite lobster place. "Sounds great. If I get through with Mr. Berry early enough, I'll meet you there. I could use a two pound lobster after the day I've had."

"Terrific. Take care." He closed the door and stepped back. When I glanced through the rear window, Chris was still staring after the car as if he didn't want to let it out of his sight.

The chauffeur turned right on Sixth Avenue, right on 57th Street and right onto Fifth Avenue where he pulled over and stopped. He opened my door and pointed to an elderly man in a blue suit.

"Reeves will take you to Mr. Berry."

Reeves lightly touched my elbow as he guided me through a door that led only to an elevator. A gold plaque next to the door discreetly announced Charpan Club.

There were no floor indicators in the elevator and I lost count of the floors. Reeves said nothing. He stared at the ceiling until the elevator hissed to a stop and the door slid open. He bowed me out of the car. Another colorless man waited.

"Ms. Doyle, follow me please."

Obviously, they didn't want the little woman wandering into any masculine nooks and crannies. I glimpsed an oak barroom with a black bartender polishing a glass, a library-like room where an elderly man dozed, and an empty dining room.

At the end of the hall my guide knocked at a door. He nodded at me and left me standing there as he retreated down the hall.

I've heard of exclusive, I thought, but this is ridiculous. I suppressed a giggle, trying to maintain a dignified mien.

The door opened. "Ms. Doyle."

"Mr. Berry, I presume."

He smiled slightly as he lightly brushed my hand and indicated an easy chair. I glanced around the room. Part of it, obviously used for playing cards, was dominated by a round poker table surrounded by comfortable leather chairs. The chair Berry indicated was in a window alcove looking out onto Fifth Avenue.

"Must be a terrific spot to watch the St. Patrick's Day parade," I said as I admired the long-range view of the avenue.

"Yes. I understand you prefer DuBoeuf's Beaujolais Villages. May I pour you a glass?"

"Yes, please." I glanced at the table. It also held fruit, crackers and assorted cheeses. I flashed back on another table that had held DuBoeuf's wine and cheese. Coincidence?

He fussed over the wine, giving me a chance to study him. He was perfectly groomed and manicured, but his knuckles gave away his working class origin; they were warped and gnarled like my father's. He was tall, heavyset, but muscular. His expression was urbane, but his eyes were shrewd. He was totally bald.

If I hadn't known anything about him, I might have been impressed, but as it was, I was just wary and worried.

He handed me a glass of wine and poured himself a glass of cola. He raised his glass in a toast. "To crime." I raised an eyebrow and he laughed heartily. "Well, admit it, Ms. Doyle, you were expecting to see an old Mafia don—at the very least, an aging enforcer."

I smiled. "Actually, I heard you were very polished. And powerful."

He accepted my remarks as compliments. "Thank you. Now, Noreen says you are her representative." He contemplated me, his head cocked slightly. "Isn't that a little out of your line? I thought you improved companies not presided over their disposal."

I shrugged. "I tried to convince Ms. Caledonia that her company can be saved, can be operated profitably . . . especially with that new government contract . . . but she's frightened. Too many accidents have happened to her trucks—drivers injured and killed." I looked at him innocently. "But surely, owning a trucking company yourself, you've heard about her problems. I assume that's why you've made these ridiculously low offers."

I leaned back, sipped my wine and stared over the rim of the glass at him. His expression didn't change, but I could see he was thinking. Suddenly, I realized that whatever Todd had left for me probably no longer existed. If it did, this man wouldn't be so confident.

"I had a nice chat with Congressman Bickers' aide, Benny Fields, today," I said conversationally. Something flickered deep in his eyes.

"I don't believe I know him."

"But you certainly know the congressman; you've been making campaign contributions to him for years."

"My companies make many contributions; I don't pay much attention to them. It's the price of doing business in America. You certainly know that."

I nodded. "Let's get back to Caledonia. Ms. Caledonia is willing to consider a sale to your company, but feels the current price is too low. After all, they do have that Superfund contract."

"Not quite." He waggled a finger at me. "That contract hasn't been signed."

"Only because the EPA believes Caledonia has a safety problem, but if I turn over Todd Mason's report, it will prove that Caledonia doesn't have an inherent safety problem—that the company has been the victim of a pernicious assault by a competitor."

He pursed his lips. "I doubt that such a report exists."

Because you destroyed it, I thought, fighting to control my temper.

"Even if it does," he continued, "I think EPA has rethought its position

and might wish to award the Queens contract to another firm. Ms.
Caledonia has demonstrated that she can't run her father's company."

I stood up. "There won't be any more accidents . . . will there, Mr. Berry?"

He shrugged. "I have no control over that." He smiled. "I think you give
me too much credit, Ms. Doyle. Perhaps, you read too many books about
all-powerful men who control whole industries and own politicians who do
their bidding." Another modest smile. "I'm just a simple businessman who
married well."

"You're too modest, Mr. Berry."

"Please sit down, have some more wine, some cheese. We can discuss this
like two civilized people." He refilled my glass and smiled at me. The smile
was only on his lips; his eyes were cold and watchful—reptilian.

I glanced out the window to reassure myself that I was indeed in the
center of Manhattan, sitting in a rich private club among people who would
protect me.

I looked straight at him. "Did you have Todd killed?"

Disbelief was replaced by hearty laughter. "Oh my dear lady, you have an
inflated sense of my criminal tendencies and power." He sipped his cola,
delicately wiped his lips, and replaced the glass precisely in the center of the
coaster.

"I admit, in my younger days, I was a rough and tumble young fellow, but
then we had to be in those days. Today, my battles are fought by lawyers and
accountants." He glanced at me shrewdly. "I won't insult your intelligence
by saying I didn't even know about it." He pursed his lips. "I assumed his
family was covering up some romantic interlude that went awry. I understand he was quite a ladies' man. Even married women."

I chewed my lip. What did I really know about the last couple years of
Todd's life. A ladies' man? Married women? Well, I had been married, but
that had been different—hadn't it?

"Perhaps," he continued, "he picked on the wrong man's wife." He whispered a famous Mafia name.

"No, no . . . I can't believe that. Todd wasn't a celibate, but he wasn't stupid either. I've seen that woman on television, following her husband in and
out of courtrooms. Not Todd's type at all. And his family didn't cover up his
death. In fact, his mother wants it solved. She wants to . . . bury him."

He clucked his tongue in phony sympathy. "I understand," he murmured.
"If he were my son, I'd be moving heaven and earth, searching for his killer.

I'm afraid I can't help you. Now, can we get back to the Caledonia situation."

"Didn't Todd prevent you from getting the Queens contract?" I persisted.

He shrugged. "That contract hasn't been signed as I said before. I understand that a report cast some doubt on our operation and I understand it was some sub-committee investigator and I suspected it might be Mason. Mason and I didn't always see eye to eye; if you've read any of my testimony in front of some of these committees, that would be obvious."

I waved a hand in annoyance. "We seem to be going in circles. Let's forget Todd for now. Noreen has another condition that must be met before she'll sell the company. Jun . . . er, Russell must be kept on in a management position."

Berry smiled. "I, too, think of him as Junior. Not half the man his father was." He pursed his lips. "I suppose we could find some position for him. I understand he likes to play tennis and golf. I could put him in charge of liaison with our Japanese associates—they like to meet on the links."

I stood up. "I don't think we have anything else to discuss. We'll get back to you. I can tell you right now, Noreen will want more money for the company."

He stood up and absently looked out the window. "The lawyers can iron out all those problems. Tell Noreen, I'm sorry for her troubles, but if it weren't me taking over, it would be some other company." His eyes softened. "She was always such a bright little girl. Her father and I were friends once . . . we both dated Noreen's mother."

For a moment I glimpsed a human side of Berry and I wondered if "date" was too weak a word. I felt that there were unexplored depths here. Was the Caledonia quest more than a business proposition? A vendetta? Revenge for a stolen love. I shook my head. Grow up, old girl, forget the romantic stuff. Money, money, money.

I was passed from employee to employee until I found myself back on Fifth Avenue where the chauffeur held the door of the limo open for me.

"No thanks, I'll walk."

At seven o'clock Fifth Avenue is almost deserted except for a few tourists wandering aimlessly. They peered in department store windows, stood on the steps of St. Patrick's Cathedral, bought pretzels from the vendors, and flagged down horse-drawn carriages.

I strode rapidly down the avenue, glancing behind me once in awhile. I zigged over to Madison and then to Lexington and fifteen minutes later I arrived at 41st Street where the lights of Ibiza beckoned me.

Pepe, my favorite waiter, greeted me at the door. "Ah, Senora Doyle, your friends await."

Chris stood up. "We were beginning to worry about you. How'd it go?"

I smiled. "A Dos Equis dark, Pepe, and a two-pound lobster . . . steamed. No salad."

I sat down and sniffed the delicious aromas. "Time flies when you're having fun," I said lightly. "Maria, long time no see. Chris . . . quit hovering and let me catch my breath."

They dawdled over coffee and dessert while I demolished my lobster. I sighed and leaned back.

Pepe removed the dishes. "Coffee, black, Senora?" I nodded.

"Well?" Chris prompted.

"Don't be so impatient . . . you remind me of your boss," I said with a grin. "Mr. Berry is very smooth . . . says he had nothing to do with Caledonia's troubles or Todd's death. His only crime . . . according to him . . . is he wants to buy Caledonia cheap." I frowned. "He also suggested that Todd had been playing around with a Mafia wife."

"Would he?" asked Maria.

"No," I snapped. Then, I remembered that Todd had been living in New York across the river from me for a year or so and hadn't called me. Had I been fooling myself, romanticizing an old flame, an old relationship, mourning what might have been? I had been carrying on as if our affair had been recent. Sometimes, it takes another woman to make you see clearly. I looked into Maria's eyes.

I chewed my lip. "I don't know, Maria, I just don't know. I don't know anything anymore. Excuse me . . . I must go." I snatched up my coat. "Put dinner on the office account," I blurted to Chris before I dashed out of the restaurant.

36

Late Monday Night

I sat at my desk listening to my phone messages. Only two were of interest. Sarnoff Agency notified me that they were holding Elvis Potter at his apartment and asked me to call. The other was from Investigator Hurley asking me to call him no matter how late I got in. Urgent.

I dialed the barracks in Kingston. He wasn't there, but he'd left a number where he could be reached. I tried that.

"Hurley."

"Doyle. You wanted me to call. What's up?"

"That's what I wanted to ask you."

"What's that supposed to mean?"

He chuckled. "Good news . . . the lid is off. When I went into my office this afternoon, all the files on your friend's death were back in place . . . including an autopsy report."

"What time exactly?"

"Pardon?"

"What time exactly did you find all this stuff?"

"Around six. I had been testifying in court all day. Nobody seems to know how the files got back."

"A congressman is dying," I muttered. "I didn't have anything to do with it, but I'd appreciate some information. What killed Todd?"

"Just what Cal remembered—an injection of lithane. He was dead before they bashed in his head. They could have just given him the injection and left him in bed . . . it would have looked like a simple heart attack."

"I think somebody was sending a message."

"To you?"

"I don't know. Who owns the inn?"

"Insurance company says Merlin Corporation. Know anything about them?"

"Sure do. Casinos, hotels, golf courses. They've pushed for casino gambling in the Catskills. Was the inn a legitimate Operation?"

"More or less."

"What does that mean?"

"Anybody who could afford it could go there, but the tab was really high. Your average businessman wasn't going to spend a weekend there. Very, very exclusive."

"I knew that . . . but Todd could afford something like that." I thought a minute. "How about Turner? Autopsy report?"

"Smoke inhalation so he was alive when the fire got him, but somebody had slipped him a mickey. He was out like a light. Probably never knew what hit him."

I pondered that statement. "I heard him scream . . . I thought I did anyway . . . maybe the wind. How'd the fire start?"

"Simple. Gasoline poured around the kitchen area. Fields must have set it and fled."

"No . . . not Fields, I talked to him . . ."

"When? Where? We want him."

"Calm down. Let me finish. I met him this afternoon. I think you'll hear from him by tomorrow. He didn't set the fire; he had already left the inn. He had a four-wheel drive vehicle parked beside the inn. He didn't even know about the cabin. And I think whoever set the fire had left a vehicle at the cabin—probably another four-wheel drive. I smelled exhaust fumes when I first got to that clearing." I hesitated. "My guess is I'd look for a slim white man."

"Terrific, some description," Hurley snorted. "The Catskills are full of slim white men."

"I don't think he's in the Catskills."

"You aren't jerking me around like you did the other day, are you, Ms. Doyle?"

"I'm sorry about that; I wasn't sure I could trust you. Your arrival seemed too convenient."

"Feeling was mutual. Your friend Standish convinced me you were okay."

"Good old Standish," I muttered. "Let me get back to you . . . tomorrow. I might be able to give you some answers then."

He sighed. "Guess I have no choice. Be careful. I suspect you're going to do something foolish. Your friend Standish said you have a death wish sometimes."

"Standish worries too much. 'Night."

37

Midnight

I called Potter's number and told my agent I'd be there soon. I called Lefty and begged for another car.

"Geez, Ms. Doyle, you've just about wiped me out. I have a pick-up I can let you have, but if you total that, I'll never, never rent you anything again."

"You won't regret it, Lefty. Bring it over as soon as possible."

I looked at the phone, debating with myself. I had promised to phone Standish, but I didn't want to waste time explaining everything to her now. I rationalized, "She's probably in bed." I patted the phone. "Later."

I was certainly overdressed to meet with Potter, but I didn't want to waste time changing clothes; besides the two most important items were already in place—my .38 and my knife.

Potter lived in a run-down apartment building on Woodhaven Boulevard. Traffic was light and it only took me fifteen minutes to drive there. It would have taken me twice as long to find a legal parking place, but Lefty's truck looked like an abandoned vehicle so I just parked it across the sidewalk.

Sarnoff Agency's Gloria Stajic let me in and said, "Boy, am I glad you're here. This guy is a sleazeball."

"Tell me about it! Stick around. Where is he? I want to talk to him alone."

"In the kitchen."

It was a standard New York apartment—a small living room, one bedroom, bathroom, and an eat-in kitchen. Potter was sitting at the table, handcuffed with his hands curled around a can of Bud. He raised it in a toast.

"Been waiting for you, pretty lady. Didn't know you were into bondage scenes. I'm ready and rarin' to go. Will this be a threesome?" His loathsome leer turned my stomach.

I forced a smile. "Same old joker, eh. Elvis? You can drop the good old boy act." I sat down facing him. I reached across the small table, grabbed the center chain of the cuffs and yanked. His rib cage slammed into the table edge and he exhaled in a whoosh.

"Hey," he yelped, "What ya doin'?"

"Getting your attention. I'm not a patient person, Elvis, so listen up." I smiled. "You didn't go to work today."

He looked sullen. "I quit. Tired of this cold weather. Going back to Alabama. Free country."

I yanked the cuffs. He winced as his ribs hit the table again.

"You aren't paying attention, Elvis. I can do this all night until your ribs won't even be worth barbecuing." I smiled. "Now . . . who did you tell where Flo and I were going? Who's the slim white man who pops up at convenient times?"

"I—I don't know."

I yanked again. Even though he was braced for it, I was still strong enough to whack him against the table. Tears sprung to his eyes.

"Jesus H. Christ, you're killing me."

"Not yet, Elvis, not yet, but I'll keep that in mind as a possibility. I suppose Russell told you he worked for the Mafia and you'd be protected . . . you could take your pay-off, move south, disappear." I laughed. "You fool. He's going to let you and your friend take the rap. Caledonia is going to sell to Berry Enterprises and Russell is going to be its manager. How do you like that?"

Elvis's eyes shifted, looking everywhere but into mine.

I smiled. "Elvis, you have two minutes to make up your mind. Either you're with me or you're against me and I hate it when people are against me." I was glad Jackie wasn't there to hear her mother sounding like a homicidal maniac.

When he broke, the words flowed like water over a dam.

"Me and Rafer worked for Berry trucking. Rafer's my cousin. He likes to hurt things. I promised my aunt I'd keep an eye on him. Mr. Caledonia said it wasn't fitten for his sister to be running the company, that was man's work and he just wanted to discourage her so she'd stay home and tend to her own business and he'd run the company like his daddy had. He figured when things got rough she'd quit." He shook his head. "Me and Rafer figured she'd give up before now. I just don't understand women today."

I smiled. "Was that Rafer who tried to run me off the road?"

"Yeh, he was only trying to scare you."

"How'd he know where I'd be?"

"After Ms. Caledonia talked about hiring you, Mr. Caledonia had Rafer follow you . . . told him to put you out of commission for a little bit."

"Using a tractor trailer to put me out of commission seems a little drastic, Elvis."

"Rafer don't have much sense."

I nodded. "How about Todd Mason's death? Rafer?"

Elvis shook his head vehemently. "No, no, no . . . Rafer didn't do that. Rafer saw them though."

I suppressed the jump of excitement in my chest and kept my voice level. "What do you mean?"

"Rafer was watching the inn after the cop took you there. Two men followed your friend back and waited outside until all the lights went off. They went in. Rafer was curious so he moved closer. A while later, he saw them dragging something out to the creek. At first, he thought it was you, but then he took a close look at the body after they left."

"Did Rafer tell you what they looked like?"

"Suits."

"Suits?"

"Yeh, he called them a couple suits. That's what he calls men who are dressed up in suits."

The two guys who had broken into the factory had worn suits. Turner wore a suit. What kind of men wore suits on a cold night in the Catskills? City men.

"Why did Rafer kill Jack Warren?"

"Accident. Jack panicked. Rafer was just trying to scare him. Mr. Caledonia told Rafer if Jack was out of the way, he could be the number one driver on the Queens job. Big money."

"Rafer has a tendency to overdo things, doesn't he? Did he follow me to the inn this past weekend?"

Elvis nodded.

"And I reckon that was just supposed to be a little fire to scare me?"

"He didn't mean to kill nobody. Rafer's just careless."

"Well, Elvis, I'm going to level with you. You're in a heap of trouble and as things stand now, there's a possibility you'll never see Alabama again." I let that sink in as I watched him. His head sunk down on his chest and tears oozed out of his eyes.

"Now . . . there is a little light at the end of the tunnel." I guess Elvis liked cliches because he looked up hopefully. "You could give evidence against Rafer." I held up a hand. "Now, I know what you're going to say—he's kin—but think about it, Elvis. You can't be Rafer's keeper forever; you've got to think of yourself. Rafer needs help and only you can help him."

I could imagine the fun Standish would have interrogating Elvis. It was almost cruel to toss this guppie to the shark.

I smiled. "What do you say, Elvis? You want to help or you want to be charged with being an accessory to murder?"

"I didn't—didn't murder anybody. I was just helping Mr. Caledonia. It was all Rafer's doing."

I nodded. "Where's Rafer now?"

"I told him to wait at the diner on Cross Bay Boulevard for me. We're leaving—we're leaving for home."

I stood up and stretched. "Gloria," I called.

"What's going to happen to me?" Elvis whined.

I smiled. "I'm going to have a friend pick you up and take you to meet Rafer. Tell her everything you know." I nodded to Gloria. "Sit on him. A Detective Standish will come for him soon. Then, you can go home. Thanks—you did a good job; there'll be a little something extra for you."

"No problem, Abby . . . always a pleasure working for you."

I called Standish. "I have a present for you." I gave her the address as I added, "He'll take you to his cousin. Better bring along some back-up. His cousin isn't playing with a full deck and overreacts."

"Where are you going?"

"I've got a couple errands to run."

"At midnight?" she snapped.

"Later, Standish. I can't do all your work for you." I hung up while she was still swearing at me.

I made one more phone call. "We have to talk—I'll be there in an hour."

38

Early Tuesday Morning

I drove along the Long Island Expressway to the Manhasset exit where I picked up a winding road that passed small estates and a horse farm. Right after the farm, I turned down an unpaved country lane.

A French Tudor, small but tasteful in a parklike setting, was at the end of the lane. The house was all lit up, welcoming. I parked the truck and sat, staring at the front door. I didn't want to go into that house.

"Let's get this over with, old girl," I muttered as I slammed the truck door. I paused, listening to the silence of a Long Island night.

The door opened. Noreen was silhouetted in the light. She looked worried.

"Sorry to bother you at this hour," I said.

"It's okay. I made some coffee." She led me to the kitchen. Kitchen was an understatement. This was a room to live in—warm red brick walls, gleaming copper pans suspended from ceiling racks, comfortable arm chairs in one corner, and a large cooking island in the center.

We sat in the chairs, facing each other over a small butcher's block table.

"You said it was important," she prompted.

I nodded. "It's about your brother."

"Russell? Has something happened to him?"

"Not yet. Russell is behind the accidents and Jack Warren's death." I watched her struggle with that statement. She had an almost resigned expression.

She rubbed her forehead as if she had a headache. "I knew he resented my being president, but I didn't think he'd do anything like that. Russell was always a spoiled boy. First mama, then Aunt Sophia who took over after mama died. He was the son and the sun, if you know what I mean."

I nodded.

"Why should I be surprised?" she asked herself. She looked up at me. "He had to have had help . . . Russell couldn't do these things."

"Elvis Potter and his cousin Rafer were hired by Russell to make accidents happen to scare you out of the business and to scare me away from helping you. Incidentally, I met with Berry and he's willing to buy your company . . . at a better price."

She stiffened. "No . . . no, it's not for sale." Her black eyes flashed. "Did he have anything to do with this? Was he behind Russell?"

I looked at her curiously. "Would that make it easier for you . . . if you could believe Russell was manipulated by the devious Mr. Berry?"

"Nothing could make this easier. What's going to happen to Russell?"

"Well, if he can give the Feds something useful on Berry, on trucking in general, he'll probably spend some time in one of those Federal country clubs, improving his tennis at taxpayers' expense. He'll have to convince them that Rafer is a nut and misinterpreted his instructions."

I chewed my lip. "It would also help if Russell turned himself in. Detective Standish has picked up Rafer by now. If I know her, she's going to do everything by the book . . . wait for the courts to open, get all the proper warrants and then pick up Russell."

"What can you do to help him?" Noreen leaned forward, looking at me intently.

I stared back at her. "You still want to help him?"

"He's my brother."

"Where does he live?"

"Staten Island."

"Call him, tell him I have to talk to him—now."

I listened to her side of the conversation. "Russell we have a problem. Ms. Doyle wants to meet with you . . . as soon as possible . . . she's here . . . I understand . . . right . . . Later."

"Well?"

"He doesn't want you to come to his home. His wife . . . his son. He'll meet you at Rockaway Beach at six." She glanced at the clock. It was already going on four. "Just go straight to the beach after you go over the bridge."

I rubbed my eyes. I was tired, but on a caffeine high. Adrenaline was pumping like it always did when I neared the end of a case.

"How'd he sound?" I asked.

"Nervous."

"Didn't he want to know why I needed to talk to him?"

"He didn't ask. He sounded almost resigned." She gave me a pleading look. "Will you bring him to the office after you talk to him. I'd like to see him before you turn him over to the police."

"No. Not a good idea." I tried a half-smile. "Call Standish and tell her to meet me on the beach at six-thirty. It will be better if Russell turns himself over to her right there. In the meantime, you'd better line up a lawyer for him—the best criminal lawyer you know."

"You sure it will go all right?"

I smiled. "I'm sure Russell is going to be sensible. He never meant for it to go this far and he's probably been trying to figure a way out."

I can only plead fatigue for my stupidity.

39

Six A.M. Tuesday

Rush hour traffic was just starting as I headed for Rockaway Beach, wondering how best to approach Russell. I didn't know him very well. What kind of man denied the existence of a twin he worked with every day? How much resentment had he built up against her over the years? How easy had it been for Berry or someone like him to manipulate Russell?

I stopped at a corner market where I bought a container of coffee and a cardboard Danish. I parked the truck across the street from the beach and carried my breakfast up to a bench on the boardwalk. After a couple sips of coffee and half of the bun, I felt too restless to just sit and wait so I walked onto the beach. I paced up and down, keeping an eye on the boardwalk.

Suddenly, he was there. He stood on the boardwalk staring at me. I waved. He looked around. The beach was deserted except for a dog walker way down at the eastern end. It was too cold for the usual early morning walkers and joggers.

He shuffled across the sand towards me, head down, right hand in his pocket. He walked by me and stopped on the edge of the water, idly digging his toe into the sand and staring out to sea. I stood to the side and slightly behind him about five feet away.

"You . . . you . . . wanted to see me. Why?"

"It's over, Russell. We have Potter and his cousin, Rafer; they're willing to testify that you hired them to cause all those accidents, including the deaths of Turner and Warren. I'm sure if you turn yourself in and give evidence, it will go easier for you."

I was having difficulties convincing myself, so how could I expect to persuade Russell, I wondered, as I looked at his profile. His face was bland, blank like a child. I wondered if he was even listening to me.

"Why, Russell . . . why did you do it?"

"They—they shouldn't have . . . made Noreen . . . president. It . . . was . . . embarrassing. I . . . just . . . wanted her . . . to stay home."

"Did Berry put you up to it? Did he offer you a position running the company after he took over?"

"Sort . . . of. Said it was . . . a shame . . . man should . . . run his own company . . . like my father . . . did."

I could just see the devious Mr. Berry patting Russell on the shoulder, offering fatherly sympathy, suggesting little things, but never coming right out and saying kill this one or that one. Nothing culpable. I thought Russell doesn't realize he was set up and his testimony won't touch Berry.

"My wife . . . my son . . . wanted me to be . . . president. They'll be so humiliated," he finished in a rush and drew something from his pocket.

A gun, a gun, my brain shrieked. I felt like I was mired in molasses as I tugged my gun from my pocket. I watched his hand come up, looked down the barrel of his gun, and heard the explosion. Ears ringing, I realized I was still standing.

Grasping my gun with both hands, I crouched and shouted. "Drop it, Russell. This is crazy. Drop it." I covered him, aiming at his chest. "Drop it, drop it, drop it," I pleaded.

He raised his gun again, aiming at me. I fired. I didn't miss. The bullet drilled him in the center of his chest and he crumpled to the sand.

40

Tuesday Morning

I watched the water lapping at the body, barely aware of a car stopping on the boardwalk behind me. I knew it would be Standish—too late.

She walked up beside me, touched my shoulder lightly as she reached for the gun dangling from my right index finger. "I'll take that."

I smiled wryly. "I know . . . probably want to check ballistics and I suppose there'll be some kind of hearing." I glanced at the windows of the high-rises along the boardwalk. "Surely, someone up there was watching the sun rise and saw our little shoot-out."

She indicated the body. "He had a gun?"

"Shot at me with something. Shouldn't you drag his body up on the sand before the tide takes the garbage out?"

I watched with idle curiosity as Standish knelt beside the body, running her hands under it and finally standing up, waving an evil, black object at me. Thank God, I thought, the tide didn't take his gun away. A smoking gun simplified things.

Standish dragged the body a few feet up onto the sand while I watched passively, thinking I should help her but not wanting to touch that body. She scattered the curious gulls who had come to pick over the trash. She pulled his wallet out of an inside pocket and glanced through it before she stuck it in her pocket along with his gun. Standish stood up, stretched her back muscles and stared out to sea. I wondered what she was thinking about.

She ambled back to stand facing me. I was staring at nothing. She waved her hand in front of my face. "Anyone home?"

I sighed. "I killed a man, Standish. Gunned him down."

"Don't be melodramatic. He shot at you first, didn't he?"

"I think so. I thought I heard a shot . . . maybe it was the clap of a breaker hitting the rocks, the sharp caw of a gull, the backfire of a car . . . who knows? I thought he fired at me." I looked at her in alarm. "Hadn't his gun been fired?"

"Yeh." She looked up and down the beach. "Why here, I wonder?"

"He came home."

"Home?"

"They used to live here when they were kids." I shook my head angrily. "The fool! He could've turned and given evidence to the Feds, gotten a token sentence in Danbury and gone on with his life." I looked at Standish, my eyes pleading for—for what—forgiveness?

"Honest to God, Standish, I didn't mean to kill him. I thought I could talk him into surrendering. I didn't know he had a gun." I dug my toe into the sand, making an aimless design. "He was like a cornered rat. Turned to fight. Drew that gun. I had no place to hide, Standish. I had to shoot."

"I know there was no other option." She pulled me close, hugging me tightly. "I know someone you can talk to, one of our department psychiatrists. Very good. Let's you get all the poison out of your system. Want me to make an appointment for you?"

Pulling away from her, I gave her the old Doyle grin, and said, "No shrinks. I'll handle this."

She shrugged. "Have it your way." She cocked her head. "Here they come."

As the sirens screamed closer, I looked at Standish who was staring at the body. "You'll tell his sister?"

She sighed. "We'll take care of it, but I think you'd better talk to her, too."

"I guess. I can think of a lot of other things I'd rather do."

"What are you going to do?"

I watched a plane roaring out to sea, climbing rapidly after its take-off from Kennedy. "That's what I'm going to do," I mumbled.

"What did you say?"

"I'm going to get on one of those jets and fly to California, spend some time with Jackie, eat seafood on Fisherman's Wharf, take a wine country tour." I grinned wryly at her. "In other words, Standish, I'm finally going to take that vacation. Forget this place." I waved my hand to encompass all of New York.

"I know what you mean. Did you ever think of just sticking to the efficiency expert game?"

"All the time, Standish, all the time."

Epilogue

Two weeks later

Nob Hill. I sat on the balcony of the penthouse apartment, enjoying the sunshine, the view of San Francisco bay and my daughter's chattering while I ate my breakfast. Electra had been properly grateful, insisting that I use one of her company apartments for my vacation.

"You were smiling," Jackie said.

"What?"

"You were smiling. You've been pretty gloomy since you got here a couple days ago. Now, you're just sitting there and smiling. Private joke?"

I waved my hand towards the skyline. "Just great to be alive. Suddenly, I just realized it's terrific to be alive, sitting here with you."

"Do you want to talk about what happened? Peg said you might have a few problems, a delayed reaction to the shooting."

"Peg? Peg who?"

"Standish."

"You discussed me with her." My temper flared, but I suppressed it when I saw the hurt expression in Jackie's eyes.

"I'm not a child," she said resentfully. "I was worried about you so I called her. She said it's hard to kill someone, hard to cope with the pain unless you're a real killer. And you're not, are you?"

I frowned. "Sometimes, I think I am, but that's nonsense. If I hadn't shot Russell, he would have killed me." I chewed my lip. "But if I hadn't been such a show-off, I could have prevented the whole situation by having Standish pick him up, but no, I had to make a grandstand play. I thought he was harmless. Good lesson to remember—anybody who's cornered can be dangerous. Remember that and always leave somebody an out—that goes for anything—a relationship, whatever."

"Can I ask you some questions?"

My daughter was getting to be as nosy as her mother, I thought wryly as I nodded.

"Why did Todd get killed? Did Berry have anything to do with that?"

"Todd's committee was investigating Berry Enterprises, but Berry didn't have anything to do with Todd's death. In the course of his investigation into organized crime infiltration of the Superfund clean-ups, he met the wife of one of the dons." I sighed. "He fell in love, they had an affair, and the don had him killed."

"Why didn't Todd and you ever get married?"

"You sound like Electra," I turned the question over in my mind. There are optimum moments in a relationship, I thought, and if you miss them, they never return. "Todd and I loved each other, but not enough. We were always too busy to take that final step in our relationship. He was my dearest friend; I would have trusted him with my life. When I look back over the last year or so, I realize we hadn't talked much. Time sort of slips away from you, Jackie. We should see more of each other."

Jackie smiled. "We will, we will. How did the don find out about Todd and his wife?"

Yes, how did the thug find out about Todd? I hadn't thought about it, but in retrospect, I was willing to bet that Berry had something to do with it. He could get rid of a pesky investigator and keep his own hands clean at the same time.

I laughed, suddenly, feeling free. I had been brooding about Berry, knowing that he was going to get off scot-free even though he had manipulated the hapless Russell. Now, I knew how to get him. A hint to Electra that Berry had set up Todd would turn her loose with a vengeance. She was an extremely wealthy woman and could destroy Berry Enterprises.

"What's the joke?" Jackie asked, eyeing me suspiciously.

"Electra. She wanted revenge and I'm going to hand her Berry on a platter. Keep an eye on his stock in the next few weeks and you'll learn how the business world works. She'll destroy him and he'll never know how it was done."

Jackie nodded in understanding. "You said you had something important to discuss with me. Is now the time?"

I watched a freighter in the bay. "Yeh, I guess so. Remember when some-one was following you and I got upset, hired bodyguards for you and you were annoyed?" She nodded. "Well, I had just about decided to give up my sideline."

"Because you think it endangers me?"

"Right. I like doing these special investigations and usually I accomplish something good. As long as you were out of sight, out of mind, so to speak, nobody bothered you and I didn't have to worry about you."

I leaned across the table and touched her hand. "I want to continue but I won't if you say not to; I can't endanger your life."

Jackie stood up and walked across the balcony where she leaned against the railing, staring out at the bay, her back to me. A few minutes later, she turned and smiled at me.

"I admit I was scared when you were investigating that dead general and I was kidnapped, and I was nervous when I discovered that creep following me a few weeks ago, but I never thought of asking you to stop your investi-gations." She frowned. "I know I act like a spoiled child sometimes, but I'm really just trying to get your attention, I guess."

"Jackie, you're always in my mind and my heart. You don't have to do any-thing stupid to get my attention. Just ask for it."

"By the way, who did hire that guy to follow me?"

"Turner, I guess, to protect you, if necessary. I wish he and I had trusted each other. This would have been resolved sooner and he'd still be alive."

"It's like a puzzle, isn't it? Putting all the pieces together." I raised an eye-brow. She laughed. "What I'm trying to say, Mom, is maybe someday, it could be a family business."

I waggled my eyebrows Groucho style and flicked an imaginary cigar. "Are you telling me that far from wanting me to give this up you might want to be my partner someday?" She nodded. I laughed. "Wait till I tell Standish!"

"I already did." She crossed the terrace and hugged me.